# the Gossip Games

ALLIE SARAH

Copyright © 2023 by Allie Sarah. All rights reserved

Published by SnowRidge Press

Cover by Ink and Laurel

Author photo by Sophie Eve Kaye

ISBN (paperback): 978-1-958412-11-4

This book or any portion thereof may not be reproduced or used in any manner whatsoever without the express written permission of the publisher except for the use of brief quotations in a book review.

This is a work of fiction. Names, characters, places, events and incidents are either the products of the author's imagination or used in a fictitious manner. Any resemblance to actual persons, living or dead, or actual events is purely coincidental

Printed in the United States of America

# Praise for The Gossip Games

"A delightfully playful romcom that feels like a sweet (gossip-filled!) treat."

— Crystal Maldonado, award-winning author of *Fat Chance, Charlie Vega* and *No Filter and Other Lies*

"Awesome read! I really enjoyed the parts about beading and Gracie's passion for jewelry making...a lot of heart in the friendships as well! Overall: *The Gossip Games* is a cute and fun YA romance debut from an awesome author with tons of potential!"

— Cookie O'Gorman, author of *Adorkable* and *Fauxmance*

"Allie Sarah's YA romance debut is full of fake-dating fun and romance from start to finish!"

— Kristy Boyce, author of *Hot British Boyfriend* and *Hot Dutch Daydream*

*To Mia and Micha,*
*who can always be found within the pages of my books.*

# Chapter One

Gracie Adams slammed her hands over her ears. "Why?" she groaned, glaring at the packed dining hall. "Why tonight, of all nights?"

Zara Ashcroft smiled sympathetically. "It's not that bad."

Gracie stared at her best friend. "Zar, we have a major chemistry test tomorrow and a group of freshmen are screaming their heads off. There is absolutely no way I can concentrate in here."

"It's karaoke." Zara flipped her book shut. "It's supposed to be loud."

Gracie rolled her eyes. "And I'm supposed to be studying."

"So why don't you go to the common room? It's a big school. There's always someplace quiet to go. I should know; my ancestors paid for it."

"Because I wanted a snack. You know the dining hall has the best late-night food." Gracie sighed as she tossed her brown waves over her shoulder. She leaned forward to take a bite of a cookie, brushing off the crumbs from her hands. "But fine. Whatever. I'll just go to the common room."

"Who needs snacks anyway?" Zara said, stealing Gracie's last cookie. "Besides, why are you worried about the test? You've been forcing me to study with you for hours. What you need is some sleep."

"I don't have time for sleep," Gracie reminded her friend. "I have to study for chem. I have math homework to finish, an English essay to write, and we're going on an overnight field trip in a few days. You know I have to keep my grades up."

"You have another two weeks to write that essay," Zara pointed out. "And you're one of the smartest people I know. You're the *smartest* English and history person I know. Dean's got some awesome science skills."

"Yes, but tomorrow I'll get even more work that needs to be done." Gracie stood up, throwing her bag over her shoulder. She gave Zara a quick side hug before pushing her way through the crowded room and ducking past a freshman who was currently shrieking at the top of his lungs.

"Don't stay up too late!" Zara yelled after her.

Gracie waved over her shoulder as she slipped through the cafeteria doors, mentally cataloging all the work she had to do. When she entered the common room a few minutes later, she wasted no time in pulling out her math textbook and heading for her favorite chair. Gracie dragged over a small circular table to rest her book on before sitting down on the velvet armchair.

The Trinity common rooms were somehow both spacious and cozy, with 400 students divided somewhat evenly between the eight dorms. Despite the large size of the rooms, the Trinity administration spared no expense with the furnishings. It was this detail alone that made Gracie's common room one of her favorite places at Trinity, and if she could've gotten away with it, she would've happily dragged a chair with her to all her classes.

Gracie worked steadily for a while, making a decent dent in her work. Finally finishing the complicated math problems, she took out the book they were reading in English and flipped to her bookmarked page. She had read *The Catcher in the Rye* before, and even though she wasn't a big fan of Holden's ramblings, Gracie figured that she could stay up long enough to get through another few chapters. It was important to always be prepared in class, and even though she had re-read the book when it had been announced as classwork, Gracie still wanted the week's chapters to be fresh in her mind. Her eyes fluttered shut once or twice as she read, but she snapped them open each time.

*Stay awake, Gracie.*

She couldn't afford to fall asleep, not without all her homework done. Turning her attention back to her book, Gracie's eyes found her spot.

✮✮✮

Dean Ashcroft walked into the student common area, his gaze scanning the room for his cousins. He didn't see anyone around, but he wouldn't put it past them to be hiding behind one of the couches. Dean walked over to his favorite fireplace spot, but unlike the last time the trio played hide and seek, no one was crouching behind the glass table. "Not funny, Jesse," he grumbled under his breath, growling at the thought of his red-headed cousin. Dean shook his head a little and multicolored glitter fluttered to the floor.

How dare his cousins prank him? Dean was the king of pranks. A bucket of glitter over the door was the most juvenile of all, and yet he had fallen for it. It was the type of trick he, Jesse, and Theo had pulled in middle school, and there he was, a high school junior, with yellow and blue glitter in his hair.

"Looking good, Dean."

Dean glanced over to see Theo snickering, his dark-haired cousin peeking out from the staircase. It was one of those staircases that curved around as soon as you hit the third step. Based on the fact that all Dean could see was Theo's stupid grin, his cousin was hanging off the banister looking as though he had just won the lottery. As soon as Theo noticed Dean's glare, he ran up the stairs as if hoping to avoid being strangled. It was a smart move, considering how inclined Dean was to hurt one of his cousins at the moment. Not actually hurt —more like pull a hasty revenge prank.

Instead of heading up to his dorm, where he would have to face Jesse and Theo's smirking faces, Dean decided the best course of action would be to hide out in the common room. When Jesse and Theo fell asleep, he would sneak upstairs and try to get the glitter out with his third shower of the day.

Exhausted, Dean headed towards the small couch in the corner of the common room. When he wanted to be alone, Dean would hunker down on the back couches where he was less likely to be spotted and drawn into conversations. It was a good place for quiet, considering that he spent the rest of his days in a school with hundreds of teenagers. A small table blocked the typically clean pathway, and Dean glanced up just in time to stop himself from gaining a bruised shin.

"What the—oh, Adams," he muttered to himself, recognizing his sister's best friend studying at the table. She was a pretty girl, exactly his type, but Zara would absolutely murder him if he tried anything. He saw her around school, hanging out with Zara, but Dean couldn't remember having a real conversation with her. Zara would occasionally drag the brunette to sit with them at lunch, but Gracie usually had her face buried in a book. Now she was sitting on the chair, eyes closed, but with a book resting on her lap.

"Mind if I join you?" He looked expectantly at her, but she didn't reply. "Adams, are you asleep?" Dean waited a second more before shaking his head. *Stupid, she can't reply if she's sleeping.* He looked up at the giant clock over the fireplace. "It's 1:45. Geez, Adams, how late do you stay up?"

Dean didn't feel right leaving her alone on the chair. He could attest that it wasn't a comfortable way to sleep. Besides, if Gracie woke up tomorrow with a stiff neck, she would probably spend the day complaining to Zara, who would spend the day complaining to

Dean, who really wasn't in the mood to listen to his sister's whinings. With a shrug, Dean slipped his arms under the sleeping girl and carefully picked her up. He was grateful the girls' dorm rooms weren't far away and that Gracie was light. Lighter than Zara, at least. Not that he would ever tell his twin that.

There were two spiral staircases in the common room, and they were mirror opposites of each other. Boys' rooms were always on the right, with six doors that led to identical dorm rooms. The girls lived on the left side, but somehow their dorms always managed to be nicer than the ones that the boys ended up with. Each dorm room had its own bathroom and a varying number of beds, but each year, Zara somehow ended up in the dorm with the largest dressers or nicest bathroom.

Dean found Gracie's room quickly. It was the one he had hauled a million boxes to on move-in day—the second on the left side of the hall. Gracie's door was ajar and Dean nudged it gently with his foot, taking care to make sure Gracie's head didn't bump into the door frame. A reading lamp glowed by the entrance, helping Dean avoid the hairbrush that was lying innocently on the black rug. A little clumsily, he made his way through the near-dark until a gasp and the sound of curtains moving caused him to spin around.

Startled, Dean stared at the wide eyes of two other girls. A phone flashlight blinked on, causing him to wince with the sudden light.

"Hello," he said once he had regained his composure, shooting them a charming grin. "Just dropping Adams off."

"Okay," one girl squeaked. Her hand reached out and tapped her friend furiously on the shoulder. Dean recognized the second girl as being in his math class. Her name was Annalie or Annie…

Well, it started with an A.

"Which bed is hers?" he asked politely. The second girl pointed to a bed on the opposite side of the room, swinging the phone light over so Dean could see.

"Thank you." Dean glanced around as he set Gracie down on her bed. His sister was lying on the adjacent bed, spread out on top of the blankets with her hair draped all over her face. Dean bit down a snicker when he saw her monkey pajamas.

He looked back, checking that Gracie hadn't disappeared from her bed in the three seconds he had thought about teasing Zara. Then he made his way out of the room, nodding at the two girls. "Ladies, have a nice night."

"Have a nice night!" the first girl said in a high-pitched voice, before turning to her friend. "OMG, Dean Ashcroft was in our dorm!"

Laughing to himself, Dean headed downstairs, crossing the common room before striding up the boys' staircase. He was determined to get a good night's sleep before waking up for classes tomorrow. Dean had to plot revenge for Jesse and Theo in the morning, and his pranks were always better when he wasn't half asleep.

✯✯✯

"Is she waking up?" was the first thing Gracie heard when she groggily opened her eyes the next morning.

"Just let her sleep," a familiar voice sighed.

"But I have to know!" the first voice complained.

"I already told you, no, it's not true!" Zara's voice exclaimed.

"What's not true?" Gracie mumbled, stretching her arms over her head. She sat up and blinked at the sudden light. Had she managed to make it to her bed last night? Gracie could've sworn she had accidentally fallen asleep while doing homework, but maybe she had woken up and walked upstairs? "Why are all the lights on? And why are you guys awake? It's only—" she glanced at her bedside clock. "—six fifteen?"

Juliet Rayne ignored her questions, her long blonde hair nearly falling into Gracie's face as she leaned forward, placing her hands on either side of Gracie's bed. "Since when have you been dating Dean Ashcroft?" she demanded.

Gracie looked past Juliet to where Zara was leaning against the bed frame, arms crossed. She glanced around the room, looking for help from her other roommate, Raina. Raina's curtains were closed, signifying that the other blonde girl was still asleep. At least someone had managed to sleep through the racket that Annalisse and Juliet were making. Gracie scrubbed a hand over her face, frowning when she noticed that her palm had glitter on it.

"I'm sorry?"

"Dean Ashcroft," Annalisse Meyers said. "Since when have the two of you been dating?"

"I haven't been dating Dean?" Gracie said, bewildered. She glanced between the three girls, rubbing her eyes. "What makes you think I have?"

"Um, he carried you in here last night," Juliet said excitedly.

Gracie scrunched her nose as her mind worked through the events of the night before. "I'm pretty sure I fell asleep in the common room. I was doing homework. He must have spotted me and brought me to my bed."

It was a little odd, but even though their interactions were limited, Dean had always been nice to her. Gracie lifted her blankets, breathing a sigh of relief when she saw her school clothes. That would've crossed the line from kind to creepy.

"Yeah, but why would he do that?" Juliet pressed.

"Because I'm his sister's best friend?" Gracie tried. "Dean and I aren't close; we only interact when we're both hanging out with Zara at the same time." Judging from the looks on their faces, Annalisse and Juliet weren't buying it.

Zara let out a sigh, running a hand through her dark red curls. She yawned loudly, never a morning person. "Look, I think both Gracie *and* Dean would tell me if they were dating, and neither of them has said anything to me. Can we just drop this? I'm meeting Jesse and Theo for breakfast, and I'd like to be at least halfway awake to deal with the terrible two. Gracie, you coming?"

"Well, I'm already awake," Gracie said, rolling her eyes. "I might as well just come and study with you at the table."

"Ooh, we'll join you!" Juliet squealed.

A twinkle grew in Zara's hazel eyes as she gave Juliet a fake smile. "Sure, why not? Jesse played a prank on me a couple of days ago; I do need to pay him back."

Juliet beamed, missing the insult. "I'm going to get my good lip gloss!" she exclaimed.

Gracie hid a snicker. "I'm taking the bathroom first," she informed her roommates.

☆☆☆

There was only one thing worse than an awkward conversation, and that was when your best friend grabbed the book out of your hand and forced you to leave it in the dorm.

"Pass the bacon, Grace," Jesse said, his mouth partially full.

Gracie wrinkled her nose, really wishing she could just pull out her latest romance and ignore him. "It's Gracie."

"That's what I said, Grace."

Gracie sighed, glancing around the cafeteria for an escape. She could go get more food, but she had barely eaten two bites of her already full plate. She had just been to the bathroom, and although she wasn't really in the mood for social interaction this morning, Gracie was too polite to run off abruptly. She wasn't a big fan of Zara's cousin, who didn't seem to take anything seriously. Not to mention, it wasn't even seven and he was way too perky. "I think I'm going to go to the library to study, Zar. I can't concentrate here."

"Oh, Gracie, you don't love us?" Jesse teased, throwing an arm around her shoulder.

Gracie ducked under his arm. "Not particularly."

Jesse looked shocked for a moment, before bursting into laughter. "I like this one, Z!"

"Yeah, yeah, I don't think she likes you very much," Zara said sleepily, cradling a mug of coffee.

"But she likes Dean," Juliet giggled.

Gracie groaned, having almost forgotten the annoying girl was there. Juliet had sat a few seats away with some girls who lived on their floor, and Gracie had been enjoying the peace and quiet that Juliet's shrill voice tended to ruin. "I'm telling you, nothing's going on between me and Dean."

"What's going on between me and Dean?" Dean asked, swinging a leg over the bench and sitting down next to Gracie. She scooted away from him. "Aww, Gracie, don't you love me?"

Gracie glared at him. She should probably thank him for carrying her to bed, but her neck ached and she'd been woken up too early.

"You know, sometimes I wonder how these idiots are related," Zara said, breaking the silence. "But then this happens."

Juliet waved Zara away, turning eagerly to Dean. "Have you and Gracie been secretly dating?" she asked in a hushed voice.

"Oh yeah, sure," Dean said casually. "Have been for months."

Gracie's mouth dropped open. "W-what?"

She barely knew Dean! He was Zara's twin brother that they occasionally sat with for meals. They had never interacted without Zara present, and even then it was usually "Pass the water" or "I'm going to get more salt." Next to her, Jesse snorted loudly and Zara dropped her spoon, splattering Fruit Loops and milk all over the table.

"It's alright, Gracie, we can tell them now," Dean said soothingly. "I've hated keeping secrets from all of our close friends!"

Juliet beamed, clearly eating up his every word. "I knew it was true!"

"It's no—" Gracie began, but Dean shoved a piece of toast in her mouth, cutting her off.

"You need to eat, Gracie. You're far too skinny. I'll see you all later." He winked at Gracie before striding away.

Gracie fumed, spitting the toast out. "How dare he!"

"It's okay, Gracie," Juliet cooed. "You can tell us now. Don't be mad at him for spilling the secret."

"What secret?" Gracie cried in exasperation.

"That you're sleeping with Dean Ashcroft, silly!" Juliet exclaimed.

Jesse spat out his coffee, making it the second casualty of Dean's announcement. This time, it was Zara's turn to hand Jesse the napkins. "I'm sorry, what?"

Zara nodded, an incredulous look on her face. "For once, I agree with Jesse. How in the world did you jump to that conclusion?"

"Well, he wouldn't just carry anyone up to bed," Juliet said matter-of-factly. "He's never that touchy with any of the girls he dates or even with you, Zara, and you're his twin sister. So clearly, they've gone further and, you know." She winked at Gracie.

Gracie blushed furiously. "Absolutely not—I never—no," she stammered. She was a virgin, for god's sake! She had only ever kissed a guy twice, and the first time she had punched the guy for kissing her without her permission. He had been too scared to go near her again, and that was the end of that "relationship." Her second kiss—an end-of-summer goodbye before his family moved to Portugal—had been much better.

Juliet giggled. "It's alright, you'll tell us when you're ready."

"I-I..." Gracie tried, before sighing and slumping against the table. If she just ignored them all, would they go away? "What class do we have first, Zar?"

"Theo!" Juliet exclaimed, cutting off Zara's response. Gracie spun around in her seat to see the wavy-haired boy approach, nodding to his cousins before sitting down next to Jesse. "Are Dean and Gracie really sleeping together?"

Theo glanced at Gracie, who quickly buried her head in her arms. "Of course Dean's sleeping with Gracie," he said easily. "Has been for months, in fact."

"The fuck?" Zara muttered as Juliet squealed. Gracie threw her arms up in the air, scowling at the three Ashcrofts.

"Wait, what?" Raina Cohen said, sliding in next to Zara. Gracie's last roommate glanced uncertainly around the table, her blue eyes blinking as she assessed the situation. "Dean and Gracie are together?"

"Oh yeah, they've been together for months," Jesse said, a gleam in his hazel eyes. "Dean tells me all the time how great Gracie is in—"

"Enough!" Gracie said loudly. "Jesse. Stop. Please."

Juliet jumped up from the table, clapping her hands. "I'm going to go tell Amaryllis," she declared, dashing off. Annalisse, who had been surprisingly silent the entire time, stuffed one last bite of pancake into her mouth before taking off after her friend.

It took Jesse all of three seconds to start dying of laughter. "I can't believe they bought that," he gasped. "Oh god, I cannot believe they fell for that."

"Wait," Raina said slowly, setting her plate down on the table. She unwrapped her plastic fork, eyeing each person for a few seconds. "You...*aren't* dating Dean?"

Gracie dropped her head on the table. Would she draw attention if she screamed?

"Of course not," Dean interrupted. Gracie jerked her head up to see him standing behind Zara. "You have my watch," he added, holding a hand out toward Theo. "I found Adams asleep last night on the couch and carried her upstairs. Those two spotted me and jumped to conclusions."

"That you didn't bother correcting," Gracie muttered in contempt.

"Aww, Gracie, don't be mad at me," Dean said with an irresistible grin. "It was just a bit of harmless fun. Besides, it's not like I said, 'Oh yeah, I carried her up here after she passed out because of how great I am in bed.'"

"Humble, too," Zara muttered, nudging her friend's shoulder. "Cheer up, Gracie. They'll forget about it in no time."

"They better." Gracie scowled, turning her glare on Dean.

## Allie Sarah

✭✭
✭

By the time Gracie settled into her usual seat next to Zara for lunch, the hall was nearly buzzing with rumors about her and Dean. Thankfully, the boys were sitting at a different table, but Juliet and Annalisse's magic had ensured that there wasn't a student who didn't know the name Gracie Adams. Everyone already knew who Dean was, but Gracie preferred to be inconspicuous. There was a reason she liked to spend her lunches in the library, and it wasn't because of the fictional characters she loved obsessing over.

"Everyone's staring at me," Gracie hissed to Zara.

"Just ignore them," Raina said wisely, dropping her plate down next to Gracie's. She tucked a strand of hair behind her ear before taking a sip from her water. "Trust me, ignoring them is the best thing you can do."

"Hey, Gracie, how did your test go?" Zara jumped in, successfully distracting Gracie from the Dean debacle.

"You had the same test," Gracie reminded her friend.

"Yes, but I don't care about it," Zara said off-handedly. She shoved a bite of pasta in her mouth. "I repeat: how did your test go?"

"I was a little distracted from this morning, but I think it went well," Gracie admitted. "I can't believe we still have lab after lunch, though. Like, we just had a test this morning. They should really give us a break."

"Gracie, if we had a break, you would spend it entirely in the library," Zara declared. "That's not a break, that's torture."

"I need to study," Gracie said determinedly. "The scholarship means my grades have to be up to a certain standard. I'm not like you, Zar. I can't afford to take time off from work."

Zara looked down, hiding what Gracie was sure was a disappointed look. "No, you're right. I'm sorry."

Gracie pressed her lips together before taking another bite of her sandwich. Sometimes she wished she was more like Zara, who could take nights off from homework to party in the common room and do sleepovers with the other dorms. She had seen firsthand how Zara got practically everything she wanted, just by throwing her last name around. But Gracie had studied hard to get into this school, and she wasn't about to throw it all away to play games and do karaoke or whatever else Zara did that caused her to stumble back into their room Saturday nights, fully sloshed. She would talk to Dean after classes and make him stop the rumors. Then she could go back to her study schedule, safely encased away from all the drama.

Gracie smiled to herself as she ate the last bites of her sandwich, grabbing a water bottle as she slung her bag over her shoulder. Talk to Dean, stop the rumors, get back to studying. Yes, it was a plan.

## Chapter Two

"Your homework is to read chapters four through six in the textbook," Dr. Jameson announced, gathering the papers on her desk together. "Clean up your stations, gather your things, and promptly and quietly—"

"—exit the room," Zara muttered next to Gracie, a smirk on her face. "Honestly, she says this after every lab. It gets so old."

Gracie smiled at her friend. "C'mon, we have a free hour before dinner. I'll play a game with you and do my homework later."

"You have a free hour," Zara said with a frown. "I have to go see Uncle Aaron."

Gracie winced. "What did you do, Zar?"

"I didn't do anything!"

"Yeah, and I'm the Queen of England," Gracie scoffed, her mind running through the plausible reasons Zara would be called to the principal's office. Since being founded by Julian and Trinity Ashcroft over 200 years ago, the number of Ashcrofts working at the boarding school had only grown. "It wouldn't be because your mom's here, would it?"

It was Zara's turn to laugh. "My mom actually show up? Please. You know she's only the 'official travel liaison' because Uncle Aaron took pity on her and made up some dumb job that doesn't exist. She's perfectly happy to use it as an excuse to stay as far away as possible."

"I suppose," Gracie said hesitantly. "But be careful, okay? He may be your uncle, but he's still the principal."

Zara nodded, smiling reassuringly at her best friend. "So, what will you be doing? Pre-Calculus? Spanish?"

"Committing murder," Gracie said casually, as if it were something she did every day.

Zara nearly choked on the gum she had just popped into her mouth. "Who-who's the unlucky victim?" she asked finally.

"Oh, he's no victim."

Zara nodded in understanding, before frowning and protesting, "Gracie, you can't just kill my brother because you feel like it."

"I will kill your brother and enjoy it," Gracie declared, huffing as a strand of her brown hair fell into her face. "As soon as I tie my hair back, of course." She grabbed a scrunchie from around her wrist and started wrapping it around her hair as she walked across the dining hall.

For anyone other than a freshman during the first week of school, Trinity was pretty easy to navigate. The administration had their offices near the main doors, to stop visitors from getting lost in the long hallways. The dining hall was connected to a large, empty room, which had multiple doorways leading to different classrooms. One door even led to a little patio, which was a nice place to eat when the weather was warm. The library was in the English wing, something which Gracie was infinitely grateful for. If it had been any further, she would have been late many, many times to Mrs. Dixon's class. Because of her tendency to eat quickly and then spend the rest of lunch in the library, Gracie knew the route like the back of her hand.

"Please don't kill my brother!" Zara called.

"No promises!" Gracie yelled back.

Five minutes later found Gracie outside of the Literature classroom, leaning against the wall and tapping her foot as she waited for class to officially end. She knew from Raina that all three male Ashcrofts were in last period English and hoped to catch Dean and make him pay.

The bell rang and Gracie pushed herself away from the wall, crossing her arms and scowling at the door.

Raina was the first one out. "Who pissed you off?" she remarked, before thinking about what she had said. "Ahh. He'll be out in a minute."

"He better," Gracie grumbled. "I have a bone to pick with him. You know, people have been coming up to me all day and asking if the rumors are true, if we're really dating, if I've really slept with Dean Ashcroft. I even had one girl ask me how much I paid Dean to orchestrate that entire scene! It's not funny," she added hastily as Raina attempted to hold back her grin.

"Admit it, that one is a little funny," Raina pointed out.

"Almost as funny when one of the older students came up to me and asked if we had used protection," Gracie said sarcastically.

Raina's mouth dropped open. "Someone really asked that?"

"Oh yeah," Gracie said. "Right in the middle of the crowded hallway. *Everyone* heard, and it somehow launched into a debate between glow in the dark versus glitter. I was ready to kill myself right then and there. *That* would've given them something real to talk about."

Raina laughed. "Want me to hold him down?" she asked, staring at the door as if it would open by itself.

"I got this," Gracie said, her gaze focused on the door as she bounced lightly on her feet.

Dean slapped Jesse on the shoulder as they exited English class. "Man, that was awesome. No homework *and* we spent half of class talking. How'd you manage that one?"

Jesse smirked. "You can get any teacher off topic if you try hard enough," he said smugly. "Mrs. D is no exception."

Theo shook his head. "Still, pretty impressive. We haven't managed to get her off Lit at all this year."

"I know," Jesse said with a wink.

"Dean Ashcroft!" a voice yelled.

"Someone's in trouble," Jesse said in a sing-song voice.

Dean turned to see Gracie Adams bearing down on him, her fists up, and an absolutely furious expression on her face. If looks could kill, he would be ten feet under right now. "Hey, Adams. What's up?"

Gracie took a step closer to him, forcing Dean to move backward. "What's up?" she hissed. "What's up?"

Dean looked around wildly, but his laughing cousins offered no help. "I thought you would be happy!" he improvised.

Gracie paused, her short ponytail whipping around. "Happy?"

Dean's shoulders relaxed, and he spoke his next words directly to Gracie's ponytail. "Yeah, we don't have to hide anymore! Look, love, I know we wanted to wait to tell people, but maybe this is a blessing in disguise!"

Gracie stalked forwards, practically pinning Dean to the wall. "Alright, then. Just one question. WHAT THE HELL WERE YOU THINKING?"

Dean laughed nervously. He'd annoyed Zara countless times, but Gracie was new territory. "Gracie. Dearest," he added as an afterthought. "You know exactly what I was thinking. Didn't I tell you all about it on our date?"

If it was even possible, Gracie's frown deepened, and Dean realized he had made a major mistake bringing up their "date." Thinking fast, he did the only thing he knew that might shut her up.

He kissed her.

⋆⋆⋆

Dean Ashcroft was kissing her.

Dean Ashcroft was kissing her, and she was kissing him back. His lips were minty and warm and slightly chapped, but it didn't really matter because he was a good kisser, and his hands were in her hair, and this was so much better than—

Wait.

Dean Ashcroft was kissing her.

*Dean Ashcroft* was kissing her, and there was a crowd of cheering students around them. His hand wrapped around the back of her neck, and that was when Gracie returned to reality.

She broke the kiss, shoving Dean away from her. He stumbled into the wall, a dazed expression on his face. "You-you—" she stammered, still catching her breath. "You kissed me!"

Dean shot her a cheeky smile. "You kissed me back."

"You kissed me!" Gracie repeated, still stunned.

Dean winced. "Yes?"

Growling, a feral glare appeared in Gracie's eyes. "You kissed me!" she shouted for the third time, using her four years of gymnastics lessons to leap on a suddenly apologetic-looking Dean.

"Don't kill me!" her best friend's brother exclaimed, shaking his head frantically as she wrapped her legs around his torso and began smacking his shoulder. Gracie shifted to hang off Dean's shoulder, using her upper arm strength to let her legs dangle free and alternate light kicks to his shins. "Jesse, Theo, a little help, *please*?"

"Oh no, cuz, you deserve this," Jesse said mildly.

"Have fun." Theo waved, backing away. "Oh hi, Mrs. Dixon," Gracie heard faintly, before Theo's words registered in her brain and she froze with Dean's hand on her wrist and one of her legs about to kick him where it hurt.

"What is going on here?" Mrs. Dixon demanded. Even though Gracie couldn't see her over Dean's shoulder, she instantly knew the stern teacher had her hands on her hips. "Young lady, get down this instan—Ms. Adams?"

Gracie dropped to the floor and put a good amount of distance between her and Dean. "I'm sorry!" She hung her head, blushing furiously. What was Mrs. Dixon thinking of her? She had never done anything like this before, and now, the strictest teacher in school just caught her attacking someone. Gracie was a good girl; this didn't happen to her!

Mrs. Dixon shook her head. "Ms. Adams, I don't even want to know why you were attacking Mr. Ashcroft like that, but regardless of the reason, you two have detention. Unfortunately, I used the last of my slips with Mr. Jesse Ashcroft last week, but rest assured, I will be finding you two later tonight to inform you of when and where it will take place."

A small whimper left Gracie's mouth, and she stared up at her teacher in horror. Out of the corner of her eye, she saw Dean arrange a chastised look on his face, but she couldn't wipe the terrified expression from her own. "D-detention?"

✯
✯ ✯

"And after they make you scrub the beakers in the chem lab, you have to help Coach Kaye organize all the balls," Dean continued. He rubbed his hands together. When Gracie had asked him about detention, Dean had happily taken the opportunity to spin a web of lies. It was too bad that Gracie was so innocent, she actually believed them.

Gracie gulped, freezing with one hand on the zipper of her backpack. "The giant cage of them in the gym closet?"

"Exactly that." Dean grinned wickedly. "You won't get back to your room until about two, maybe three in the morning."

"They can't do that."

"Sure, they can."

"No, they can't." Gracie turned to his cousins. "Jesse? Theo? Does that actually happen?"

Theo opened his mouth before closing it. "We-ell," he hedged, glancing between the two.

"What lie did you tell her this time, idiots?" Zara demanded, barging in between her two cousins.

"Nothing!" The trio of boys protested in unison.

Gracie shook her head. "Please tell me they're ly—wait, you're back. How was Principal Ashcroft?"

"You got sent to Uncle Aaron?" Dean's head whipped around to stare at his twin. His uncle doubled as the principal of Trinity High School, but he only called his nephews and niece to his office when he was upset or wanted something. In most cases, it was to yell at Zara for whatever idiotic stunt she had pulled.

Zara scoffed, tossing her hair over her shoulder. "Wanted to convince us to go home for Christmas."

"So why didn't he ask me?" Dean frowned. Thinking it over, he knew why he hadn't been asked. Dean would agree just to keep the peace, but Zara was the one that needed to be convinced.

"Because he tried to bribe me with new dresses and makeup."

Dean smirked. He knew his sister, and while she would get dolled up for special occasions, Zara hated the feeling of anything on her face. "You? Makeup? Please."

"I can wear makeup if I want," Zara argued, crossing her arms.

"So do it."

"I don't want to."

"I'm going to go to the library," Gracie interrupted the argument. She zipped her bag and slung it over one shoulder, picking up her water bottle and book from the floor. "Zara, I'll see you later."

"You're not going to eat?" Dean asked. "We're all going to get a snack."

"I'm not hungry."

Dean's eyes tracked the brunette as she headed down the hall, clutching a worn book to her chest. He had never really thought of Gracie Adams before, but now he found himself...fascinated by her.

"You're staring."

"Am not," Dean huffed, but he still shot one last look at where Gracie was disappearing around the corner. It had been a short kiss, and Gracie had been trying to kill him both before and after, so why was it the best kiss he had ever had, and one that he definitely wanted to repeat?

✯✯✯

"Your detention will be tonight with Dr. Patel," Mrs. Dixon informed Dean that evening at dinner, handing him one of the pink detention slips she was holding. "Please report to the physics classroom at 7pm, Mr. Ashcroft."

Dean groaned internally but shot a charming smile at his English teacher. "You got it, Mrs. D."

Zara snickered, watching as their teacher walked away. "How did you manage to get detention again? And so soon?"

"It's all your little friend's fault, actually," Dean informed her. "She attacked me after class."

"Gracie attacked you after class? You didn't tell me that. Hell, *Gracie* didn't tell me that."

"Oh yeah, everyone was watching," Jesse chimed in. "Dean got his ass kicked by a girl."

"What's wrong with being a girl?" Raina asked, putting her hands on her hips and glaring at him.

Jesse gulped. "Nothing. Absolutely nothing. I love girls!"

A mischievous look appeared on Raina's face. "You know, if you didn't, that would be okay," she said soothingly. "We'll accept you and support you in any...life decisions you want to make."

"Thank—wait, what?" Jesse said. "I don't get it." Theo smirked before leaning over and whispering something in his cousin's ear. Jesse's mouth fell open. "I'm not gay. I'm not gay! Dean, please tell Raina that I'm not gay."

"Are you saying there's a problem with being gay?" Zara cut in. She raised her arm, showing off the pink, purple, and blue bracelet that dangled from her wrist.

"No! Of course not!" Jesse exclaimed. "But I'm not. I'm very straight," he rambled. "Very, *very* straight."

Raina kept her poker face for all of three seconds before bursting into laughter. Jesse grinned at her sheepishly from across the table. Dean narrowed his eyes as he glanced between the two, catching a hint of something that hadn't been there a few days ago. He knew that the duo had hung out together last weekend when everyone else was busy, but Jesse hadn't mentioned any new developments in their relationship. He did know, however, that Raina was an extremely shy girl, and that nothing would happen with Dean, Zara, and Theo at the table.

"This is why we keep you around," Zara declared, holding up her hand up for a high five. Dean quickly intercepted the motion, smacking Zara's hand. "Ow! What was that for?"

"We have the *thing* to work on."

"No, we don't," Zara said, confused.

"Yes, we do," Dean countered. "Theo said he'd help us with it."

Dean could tell the exact moment that Theo understood. "Yes, I did! Come on, Zara."

"But–" Zara protested, flailing helplessly as Dean seized her arm and began dragging her away. "What was that for?" she cried when they were outside of the cafeteria.

Theo rolled his eyes. "You idiot, they *like* each other."

"Who?" Zara asked dumbly.

"Gwen Stefani and Blake Shelton," Dean said sarcastically. "No, the only other two people at the table!"

"No, they don't," Zara argued. "Jesse would tell me. Jesse tells me everything."

"Likely he hasn't realized it yet," Theo said.

Dean shook his head. "Sometimes I wonder how we're related."

"Because you're both idiots." Zara stuck her tongue out at her twin.

Dean ignored her. "A pretty girl likes me? I would know in seconds."

"And that's why you're two different people," Theo said smartly. "Because every person, no matter how alike they look or the genetics they share, is different. You can give two people the exact same situation, and they'll react differently."

Dean studied his cousin for a second. If Theo straightened his hair and added colored contacts, they would probably be able to pass as identical twins. But despite their similar looks, he would be the first to admit that he and Theo had very different personalities. "You know, I might be a science person, but I never really got into bio and genetics. Chem is just so much more interesting."

"I think they're all boring." Zara turned around and peered through the cafeteria doors. "Look, they're talking to each other! Oh, now Juliet's going over, surprisingly, without Annalisse. Ugh, she's going to ruin all our plans!"

"What plans?" Dean and Theo chimed in at the same time.

"We don't have any plans," Dean added.

"Well, now we do," Zara declared, huffing at the two boys. "Look, she's making Jesse get up and leave! Come on, let's go back in and let Juliet know she's not wanted there."

"I thought we wanted Jesse and Raina alone?" Theo frowned.

"Yeah, but if Jesse's leaving, there's no point in Raina being alone with Juliet," Zara explained. "I wouldn't wish that upon anyone. Now come on. I need partners-in-crime for this plotting."

Dean tuned his sister out as he followed her back into the cafeteria, barely paying attention as she and Juliet started arguing with each other. He was drawn back into the present when a loud bang echoed through the hall; the doors slamming against the walls a moment later.

His head, like everyone else's, shot up to take in the girl standing in the doorway. She was a familiar sight to the Trinity High students with curly hair that rivaled Zara's pulled into a tight ponytail, ebony eyes that matched both her hair and her disposition, and a smirk that was slowly curling across her painted red lips. She was wearing a leather jacket that seemed to be tailored to fit her perfectly—Dean knew for a fact that it had been—and a pair of studded tight black jeans that Dean figured cost more than his entire wardrobe. It was most certainly not the school uniform, and Dean could almost sense his uncle foaming at the mouth.

Glancing to his side, Dean caught the open-mouthed expression on Jesse's face, before it was quickly replaced by a look of sheer delight. Clearly, Jesse's best friend had kept her arrival a secret. It was the kind of thing she'd do, hoping to create the maximum surprise effect. She had clearly succeeded, with an entire room focused on her triumphant return.

Nicole Lawrence grinned wickedly as her eyes scanned the silent cafeteria, her smile stretching even wider as she spotted the teachers' table where the adults also sat in stunned silence.

"I'm back, bitches!"

## Chapter Three

"I can't believe I have detention. I've never had detention before! What if this goes on my permanent record? Will this go on my permanent record? I can't have this," she rambled, wringing her hands.

Dean rolled his eyes, walking alongside the shorter girl. "Chill out, you'll be fine."

"But they'll have us do some terrible task for hours and I won't get any sleep," Gracie said worriedly.

Dean sighed. "I was just kidding with you. We won't be doing anything bad. Probably just lines or cleaning."

"Lines," Gracie repeated. "I can do that."

"Thank god."

"Ahh, Mr. Ashcroft, Ms. Adams," Dr. Patel said from the door of the physics classroom, his arms folded over his chest. "You'll be cleaning for me tonight. I have to drop something off with another teacher, then I'll be back to supervise. I expect the tables cleaned, shelves dusted, etcetera. You know what to do, Mr. Ashcroft."

Gracie glanced sideways at Dean, wondering how many times he'd had detention before if he knew exactly what to do. Judging how he walked straight to the dark closet and pulled out supplies, she assumed plenty. He knew to head to the sink and wet a few of the rags, and she tracked the movement of his hands as he wrung one of them out, water dripping onto the button down he was wearing. Unlike her, he hadn't changed out of his uniform shirt, and Gracie watched, unable to look away as he shoved his sleeves up to his elbows. Her eyes stayed glued to his forearms as he wet another cloth, and she tracked a droplet of water as it ran down his skin.

"Adams," Dean said suddenly, breaking her out of her thoughts. He held out a dust cloth, and Gracie wrinkled her nose as she took it. "You do that half, I'll do this half," he instructed, not waiting for an answer. Gracie scowled at his back before reluctantly walking over to the windowsill. She began dusting slowly, taking extra care to make sure Dean wasn't in her line of sight.

"Alright, I'm leaving now," Dr. Patel announced. "I'll be back shortly. Try not to get into trouble, please." Gracie nodded, her heart sinking as she realized she'd be left alone with Dean.

"So," Dean began the moment the door closed, "how are you doing?"

"Fine, thank you," Gracie said stiffly, both wanting to be polite and to tell him to stop talking to her. The room was silent for a minute.

"Aren't you going to ask me how I'm doing?"

"No."

Dean huffed. "Well, you're a feisty one," he declared, dropping his rag on Gracie's table. She looked up, startled, to see him standing next to her. "So, Gracie Adams, how did you meet my sister?"

"You dyed her hair, and I helped her get the color out," Gracie answered.

It was Dean's turn to be surprised. He grabbed his backpack from the floor and set it on a chair, digging inside until he found a navy sweatshirt. "That was you? She never said who helped her."

Gracie shrugged, averting her eyes as he pulled the hoodie over his head. His hair was mussed when she glanced back at him, and she had to force herself to take a step back to stop her hands from smoothing it down. "That was a mean thing to do, anyway."

"I didn't know it would stain her hair," Dean said after a minute. "Well, I also didn't know it was kool-aid. I thought it was just water, but Jesse is an idiot and couldn't find the water bottles, so he put kool-aid in instead."

"Still, you shouldn't rig a door to dump water on people's heads," Gracie insisted.

"Hey, Zara deserved it. She was the one who stole our towels from the bathroom. We had to walk through the halls naked."

Gracie blushed. "I don't remember that happening in freshman year," she said after a moment.

"You wouldn't," Dean said smugly. "Theo borrowed a towel from someone else and told everyone to clear off the hallway because of a gas leak or something, and then we made a run for it."

"I remember that!"

"One of our better pranks," Dean said proudly. "The best type of prank is when you're not even trying to prank and you still do it anyway, you know?"

Gracie wrinkled her nose. "I'm not much of a prankster."

Dean stared at Gracie for a second. "Okay, we're going to change that this year," he decided.

"When?" Gracie asked, lifting an eyebrow. "In case you haven't realized, we're in detention right now."

"Well, not now, obviously," Dean said. "Speaking of now, though, you're doing it wrong."

Gracie looked down at the table. "What?"

"Here," Dean slid closer, making her gulp slightly. "Don't use a really wet one on the table. It's made of wood. Use the slightly damp one and then the dry one right after." He picked up one of the cloths and handed it to her.

"Thanks," Gracie murmured. "You seem very well versed in how to clean a table."

Dean laughed. "Yeah, I've done this before. I also have class in this room, since I'm taking both chem and physics this semester. So I know this room well."

"Do you get detention often?" Gracie asked curiously.

"Kinda," Dean admitted. "Jesse, Theo, and I have played a bunch of pranks, and, well, we got caught on some of them."

"Like your prank war last year." She winced at the memory. "Zara was in detention for days after that."

"So were we." Dean laughed. "But it was so worth it."

Gracie shook her head. "Nothing is worth detention," she declared. "Doesn't it go on your permanent record?"

Dean shrugged. "Not sure, but I don't really care. As long as I've got good grades, I don't need to worry about the rest of it."

"Oh." That was a foreign concept to her, not having to worry about what she would do past high school. Gracie always had to work for everything in her life, and she never gave anything less than 110 percent.

"School's pretty important to you, though, isn't it?" Dean asked after a moment.

Gracie nodded before realizing that he wasn't looking at her. "Yeah. I'm here on a scholarship, so I have to keep my grades up."

"Still, you're always studying," Dean insisted. "I see you in the common room late at night."

Gracie blinked. "I didn't know anyone else was awake then."

"I don't really sleep well," Dean said in a low voice.

"I'm sorry."

"It's fine. I'm used to it."

They both fell silent again, cleaning opposite sides of the same table and sneaking glances at each other every few seconds.

Gracie scrubbed her side of the table harder, wishing that Dr. Patel would return so detention could be over. Even if he kept them longer, there would still be another person in the room to counter the tension. She was consciously aware of Dean moving closer to her with every swipe.

"Hey, what did the table do to you?" Dean joked. Gracie looked down, surprised, to see that she had been furiously wiping the table to the point that the pink sharpie had partially come off.

"Nothing," she muttered, turning pointedly away from Dean.

Dean took a step closer, placing a hand on her arm. "Hey, you—"

"Don't touch me!" Gracie exclaimed, ripping her arm out of his grasp.

"Sorry."

Gracie looked up just in time to see him take a step away. "It's not you," she muttered, feeling bad at seeing the hurt look on his face. "I...I just..." Her voice trailed off. "I don't know."

"Are you not okay with people touching you?" he asked her.

Gracie shrugged. "It comes and goes. Depends on the person. Anxiety. It's fun, right?"

Dean's lips twitched. "You're rambling."

"Am I?"

His face turned somber. "I'm sorry about earlier. For kissing you without warning and all that. I just... well, there's no excuse. I shouldn't have done that."

"It's okay," Gracie told him, realizing a second later that it really *was* okay. For some reason, she felt comfortable around Dean. Was it because he was Zara's brother? But Gracie didn't want to kiss Zara.

Not that she wanted to kiss Dean either.

Or did she?

"Your hands are shaking," he said gently, moving his own to hover over hers. "Can I touch them?"

After a few seconds, Gracie nodded, the tension leaving her as his warm hands settled on top of hers.

"What are we doing?" Gracie whispered so quietly she wasn't even sure she had spoken.

But she must have because Dean breathed, "I don't know." His gaze flickered down to her lips, which Gracie only caught because she had been staring into his hazel eyes. His irises darkened as he gazed at her, an unmistakable look of desire on his face. His hand wrapped around her back, before snaking up to leave ghost-like touches on her neck.

"Miss Adams! Mr. Ashcroft!" the surprised voice of Dr. Patel exclaimed.

Gracie let out a small *eep* as she disentangled herself from Dean and shot to the other side of the room.

"Dr. Patel!" she squeaked, chancing a glance at the boy she had almost been about to kiss. Dean was leaning against the table she had just been pressed against, a nonchalant expression on his face.

"Hey Dr. P," he said casually, crossing his arms. "What's up?"

Dr. Patel stared at him for a second. "You. On your way to Mrs. Dixon's office."

A slow grin appeared on Dean's face. "Awesome, I love visiting Mrs. Dixon. What's the occasion?"

"Handing her your detention slip for tomorrow," Dr. Patel replied, grabbing a pad from inside his desk. He scribbled something on the paper before ripping it off, tearing it in two, and handing one of the pieces to Dean. "Miss Adams?"

Gracie walked slowly to the front of the room and took the paper.

"You two can go now," Dr. Patel announced. "Go give those to Mrs. Dixon, please. I'll see you both back here tomorrow, same time."

Gracie walked three steps out of the classroom, waited until the door shut, and spun around to glare at Dean. "I hate you," she hissed.

Dean laughed. "You love me."

"No, I'm pretty sure I hate you."

"There's a fine line between love and hate," Dean said in a sing-song voice.

Gracie growled at him before storming ahead, crushing the detention slip in her fist as she stomped away. The students she passed glanced at her curiously, but Gracie ignored them, intent on getting as far away from Dean Ashcroft as possible.

"Hey!" Dean called from behind her. "Hey! Adams! Gracie!"

Gracie huffed. "What do you want?" she cried, spinning around.

"You already got me detention, twice! What more do you want from me?"

A hurt expression flashed across Dean's face, but it disappeared in an instant. Gracie glanced around the halls desperately, trying to figure out a way to escape from the conversation, but the crowd of unfamiliar girls seemed unlikely to help her.

"Why Gracie," Dean cooed, taking a step closer as a sly grin appeared on his face. "That wasn't what you were telling me a couple of minutes ago. In fact, if I recall correctly, you had no problem with the reason we got detention again, isn't that right, sweetheart?"

Gracie flushed. "Don't call me sweetheart," she hissed.

"So you're saying you enjoyed our kiss," Dean said triumphantly.

"I will hurt you," Gracie threatened.

Dean smirked at her, running a lazy hand through his dark hair. "You didn't deny it."

"I, uh, ah," Gracie spluttered. "I hate you!"

☆☆☆

Dean plopped onto his bed with a cheerful grin, beaming at his cousins. "Good evening, Jesse, Theo," he said brightly, grabbing a squishy ball from his nightstand and tossing it up in the air. "Isn't it a lovely day today?"

Theo eyed him skeptically. "What's put you in a good mood?"

Dean sighed happily, not wanting to admit that it was because Gracie had almost kissed him for the second time. "Oh, the enjoyment of Gracie Adams' face earlier."

"You know Zar's going to kill you for messing with her best friend," Theo pointed out.

"Ugh, why do you always have to be the voice of reason?" Jesse snorted.

"Well, somebody's got to be, and it's most definitely not going to be you," Theo shot back. Jesse stuck his tongue out at Theo. "Oh, how mature!"

Dean dropped the ball onto his bed, sitting upright and stretching out his legs. "Don't worry guys," He spoke over his two arguing cousins. "I'm sure it'll all blow over tomorrow, so there's no need to worry about Zara's wrath. Hey, are you guys going home for Christmas?"

Theo stopped arguing immediately. "I don't know yet," he said. "On one hand, Mom's home, but on the other hand, Dad's got to stay as vice principal and Mom can just come up here if she wants."

"I'm going to stay," Jesse chimed in. "My parents are going to be gallivanting throughout Europe or something, and I'd rather not spend Christmas in a hotel room by myself."

Theo snorted. "*Gallivanting*. Where the hell do you get a word like that?"

Jesse flushed and turned to Dean, ignoring Theo. "Are you?"

"Well, I've kind of got no choice," Dean admitted. "Mom's not going to be here because, well, why would she want to spend a family holiday with her family? Uncle Aaron and Aunt Becky will be here for sure, and I know Zar's considering staying."

"What's her other option?" Jesse asked curiously.

"Go home with Adams," Dean replied. Jesse nodded, and it seemed to be the end of the conversation as the trio separated. Dean brushed his teeth and headed back into the main room, more than ready to go to sleep.

A hand on his arm stopped him from his date with his pillow. Dean tossed a glance over his shoulder before grinning. "Now, Theo," he teased. "If you wanted to climb into bed with me, all you had to do was ask."

Theo nodded his head towards the bed, ignoring the joke. "In," he ordered. "SCT."

Dean nodded seriously and sat down, crossing his legs. Years ago, he and Theo had a major argument because Dean thought Theo was joking about something when it turned out he was being serious. After they had both lost television privileges for a month, they had agreed to figure out a code so it wouldn't happen in the future. From then on, when either of the two called SCT, or Serious Conversation Time, all joking and pretenses stopped immediately.

When they were younger, Dean and Zara had been as thick as thieves. As they grew older, Dean, Theo, and Jesse gravitated towards each other, wanting to play cars and trucks without an annoying girl bothering them. Zara had often been left to play dolls alone, but after Dean and Theo started actually talking to each other instead of just arguing and playing pranks, Jesse had joined her at the tea party table. Even though the trio were best friends and would defend Zara in a heartbeat, Dean and Theo had formed a special bond, while Jesse and Zara would always stick together.

"What's up?" Dean asked. "You, or me?"

"You," Theo said, a serious look on his face.

Dean sighed, banging his hand against the bedspread. "My mom," he said, Theo's nod confirming the reason for the SCT. "You want me to give her another chance?"

"Bingo. I know she doesn't deserve one. But she's still your mother."

"A mother who left us with our aunt and uncle for three years while she ran off to California," Dean reminded him. "We were *three*, Theo. Do you know what it's like to be a three-year-old, dropped off at your aunt's and uncle's, and all you want is your mother, but she's not there?"

"I was there," Theo pointed out. "I was the 'aunt's and uncle's' you were dropped off at, Dean. I remember."

Dean groaned, scooting back until he was leaning against the wall. "Sometimes I wish I knew who my father was," he confided. "It's got to be impossible now though, finding one of my mom's one-night stands from nearly seventeen years ago."

"Well, you've always got me," Theo said firmly. "I'm way better than any dad."

Dean chuckled. "Thanks, Theo."

"Plus, there's Uncle Aaron and Aunt Becky and my mom and my dad and sometimes Uncle Jonas and Aunt Lisabeth when they're not traveling, and Zara and Jesse and—"

"Who set him off?!" Jesse cried in frustration as he exited the bathroom, a towel slung over his shoulder. "No! Dean, you know how he gets when he lists the Ashcroft family! What did you say?"

"Nothing!" Dean exclaimed, throwing his hands up, the perfect picture of innocence. "He started all on his own."

"—and cousin Marley, and her children, and second cousin Ryder—"

Jesse groaned. "Theo, shut the fuck up!"

Theo just grinned at him. "—and of course, great-uncle Aaron the first and great-aunt Sarah—*oof*!" he was cut off by a pillow smacking into his head. "Jesse!"

Dean laughed and grabbed the nearest pillow, the SCT over for now. He knew the topic would come up again later, but for now, he was happy to join in on the pillow fight between his two cousins.

## Chapter Four

"Wakey-wakey," a familiar voice sang. Gracie groaned, rolling over and shoving her pillow over her head.

"No," she mumbled, flopping an arm over the side of the bed. "Tired."

"Jeez, girl, how late were you up?" the voice exclaimed.

"Not late," Gracie muttered sleepily. Was she dreaming? If so, why did she respond in her dream? And why would her dream snatch away her pillow? That wasn't a dream, that was a nightmare.

"Don't lie to me, girlie."

Gracie peeked open one eye. "I think I'm dreaming," she said, her voice riddled with sleep. "Look Zar, Nicky's here. But Nicky's in California, so I'm dreaming." She rubbed her face, unsure whether it was her eyes or her mind playing tricks on her.

"Not a dream," Nicole said cheerfully, tossing Gracie's pillow onto the bed. "Wake up, bitch."

Gracie's eyes widened, and after a moment of staring at the girl in front of her, she shot up in bed. "Nicole? What are you doing here?"

"Going to school, duh," Nicole rolled her eyes, checking her nails for imaginary chips as she moved to the foot of Gracie's bed. "I convinced daddy dearest to transfer me back. You fell asleep before I got back to the room last night."

Gracie nodded, yawning as she swung her feet out of bed. She accepted the explanation without question, knowing that Nicole had her parents wrapped around her finger. "'Kay. I'm going to use the bathroom. You should get dressed," she added, noticing that Nicole was still in her pajamas.

By the time Gracie returned to the room, Nicole's velvet shorts and tank top had disappeared, replaced by the pleated skirt and white top that all Trinity girls were required to wear during class hours.

"It's only been two months and I've forgotten how to tie a tie," Nicole was complaining to Zara, who was standing in front of her, looping the fabric around the other girl's neck.

"And you managed to get detention before you even made it to your dorm room," Zara added with a chuckle. "Even I've never done that."

Nicole shrugged. "In retrospect, cursing at the teachers was not one of my brightest ideas. But what are they going to do? Daddy dearest is one of the biggest donors here. They can't exactly expel me. They were practically begging for me to come back."

Gracie slipped her arms into her own button-down shirt, carefully knotting the buttons. "Where are Juliet and Annalisse?" she asked.

Zara smirked, a wicked grin flashing on her face. "*Somebody* told them that Theo was off to breakfast early. They left so quickly Juliet almost forgot to apply her lip gloss."

"Almost," Nicole chuckled. "She ran back here, complaining the entire time about how Annalisse would have Theo all to herself."

Gracie snorted. "And where is Theo?"

"Hell if I know," Zara said airily. "Come on, I want food." Gracie nodded in agreement, following her friend out of the room. The trio walked into the spacious common room, and Nicole immediately let out a squeal of excitement.

"Jesse!" she cried, flinging herself at the redhead.

*The Gossip Games*

Jesse spun around from where he was standing with his cousins by the fireplace. "Nicole!"

Gracie grinned at the two of them. Nicole had been moaning for weeks about how she had been separated from her best friend due to switching schools.

"Are they dating?" Raina asked, appearing behind Gracie.

Gracie let out a small squeak, placing a hand over her heart. "You scared me!"

"Sorry," Raina said, not sounding sorry at all. She ran a hand through her pale hair, watching Nicole and Jesse with a frown. "Are they?"

Zara glanced between the two. "No, they're just best friends. Oh, you haven't formally met Nicole yet, have you? You were already asleep when she got back. She's the sixth person in our dorm. Her parents transferred her to another school for this year, but she managed to convince them to transfer her back. You saw her arrival at dinner last night, but she had to go speak to Uncle Asshole immediately."

"Don't worry, she and Jesse are just friends," Gracie chimed in. "They're very close, but they've never given any indication of it becoming something more."

"Plus, Jesse seemed really into you yesterday," Zara added.

"Okay," Raina said uncertainly, her delicate fingers playing with her Star of David necklace. "If you're friends with her, she must be nice." Zara and Gracie exchanged looks and snickered, Raina's eyes flickering between the two of them. *Nice* was the last word they would use to describe Nicole. Sometimes they forgot Raina had only transferred to Trinity this year. She fit into their group so well it was as if she had been there since freshman year, just like the rest of them.

Zara turned to Gracie. "So how was detention last night? I meant to stay up, but I fell asleep in the middle of reading my English book. I'm telling you, they choose those things just to torture us."

Gracie winced, focusing on Zara's first sentence instead of

getting into yet another argument about schoolbooks and whether they were decent reading material. "We-ell," she hedged, "I've got detention again tonight."

"How'd you manage that?" Zara asked, looking impressed.

"Dean," was all Gracie said.

Zara nodded knowingly. "I love him, but he can be a real pain in the ass."

"Oh, talking about me again," Dean cooed, approaching the three girls and slinging an arm around his sister's shoulder.

"Eww, get off me," Zara shrieked, batting his hands away.

Dean shook his head, grinning as he backed up. "Well, hello, on this lovely, lovely morning, Gracie," he said pleasantly. "Raina. Sister."

"Idiot," Zara responded in greeting, crossing her arms.

"Well, somebody's in a good mood this morning," Dean commented.

"I'm in a good mood every morning," Zara corrected. "Seeing you just ruins it."

An offended look appeared on Dean's face. "I'm very hurt."

"I very much don't care," Zara said bluntly, before walking towards the door.

Dean sighed. "Ahh, the joys of having a twin sister. Don't you just love the constant strife?"

Gracie rolled her eyes and followed Zara.

"I wasn't finished speaking!" Dean yelled after her.

"Well, I was finished listening!"

☆☆☆

"See no one told you life was gonna be this way," Nicole warbled a couple minutes later.

Zara groaned, shoving her head into her hands. "Nicole. Hun. You have many talents, but singing is not one of them."

Nicole pouted. "But I want to sing for my next TikTok!" she exclaimed. "I just hit 25k followers."

"Do *not* sing that song," Gracie chimed in, grabbing a piece of toast from the plate in front of her. "Or any song."

"But it's perfect since I have so many new friends!" Nicole protested.

Gracie sighed. "Trust me. Don't sing."

Nicole ignored her friend, setting up the phone again. "Gracie, want to make a TikTok with me?"

"I'll pass, but thanks," Gracie replied.

"I think you should."

"I think I shouldn't."

"Gracie would love to," Dean cut in, sliding in next to Raina. He snatched the apple from Jesse's plate and took a bite, chewing, before directing his next question to Nicole. "What's Gracie doing?"

"TikTok," Nicole said.

"*Nothing!*" Gracie said loudly, hoping to drown out Nicole's words.

"I'll make a TikTok with you," Dean continued, as if Gracie hadn't spoken. "Your fans will love me."

"They're called followers," Nicole said. "But sure. You're cute, I guess."

"I am extremely sexy," Dean declared, putting his hands up as if to emphasize his point. "How dare you call me anything less."

Grabbing an apple as an excuse to hold her hand up to her mouth, Gracie bit back a snicker.

"I can see you laughing, Gracie Adams," Dean said. "But don't worry. We all know you're in love with me. It's only a matter of time before you admit it."

Eyebrows raised, she cocked her head. "Really?"

"Mhm."

"I think it's the other way around."

"You wish."

"Do I?"

"Course you do."

"Better watch yourself," Gracie shot back.

Dean paused. "What's that supposed to mean?"

Gracie grabbed her bag as she stood up. "Figure it out."

✯✯
✯

Gracie had no idea what had come over her back in the dining room. Arguing and threatening someone? Those behaviors weren't like her at all! She stormed down the hallway, barely even noticing where she was going until she bumped into something hard.

"Whoa!" an amused voice said. Gracie lifted her eyes to see a tall, well-built boy standing in front of her. He looked similar to Dean, actually, with dark wavy hair and a warm smile that wouldn't look out of place on her "boyfriend's" face.

"Sorry," she squeaked, hurriedly taking a step back. "Um, sorry."

"It's fine," the boy chuckled.

"Still bumped into you, I'm sorry," Gracie babbled, wringing her hands.

"Hey, no worries." The boy shot her a smile, and she had a sudden urge to spill her deepest, darkest secrets. "Sadly, I'm kinda used to girls throwing themselves at me."

Gracie laughed nervously, pushing a strand of hair behind her ear. "Well, I better be going," she said, looking down at her shoes.

"Wait," the boy stopped her as she made to move past him. "What's your name?"

She blushed. "Gracie."

"Well, it was lovely to meet you, Gracie," the boy smiled. "I'm Blake."

The bell rang, and Gracie instinctively looked up at the speakers with a gasp. "Oh, no, I'm late!" she exclaimed.

"What class do you have?" Blake asked curiously.

"English. Mrs. Dixon," Gracie said quickly, before waving and running down the hall.

"See you later!" Blake called after her.

※

Gracie slid into her seat just as the second bell rang, giving Zara a relieved smile.

"Just in time," her best friend commented, reaching out to squeeze Gracie's hand. "What took you so long? You stormed out of breakfast and I couldn't find you, so I thought you came here."

"Oh, I ran into this guy," Gracie said. She leaned closer so Zara could hear her in the crowded classroom. "He was really cute. I bumped into him and I couldn't speak at all and ended up stumbling over all my words. His name is—"

"Good morning," Mrs. Dixon announced, setting her bag on the desk. "A reminder, you have your essay on *The Catcher in the Rye* due next week. You will not have any more class time to work on this." Zara groaned from Gracie's right side. "Today, we'll be partnering up and discussing where we see the title in the novel and what it means. You may pick your partners, but if I see you chatting, you'll be doing this for homework tonight."

Gracie turned to Zara instantly. "So, have you actually read the book?"

"We-ell," Zara hedged. "I know what happens."

"Zara!"

"It was boring!" Zara defended herself. "I read like 50 pages, but then I fell asleep and ended up just looking at SparkNotes for the rest. Don't shoot me, Gracie. You're like the only person who actually reads the books."

Gracie huffed but didn't contradict her words. "Fine then, tell me what we're talking about."

"We're talking about the scene in *The Catcher in the Rye* where

Holden sees a kid playing and singing a song about bodies in the rye," Zara said smugly.

"He wasn't playing, but I'll give it to you. And I think that Holden just wants to keep everyone young forever."

"Like Peter Pan."

"Yeah, like Peter Pan," Gracie agreed. "He wants to preserve the innocence of childhood and stop children from 'falling off the cliff' of being an adult, as the book says. Because he couldn't save Allie and he can't save himself."

"Very good, Miss Adams," Mrs. Dixon said, stopping by their desks. "Continue the discussion, and could I have a few minutes of your time after class?"

Gracie exchanged a nervous look with Zara. "Um, okay."

"What do you think she wants?" Zara asked in a hushed tone as soon as the teacher was out of their earshot.

Gracie shrugged. "I have no clue. I've done all my homework, I've never been late to class, I never had detention until—" she dropped her pen on her desk, her mouth wide open in shock. "Oh my god, do you think it's because I got detention?"

"Doubt it," Zara reassured her. "I've had detention multiple times, and I've never had to speak to Mrs. D."

Gracie worried through the rest of class, ignoring Zara's attempts to calm her. When the bell rang, she almost fell out of her seat in her hurry to reach Mrs. Dixon's desk. It took pushing past multiple classmates, nearly stepping on a stray pencil and a dropped notebook, but Gracie managed to make it to the front just as her teacher stood.

"Am I failing?" she blurted out.

A surprised look appeared on Mrs. Dixon's face. She wasn't a teacher that was easily rattled, and her graying hair, perpetual stern expression, and narrowed eyes led to the impression that she wasn't a teacher to be messed with. "Failing? Of course not. I just wanted to talk to you about some rumors I've heard lately."

"Oh," Gracie breathed a sigh of relief. She moved slightly to the

*The Gossip Games*

side as one of her classmates hurried out of the room, before tensing up again. "What rumors?"

"There have been rumors about you and Dean Ashcroft circulating the school," Mrs. Dixon explained. "And after the scene I witnessed the other day, I wanted to check in with you."

Gracie flushed, looking down at her shoes. "Everything's okay. Dean and I..." she paused, not sure how to phrase her next words.

"Are...are you two using protection?" Mrs. Dixon asked carefully.

"What? No!" Gracie exclaimed. "We're not—I haven't, that is, um..."

"It's okay for teenagers to explore themselves and their bodies," Mrs. Dixon continued, talking over Gracie's sputterings.

"Dean and I aren't together! I just fell asleep, and he carried me to my bed so I wouldn't sleep in a chair all night. The next day there were all these rumors about us! Nothing's going on between us."

Mrs. Dixon frowned. "You know some of those rumors came from Mr. Ashcroft himself, right?"

"Yes, he's having a great time encouraging all this," Gracie said dryly. "Seems to think it's funny."

Mrs. Dixon let out a small chuckle, moving to sit behind her desk. "You know, when I was younger, if a boy messed with us, we just messed with him back."

"Messed with him back?"

"Oh yes," Mrs. Dixon nodded. "And since I've been working here, there have been several girls wanting revenge on various guys. Have you heard of the *Mean Girls* incident?"

Gracie racked her brain, before remembering something Zara had told her in their first year. "Not really," she said hesitantly. "Just that there was a guy and a girl who pranked each other with stuff from the movies."

"The guy had just seen *Mean Girls* and decided to cut holes in a girl's t-shirts," Mrs. Dixon explained. "Like they did to Regina in

*Mean Girls*. She got revenge by collecting awful photos of him to make a burn book before pasting the pictures all over school."

Gracie laughed.

"That was the last time the administration showed *Mean Girls* as a movie night," Mrs. Dixon added. "Gracie, you're a very responsible girl and I trust that you'll act admirably in the coming weeks, but don't let Mr. Ashcroft have all the fun. You're only young once, you know."

Gracie's mouth dropped open, shocked at her teacher's words. Was she really encouraging her to play pranks on Dean? Besides, that was his specialty, not hers.

"B-but you're a teacher! Shouldn't you want to keep peace between your students?"

Mrs. Dixon chuckled. "I think we all knew that peace was lost the minute the Ashcroft children entered Trinity. Besides, I can't see any harm in encouraging you to have a little fun. You're an extremely hardworking student, and I think Mr. Ashcroft's influence would be good for you."

Gracie stared at her teacher. Had she *met* the Ashcrofts? No one would ever call them a good influence. "Um, thank you. I have to get to lunch."

As quick as she could, Gracie gathered her bag and practically raced out of the classroom, leaving Mrs. Dixon and her odd comments alone.

She didn't want to get pulled into a prank war. Gracie knew firsthand how terrible those were and wanted to avoid one at all costs. But revenge? Plotting was never really her thing. That was more Zara's style than hers.

Although, she was really mad at Dean, and if anyone deserved to be revenged against, it *was* him. Gracie nodded to herself, the beginnings of a plan forming in her mind. Peeking into the cafeteria, a smile appeared on her face as she noticed Juliet sitting down at a table which held Dean, Theo, a couple of boys she recognized from the dorm, and a frustrated-looking Zara. Her red-headed best friend had a fork dangling halfway from her fingers and a scowl on her face as she had to move over to make room for Juliet. Theo was ignoring the cafeteria chaos, smartly keeping his earbuds in as he ate his pasta. Deciding she wasn't really hungry, Gracie skipped the buffet and headed straight for her friends' table. She tuned out the noise of the 200 plus people in the room and focused her full attention on Dean, giving him her best innocent smile.

"Hello Dean."

## Chapter Five

"Hello Gracie," Dean said hesitantly, not sure what she wanted. Gracie wouldn't talk to him without a reason, especially not with that sly grin of hers. Something had to be up, and he would bet money that it had to do with the way she daintily crossed her legs and turned her body to face his.

"You know, Dean," Gracie said, snagging one of Zara's pretzels and ignoring the redhead's glare. "I've been thinking."

Dean nodded. "Well, that's only natural, Adams. I would hope that you would learn to think by now."

"And I was thinking," Gracie spoke loudly over Dean, "you were right."

Dean blinked at her. "Sorry, say that again?"

"You were right," Gracie repeated. Dean glanced between the occupants of the table, wondering where she was going with this. "Guys, I have a confession to make. Dean and I *have* been secretly dating. We didn't tell anyone because we weren't sure how people would react, but Dean had the right idea. I want people to know about us."

Zara dropped the cup she was holding. Water splashed all over her fingers, but she ignored it. "What did you just say?"

"Dean was telling the truth," Gracie continued patiently. "I'm sorry for lying, guys. We just weren't sure how everyone would react."

"Whoa, whoa, hold on," Dean tried, but Gracie cut him off, wrapping an arm around his shoulders and pressing a kiss to his cheek. He leaned closer unconsciously, his nose catching a whiff of strawberry. Her shampoo, maybe?

Gracie pulled away and stood up. "I'll see you around," she said, before winking at Dean and walking away.

Dean sat in his seat for a minute, dumbfounded. Had Gracie just told everyone that they were dating? He hadn't sleep-asked-her-out, had he? He wasn't sure what to make of this new development. When Zara began laughing, he grabbed his bag, untangled himself from the table, and shot her the finger before running after Gracie.

"Adams! Hold up!"

✯✯✯

Gracie grinned as she walked out of the lunchroom, mentally counting. As she reached ten, she heard footsteps hurrying behind her, before a shout echoed in her ears.

"Adams! Hold up!"

Gracie spun around to face Dean, a sly smile on her face. "Why hello, boyfriend," she said in a sickeningly sweet voice. "Did you forget something?"

Dean growled. "You know that's not the truth."

"That's not what you've been saying," Gracie said innocently, batting her eyelashes at him.

"You know what happened," Dean hissed, stepping closer. "It was all just a joke!"

Gracie tilted her head to the side, her hair falling over her shoulder. "Okay then, why don't you go tell everyone that?" A slow smirk spread across her face as she watched Dean's expression change, realization dawning on him.

"Sneaky," he said somewhat admiringly, taking another step closer. "But I would *never*. If anybody's giving up, it's going to be you."

"Are you sure about that?" Gracie asked, dropping her voice so no one could hear. With how close they were standing, any bystander would assume that they were about to lip-lock.

"Oh, I'm sure," Dean said confidently. "You know, Gracie, it's surprisingly hot to see you like this." Gracie flushed, mentally kicking herself. She knew that was exactly what the infuriating boy wanted. True enough, a cocky grin appeared on Dean's face. "Dean, one," he said slowly. "Adams," he paused for dramatic effect, "zero."

Gracie crossed her arms before taking a step closer to Dean. "Are you sure about that?" she whispered, tilting her chin up. Purposefully, she turned her gaze to Dean's lips. It was Dean's turn to swallow as her lips almost met his.

"Gracie, one; Dean, one," she said, spinning on her heel and walking away.

☆
☆ ☆

D ean blinked.
He blinked again.
He looked around the hall, but Gracie was gone.

A small smile crept onto his face and Dean pushed it away. He shook his head, getting rid of all the thoughts of Gracie's soft, inviting lips and the smell of her strawberry hair.

"You won that one," he admitted quietly as he raced down the hall. Dean spun around, made a quick stop in the cafeteria to grab his two cousins from their tables, and then dragged them to their shared dorm.

"Why are we here?" Theo complained once they reached the

room. "I was listening to my music."

"Seriously, I was eating lunch with Nicole." Jesse flopped down on Theo's bed, causing the brunette to let out a yelp.

"I need to beat Gracie Adams," Dean said determinedly. He paused, but neither Jesse nor Theo responded. "This is the part where you talk."

"Oh, of course, you need to," Jesse said sarcastically.

"I'm not taking part in any sort of physical violence," Theo added.

"No, no," Dean said hurriedly. "Win against her, not physically beat her."

"Okay," Theo said. "Nope. I still have no idea of what you're talking about."

Dean huffed. "Gracie Adams. Zara's best friend."

"Yes, we know who she is," Theo said patiently. "I just don't know why you want to beat her and what you want to beat her in."

Dean paced back and forth across the room. "What do you know about this whole 'me and Adams dating' thing?" he asked, making quotation marks in the air. "People shut up when I come near, but you guys must have heard some of the rumors."

"The entire school thinks you're dating," Theo said. "Actually, they all think that you're sleeping together, but the majority won't say that to my face. I walked out of our room earlier and there were a bunch of people in the hall, and they all wanted to know when you two got together."

"Someone asked Gracie how much she paid you," Jesse chimed in.

Dean and Theo turned to stare at him. "Why—" Dean started, before shaking his head. "Okay. Whatever. You two know it's all fake, right?"

"Course," Theo said easily.

Jesse frowned and said, "You know, if you two really were dating, you could tell us."

"Jesse!" Dean exclaimed. "We're not dating!"

"Alright, alright," Jesse threw up his hands. "Yes, I know," he sighed dramatically.

"Good, because I played along as a joke and Gracie got mad," Dean continued. "So she said that it was all real, just to get me to admit the truth."

"Did it work?" Theo asked at the same time Jesse said, "Did you fall for it?"

"No," Dean snorted. "Give me some credit. But now I need to beat Adams at her own game."

"You're going to trick her into telling the truth," Theo realized.

"Brilliant deduction, Sherlock!" Dean exclaimed, jumping onto his bed and thrusting a hand in the air. "I will be victorious!" He stabbed the air, accidentally punching his hand into the ceiling. "Ow, ow, fuck, that hurt," he whined. Jesse and Theo snickered. "We'll see who's laughing when Adams tells everyone she was lying," Dean mumbled to himself, cradling his arm against his chest.

☆☆☆

Gracie sat down on Zara's bed, her arms crossed. "I don't think this is a good idea," she said hesitantly.

Zara rolled her eyes, sitting down next to her friend and throwing an arm around her shoulders. "Gracie, Gracie, Gracie, Gracie," she sighed. "Dean *will* be trying to get back at you. There's no denying it. He's my brother, unfortunately. I know how his mind works."

Nicole snorted, pushing herself off of the wall to lie down on the bed next to Gracie. "Pass me the black nail polish. And c'mon Gracie, wouldn't it be fun to one-up Dean for once? It's been a while since someone pranked him."

Gracie shrugged. "That's not really me, though."

"Gracie, that trio has been on top of everything for as long as we've been here," Nicole said. "Everyone adores them. They can do no wrong. As their friends, it's our duty to knock them down a peg.

Have you heard some of the names they've been called? Seriously, we'd be doing them a favor. We can't let their heads get too big."

"Oh my God, the Unholy Trinity just waved at me," Zara mocked, standing up and fanning herself with a book from her bedside table. "Oh, they're so cute!"

"Please," Nicole rolled her eyes. "That name isn't even good."

Gracie bit her lip. "I don't know. I know I told him it was on, but now that I think about it, I'm not sure it's the best idea. I really have to keep my grades up. I don't have time to get into a whole prank war thing or whatever this is with Dean."

"So just keep doing what you're doing," Zara encouraged. "Only tease Dean every once in a while."

"I'll think about it," Gracie said after a minute, shooting her friends a look that said that she wanted to end the conversation.

Before Nicole could object, the door opened and Raina walked in.

"Hey guys, what'd I miss?" She waved to Annalisse, who was working at her desk with a pair of purple earbuds in.

"Oh, we were just talking about Gracie and Dean," Nicole said lazily, draping herself all over Zara's bed, her body squishing Gracie as well.

"Hello, I'm right here," Gracie coughed, squirming under Nicole's arm.

"Tough," Nicole shot back.

Raina glanced uncertainly between the three friends. "Um, okay." She tiptoed to her bed and sat on top of the covers, a notebook on her lap.

Zara sat on Nicole's legs and, ignoring the shriek of protest, turned to Gracie. "Are you excited for the field trip tomorrow?"

Gracie nodded eagerly. "We're going to a museum to look at gemstones. How could I not be excited?"

Zara laughed. "I'm buying you stuff from the gift shop," she said matter-of-factly. "I want one of those tree necklaces with the pretty stones."

"You can't just buy me stuff all the time," Gracie protested.

"Course I can," Zara waved it off. "Besides, I'd much rather spend it on you than have my mom waste it on more wine."

"Still," Gracie insisted.

"And that's why you'll make me some jewelry from it," Zara said triumphantly. "So you can say that I'm paying you in gemstones."

Gracie hesitated. Zara made no secret of the amount of wealth her family possessed, and even though she would happily pay for everything, Gracie didn't feel right taking money from her. "Alright," she finally agreed. "In exchange for jewelry."

"You've gotten really good at it," Zara commented idly. She climbed off the bed and stretched, before grabbing a notebook from her bag.

"I practice," Gracie shrugged. "You know what, I'm going to make something now." She quickly stood up, kicking a grumbling Nicole off her body, and took a seat at the wooden desk she and Zara shared. Gracie's jewelry making supplies were on the left side, and she pulled open the drawers and took out the items she needed.

"Can someone explain how to find $x$?" Zara called out to the room.

"If the *sine* of $x$ is equal to a number, use the *arcsine* to find $x$," Nicole said from her position on Zara's bed. She sat up, her hair flying around her. "That reminds me, I should probably do *my* math homework."

"Thanks," Zara murmured, sticking her pencil in her mouth. "Wait, what about *cosine*?"

Nicole huffed but walked over to help. "It's the same, you just take..."

Her voice trailed off as Gracie put her earbuds in, preferring music when she worked. Picking up a pair of pliers, she began twisting beads onto her wire, years of practice allowing her to know where each one went without using a pattern.

Gracie noticed movement on her right and turned to see Raina sitting down at the desk she now shared with Nicole.

"Ooh, are those for me?" Zara's voice asked from right next to Gracie's ear, wrenching Gracie's earbuds out as she spoke. Gracie jumped, dropping the earring onto the desk.

"Zara, don't do that!" she gasped, bringing a hand to her chest. "You scared me!"

"Sorry," Zara said, not sounding sorry at all. "But are those for me?"

Gracie shot a quick glance at her friend, mentally comparing the gemstone colors with Zara's skin tone. "No," she said after a moment. "They're not your color. Besides, I used gold posts."

"Never mind then." Zara nodded. "Speaking of which, my mom *still* hasn't learned that I'm allergic to gold. Please take the earrings she got me as an 'I'm-sorry-for-not-being-in-your-life-for-the-past-two-months-let's-pretend-to-do-better-this-month-even-though-nothing-will-change' present," she said, digging out a small jewelry box from the desk drawer. "I shoved it in here when it came last week."

Gracie took the box carefully, flipping the lid open to reveal a pair of shiny gold earrings. A little diamond heart dangled inside a larger golden heart, and Gracie knew without a doubt that both the diamond and gold were real.

"I can't take this," she protested. "This is expensive."

"Course you can," Zara said easily. "Are you really going to make me go all the way to Paris to return it?"

Gracie's jaw dropped. "These came from *Paris*?!"

Zara shrugged. "Either Paris or London. Mom's jetted off to both in the past month. I wonder what Dean got."

"Nu-uh," Gracie shook her head emphatically. "I'm not keeping these." She thrust the box back at her best friend, who took it reluctantly.

"Fine," Zara huffed. "But if you won't accept the thousand-dollar earrings I'm offering you for free," she said, her tone making it clear how ridiculous she thought Gracie was being, "then will you at least help me with my math homework?"

Gracie laughed. "I thought Nicole was helping you?"

"She was, but I'm hopeless," Zara smirked.

Gracie shook her head but agreed, following her best friend over to where she had spread out her math pages.

✶✶✶

Dean groaned to himself, throwing his pencil down in frustration. "Can we just agree that math completely and totally sucks?" he asked the empty room. As he glanced around, wondering where his cousins were, the door slammed open and Jesse entered.

"I seriously love not sharing a room with anyone," he declared, throwing himself onto his bed. "God, the amount of people who were just begging me to let them use my bathroom is insane."

"Um, hello," Dean said, his eyebrows raised. "Person you share a room with over here."

"No, no," Jesse said, waving him off. "Like it's just the three of us in here, while the other dorms are built for five or six."

Dean frowned, looking around the room. "Hey, you're right," he said thoughtfully. "Why is that?"

"Because our family basically runs the school." Jesse rolled his eyes. "Also, there weren't enough boys in our year to fill the dorms. They barely have five in the other rooms as it is."

"Both accurate answers," Dean agreed.

Jesse jumped off of his bed, walking over to where Dean was sitting at his desk. "Are you doing the math work?"

Dean winced. "Attempting to. It's not going so well."

"Wait for Theo to get back," Jesse advised. "He's the nerd in the family."

"I heard that," Theo called, entering the room and tossing his bag on the floor.

"And you deny it?" Jesse asked, pulling his shirt off and grabbing his towel from the hook by his bed.

Theo rolled his eyes at his cousin before walking over to the desk area. "You need to take the *inverse sine* in order to get $x$ by itself," he said. "Right now, you have what $x$ equals, but you need to find $x$."

"Oh, that makes sense," Dean realized, quickly scratching out his previous work and jotting down a new answer. He plugged the numbers into his calculator, nodding when his answer came out correctly.

"Well, now that you only have another seven problems to puzzle through, I'm going to take a shower," Theo stated.

"Jesse's in there," Dean said, not looking up from his paper.

Theo groaned. "Seriously? Since when does Jesse shower at night? He takes hour-long showers; that's why he needs to shower in the morning! If he doesn't wake up in time, he doesn't shower. Why is he taking *my* shower time?"

Dean laughed. They had worked out a shower schedule in freshman year, with Theo showering early in the night, Dean showering at around midnight, and Jesse waking up early to shower. It was the perfect incentive to get Jesse awake in the mornings, and even though Theo and Dean hated being woken up every morning by a pillow in the face, they wouldn't complain for fear of Jesse switching his shower and pampering routine to the night.

"It's because of the field trip tomorrow," Dean responded.

"Shit, I have to pack," Theo cursed, glancing around the room frantically. "What do I need?"

"Something to sleep in and clothes for the next day," Dean replied. "Toothbrush, toothpaste, the stuffed animal you need to sleep at night."

"Ha-ha, hilarious," Theo said, crossing his arms as he made his way over to his bed.

"I know I am." Dean made a mental note to pack his own bag as he turned back to the math homework.

## Chapter Six

For a group of three teenaged boys who lived in a dorm, getting out of bed, dressed, and ready for the school day was normally a challenge. Getting dressed, ready, and with a properly packed overnight bag was nearly impossible.

"Why the hell would you need flip flops and a tie?" Theo cried the next morning after he tripped over Jesse's bag on his way to the bathroom, spilling its contents all over the floor.

"Hey, that's where my bag went!" Jesse exclaimed, rushing over. He bent down and began shoving various items into the small bag, miniature shampoo bottles and little boxes of Nerds falling back out every few seconds.

"One, why was your bag in the middle of the floor, and two, who taught you how to pack?" Theo screeched the last words as he made his way into the small bathroom, slamming the door shut behind him.

"My mother," Jesse offered.

"Yeah, okay, that makes perfect sense," Theo called through the closed door.

Dean rubbed his eyes, groaning as he dragged himself out of his comfy bed. He walked to his dresser and pulled out a shirt and a pair of pants, yanking them on as he looked over at his cousin wearily.

Jesse danced around the room, twirling a pair of his boxers on one finger. "Come on, Dean, up and at 'em!"

"You realize I'm awake, right?"

"Yes, but you don't look awake," Jesse said mischievously, one hand hidden behind his back.

Dean eyed him suspiciously. "What is that?"

"Oh, nothing," Jesse said in a sing-song voice, before darting forward and launching a water balloon at his cousin's shirt.

Dean yelped and ducked. He wasn't quick enough, and the balloon slammed straight into his nose, exploding and soaking his hair, face, and shirt. Pursing his lips, Dean wiped the water from his eyes, flicking his dripping fingers at his cousin. "Seriously?"

"It was absolutely necessary," Jesse said, straight-faced.

Theo opened the bathroom door, took in the room, and sighed. "Did you fall for the water balloon trick again?"

"It's the *morning*," Dean defended himself. "You can't expect me to be on alert for pranks in the morning. Scratch that, it's not even morning. It's five o'clock. That's like, still nighttime."

"It doesn't matter. We've only got fifteen minutes before we need to be downstairs," Theo reminded him. "And Jesse, you still need to pack."

"I packed," Jesse protested, holding up his open bag. A pair of SpongeBob SquarePants boxers slid out onto the floor.

"Right. Packed. Dean?"

"Already got it," Dean called, tossing Theo an empty duffel. After their very first field trip, where Jesse ended up wearing Theo's sweatshirt and Dean's pants their second day, the two cousins had begun packing some of Jesse's clothes along with theirs. Even though his childhood had been composed of trips to Europe every other weekend, Jesse had never learned to pack properly, relying on other people to do it for him. Dean and Theo found it was easier to pack spare clothes rather than argue with Jesse, and so while Jesse brought bags full of random things he would never need, Dean and Theo would make sure that he had enough clothes to get him through the trip.

"You don't need shaving cream," Theo was saying when Dean exited the bathroom five minutes later. "Seriously, you don't even shave. Why the fuck would you need shaving cream?"

"Well, what if I need to shave? Or what if Zara needs shaving cream because she didn't bring her own?"

Theo threw his head back, groaning. "For the love of god, Jesse, you don't need shaving cream! And I guarantee you, Zara can go two days without it!"

Dean smirked as he walked past his arguing cousins, shoving his toothbrush in his bag and double checking to make sure he had everything he needed. "I'm ready to go," he said. "You guys coming?"

"Yes," Theo huffed, swiping the shaving cream from Jesse's bag as soon as the redhead turned away. It made a clattering sound as it landed on the floor, but none of the boys bothered to pick it up. "Let's go, *please*."

☆☆☆

Gracie blinked, opening her eyes just as something hit her in the face. She turned, glaring suspiciously at Zara just as her best friend smacked her cheek. "I'm trying to sleep here," Gracie grumbled, knowing that it wouldn't do her any good. Years of sleepovers had taught her that Zara moved around a lot in her sleep and would kick at anything even remotely near her—Gracie included.

Huffing, Gracie glanced around the bus for an empty seat she could move to. Zara had insisted that they sit in the back, promising that she wouldn't fall asleep. Not even ten minutes into the bus ride, Zara had conked out on Gracie's shoulder, leaving Gracie to cross her arms and attempt to sleep through the constant jolting.

"Alright, enough," Gracie hissed, standing up just as the bus turned sharply. She lost her footing, stepping forward a few rows and falling on top of a hard body.

"Ow," Dean Ashcroft's familiar voice groaned.

Gracie jumped up. "Sorry!" she exclaimed. "Sorry, the bus swerved."

Dean stretched, sitting up from where he had been lying across two seats. Gracie averted her eyes from the stretch of skin shown at his waist when he lifted his arms above his head. "Weren't you sitting next to my sister?"

"I was." Gracie rolled her eyes. "But she fell asleep."

"Say no more," Dean said wisely, swinging his legs around so Gracie had room to sit. "I know how sleeping Zara is."

Gracie eyed him for a second, wondering if he had any ulterior motives before sitting down. "Thanks."

"No problem," Dean said with a wink. "Besides, can't have my girlfriend all black and blue."

Gracie flushed. "We are not together!" she hissed, smacking him on the shoulder.

"Ow, woman, that hurt," Dean complained. "And fine, if we're not together, then tell them that." He gestured to the bus at large.

"No way," Gracie said stubbornly. "You admit the truth."

"Not on your life, sweetheart."

Gracie growled at him under her breath, before crossing her arms and turning away. She heard Dean's chuckle as he shifted to lean back in his seat, tucking a sweatshirt under his head. Gracie shot a quick glance at him before pulling out her phone and a pair of earbuds from the pocket of her hoodie.

☆
☆ ☆

When the flashing notification telling her she had twenty percent battery left appeared on the screen, Gracie reluctantly put her phone away. She turned to her seat partner, noticing that Dean's breathing had evened out and he had fallen asleep. Bored, Gracie glanced around the bus, but everyone else was sleeping, attempting to, or watching something on their phones. She wished she had her beading supplies, but Zara had insisted that she leave them at school.

Gracie glanced at Dean again. He looked much more peaceful and innocent in his sleep. Zara's words rang through her head, telling her to get revenge on him. "What the heck," Gracie muttered to herself. "He deserves it anyway." She tentatively leaned her head against Dean's shoulder. He shifted an arm to wrap around her and Gracie smirked triumphantly before giving a swift kick to the seat in front of her and closing her eyes.

Juliet's complaints quickly turned to squeals as she took in the scene on the seat behind her—Gracie wrapped up in Dean's arms and both of them seemingly asleep. Gracie could hear the clicks of a camera and white filled her vision for a second. She peeked just in time to see Juliet turning away to nudge Annalisse on the shoulder. Gracie grinned to herself, knowing that the pictures would be spread through the gossip grapevine soon enough.

Gracie yawned, figuring that she would just close her eyes for a minute. She squirmed a bit, but Dean's arm refused to move. Sighing, Gracie leaned her head back against Dean's shoulder, resigned to her new sleeping position.

✯✯✯

The first thing Dean noticed when he woke up was that Jesse had fallen asleep on him again. The second thing he noticed was that the person asleep on top of him wasn't Jesse.

Dean shrieked, and then the person shrieked, and only then Dean realized it was Gracie Adams who was glaring at him, wavy hair a mess and eyes still sleepy.

"What are you doing here?" he whispered furiously, not wanting to wake up the rest of the bus. Judging from the sleepy frowns and confused looks that turned toward them, he failed miserably. Dean glanced to the front, but miraculously, they hadn't woken up any of the chaperones. If they had, Dean and Gracie would probably be glaring at each other from opposite sides of the front row by now.

"You said I could stay," Gracie hissed. "Zara was kicking, and I accidentally fell on you."

"Was I half-asleep?"

Gracie tilted her head to the side. "Yes," she said after a minute.

"Well, that's it," Dean declared. "You can't listen to a single thing I say when I'm half-asleep."

"That explains the civil conversation we had," Gracie said sarcastically.

"Now that's cleared up, go back to getting kicked by my sister," Dean said, nodding his head to where Zara was still fast asleep, draped across two seats.

"No way." Gracie shook her head. "I'm not moving."

"Yes, you are," Dean argued. "This is my seat and you're intruding on it. Intruder! Intruder in my seat!" he called softly, debating whether to yell and annoy the rest of the bus as well. He decided against it, turning back to the girl next to him.

Gracie reached out and swiped a pair of earbuds from the pocket of the seat in front of him. It took until she had placed the first one in her ear before Dean realized that the black and silver earbuds were his own, and he angrily tugged it out of her ear.

"That's mine," Dean said, moving closer to grab the cord from her.

"Actually, they're Zara's," Gracie shot back. "I know because I saw her using them last week."

"That's because she stole them from me," Dean corrected, giving the cord a firm tug. Gracie yelped as the force pulled her forward, letting go of the earbuds just as she landed on top of Dean.

"Oh." Gracie blinked, before registering that her face was mere inches away from Dean's. "Hi," she offered after a minute, neither of them making a move to separate.

Dean let out a low chuckle. "Hello, Adams. Now would you mind getting off me?"

"Right," Gracie said dumbly, scooting backwards. "Um, sorry."

"No worries. I know I'm irresistible." Dean flashed her a charming grin. "All the ladies fall for me."

"Well," Gracie said sweetly. "They might fall for you, but nothing is ever going to happen between you and them. You have a girlfriend, remember? Unless—" she widened her eyes innocently. "—there's something you'd like to say to everyone?"

Dean clenched his jaw. "Never."

Gracie shrugged. "Guess you're stuck with me. The one girl who doesn't actually want to date you. Pity."

"Oh, yeah?" Dean challenged, grasping her wrist. "Let's see you try to resist this." He tugged Gracie forward and connected their lips. After a few seconds of kissing, his arm wrapped around her waist as he pushed her backward until she was nearly lying against the seat. A self-satisfied smirk spread across his face as he broke the kiss. "Changed your mind yet?" he asked, wiping his mouth with the back of his hand.

Gracie's eyes narrowed, strangely happy to see her gloss all over Dean's mouth. "Not yet." This time, it was Gracie who started the hungry kiss, both their tongues battling for domination as they fought to get hands all over the other.

"Break it up, break it up," a familiar voice hissed. Gracie broke apart from Dean, one hand still tangled in his hair as she turned to see Zara standing in the aisle, arms crossed and a disgusted look upon her face. She wrinkled her nose, miming a gagging motion. "I don't need to see my best friend and my brother attempting to shove their tongues down each other's throats. *Nobody* needs to see that." Zara shivered.

Gracie pushed Dean away as quickly as humanly possible, almost slipping off of the carpeted bus seat in her attempts to get away. "This changes nothing," she said hotly. "I still hate you, and I'm going to win."

Dean smirked, stretching out his long legs as he lounged in what had been *her* seat. "Two out of three isn't bad, Adams," he said casually. "But you got one thing wrong. *I'm* going to win."

"I. Will. End. You." Gracie growled and Zara's arm on her wrist was the only thing stopping her from attacking Dean.

"Okay!" Raina said brightly, leaping forward to latch onto Gracie's other arm. "Come on, Gracie, let's go sit down and eat some Oreos. How does that sound?"

Gracie shot one last glare at Dean before following her friends back to their seats. Dean's laughter rang in her ears as she sat down, pouting like a toddler.

Nicole turned around from her seat in front of Gracie and Raina, Zara plopping down next to her. "So are you sure you don't like Dean? I know you say you don't, but I was gone for two months and a lot can happen in that amount of time."

Gracie's mouth dropped open. "I don't like Dean!" she insisted, tucking a stray piece of hair behind her ear. "We just end up kissing every other day."

Nicole snorted, wrapping her arms around the seat. "Girl, you fucking like him. But you know what? It's very amusing for the rest of us to watch the two of you attempt to hide your feelings, so please, continue with your little game."

"And don't tell him you like him before Christmas," Raina added. "I've got ten dollars on it happening after."

"People are betting on us?" Gracie exclaimed, outraged. She looked from Zara to Raina, before glancing at Zara again. "Zara, please help me here. Tell them they can't just bet on us!"

"No can do." Zara shrugged, leaning against the window. The

bus jerked and she grimaced before pulling out her phone. "But while you're at it, please confess your undying love for my brother *before* Christmas, or else I owe Raina ten bucks."

"Your family are millionaires," Gracie shot back. "You can spare ten dollars."

"Well, of course I can," Zara said matter-of-factly. "But then I'll have lost, and Ashcrofts don't do losing."

Gracie stared at her friend before shaking her head. "Well, you Ashcrofts better get used to it," she announced. "Because you're both losing that bet since the only feeling I have for Dean is the desire to kick his ass."

## Chapter Seven

"Adams, Ashcroft, Cohen, Lawrence," one of the parent chaperones said boredly. He waved an envelope in the air.

Raina squealed from next to Gracie, grasping her hand. "Yay, we're together!"

Nicole rolled her eyes. "Well, yeah, there wasn't much doubt about that," she said. "They typically put roommates together, and I know for a fact none of us requested Juliet and Annalisse."

"Should we go find our room?" Gracie cut in, noting that Raina's face had fallen.

"Yes, let's do so," Zara said, grabbing the handle of her suitcase. She tugged it toward the elevators, Nicole and Raina following. Gracie sighed at her friends, before going to get the room cards. Surprisingly, there wasn't a crowd in front of the chaperones, and she was holding the plastic key in her hand before the elevator arrived. Gracie thanked the chaperone, before dragging her bag over to where Zara was impatiently tapping her foot outside of the elevator doors.

"What took so long?"

"Zar, I was gone for all of three seconds. And it was to get the keycards to open up the room you're so eagerly rushing to."

"Okay." Zara shrugged, reaching out to press the elevator button again. The doors opened and she grinned triumphantly at Gracie before all four girls lugged their bags inside.

"Wait for us!" Theo's voice exclaimed. Gracie turned to see Dean, Theo, and Jesse rushing toward the open elevator, each holding a duffel bag.

"Quick, close the doors," Gracie said frantically, jabbing the button multiple times.

"Aww, Gracie, trying to shut the doors on us?" Dean cooed, leaning against the elevator wall.

Gracie gave him a sweet smile. "No, just calculating the ideal time to cut off one of your hands."

Jesse gulped. "Okay, she's scary," he announced, before scooting closer to Nicole and throwing an arm around her shoulders. "Nicky, how's my bestest friend doing today?"

Gracie glanced uncertainly at Raina as Nicole shoved Jesse, sending him into the wall. Raina's eyes had dropped to her black flats at Jesse's words, clearly hurt that he hadn't even acknowledged her.

"Hey, chin up," Gracie whispered quietly to her friend.

Raina gave her a small smile as she brushed invisible dust off of her purple cardigan, before pretending to fix her hair in the mirror. Gracie pursed her lips, mentally cursing Dean's cousin. He might be Nicole's best friend, which made him best-friend adjacent, but he could be extremely dense sometimes.

A duffel bag nudged her thigh and Gracie looked up to see Dean with an apologetic look on his face. Had someone else picked up on the tension between Raina and Jesse?

"Your bestest friend is wondering who dared to speak to her before ten o'clock without bringing her coffee," Nicole said snarkily.

"Oh, how could I forget!" Jesse exclaimed, before reaching into his bag and pulling out a small glass Starbucks bottle. "One mocha frappuccino, bus temperature."

Dean threw his hands up in the air. "So he remembers to pack coffee for Nicole, but not deodorant or socks," he declared. "I give up."

Nicole squealed in a way that was very unlike her. "I fucking love you, Jesse. Like, have I told you how much I love you lately?"

A bell dinged, and the doors opened, everyone shoving to get out of the elevator. Gracie slipped an arm around Raina, hugging the taller girl tightly.

"Are we doing that girl thing again?" Jesse complained. "You know, the one where you girls hug each other at random times for no reason."

Zara smirked. "Sure, Jesse. We're doing that. And congrats, you've become an honorary girl. Now go give Raina a hug."

Jesse shrugged, crossing the hall in two steps and wrapping his arms around the blonde. After an awkward pause, Raina hugged him back.

"Lovebirds," Dean sang quietly enough that only Gracie could hear. "Now," he said, "we're right here, boys, and you girls can have fun finding your own room."

"Wow, so helpful," Gracie said sarcastically.

Dean smirked at her. "You're very welcome."

✯✯✯

Dean followed his cousins into their hotel room. "Man, we lucked out again. I can't believe we don't have a fourth roommate."

Jesse shrieked girlishly. "Shot the single bed!" he exclaimed, dashing across the room and leaping on the bed closest to the window.

"Seriously?" Theo complained, almost tripping over Jesse's dropped bag as he made his way to the other bed. "We can't, like, draw straws or something?"

"Nobody draws straws anymore." Jesse snorted, stretching out on his newly claimed bed. He smirked at Theo. "Ahh, this is so comfy."

Theo growled at him before setting his duffel on the desk chair and storming off to the bathroom.

Dean walked over to the empty bed, throwing his own bag onto the desk. "I'm tired," he sighed, running a hand through his hair. "How long do we have until we're forced to go to a group activity or some other dumb shit?"

"Half an hour," Jesse responded, tossing a ball up in the air and catching it.

Dean blinked, vaguely wondering where Jesse had gotten the miniature basketball from. He shook his head. It didn't matter.

"So have you decided what to do about Christmas yet?" Jesse asked, throwing the basketball up again.

Dean shrugged. "Not sure. On one hand, I could just stay at school. Aunt Becky's coming, and our dear old cuz," he said sarcastically, "will be there as well."

"Ugh," Theo made a face as he exited the bathroom. "Well, that's a giant negative. What's the other option?"

"Go home with you, idiot," Dean said, rolling his eyes.

"Well, I don't even know if I'm going home or not," Theo pointed out. "Mom might come up to school."

"So it's Aunt Becky and possibly your mom, but also Voldemort," Dean said with a sigh. "Not sure if the pros outweigh the cons."

"Don't you need to talk to Zara before you decide?" Jesse asked, turning over on the bed.

"I think she still wants to go to Gracie's."

"Well, it's the middle of November," Theo said, sitting down at the desk and grabbing one of the notepads. "You've still got a couple of weeks."

Jesse jumped off of the bed and peered over Theo's shoulder. "What the hell are you doing?"

"Nothing," Theo said, tearing the paper off and crumpling it into a ball.

Dean glanced at his cousin curiously, before an alert from his phone captured his attention. "Text from the school," he announced. "A reminder that we're supposed to be downstairs in twenty minutes, and that the bus will be leaving in exactly twenty-one minutes—without us—if we're late." Dean swung his legs off of the bed. "We might as well go pick up the girls early. Anything's got to be better than this conversation."

✦✦✦

"Alright, we're going to be giving you your groups now!" the chaperone called loudly, waving her hands in the air to make sure she had everyone's attention. "You won't need to stay in your groups, but there will be assigned check-in points, and you'll need to meet with your group for lunch. Each group will be visiting a different museum, so please make sure to stay inside and don't run off. We'll be splitting you up by last name. A through E, with me. We'll be going to the Museum of Natural History first. F through M, will be going to the Museum of American History. N through R, to the Museum of African American History. And S through Z, you'll be at the Air and Space Museum. Oh, and Ashcrofts?"

Zara groaned from where she had been about to drag Gracie over to group one. "Damn, I hoped they would have forgotten."

Gracie snickered. "Zar, you guys toppled a half a million-dollar statue—"

"We didn't break it!" Zara said quickly.

"—do you really think the chaperones would let all four of you be in the same group for field trips ever again?" Gracie finished, as if her best friend hadn't interrupted her.

"No," Zara muttered, sulking as she crossed her arms.

"Go get your group assignment." Gracie nodded her head toward where the other three Ashcrofts were gathering, giving her friend a small shove.

"I hate you!" Zara called, as she danced out of Gracie's reach.

"Love you too!"

Gracie joined Raina, the rest of their group congregating around them. "So how are you finding DC so far?" she asked her friend.

Raina let out a small huff. "There is a lack of decent food I can eat," she complained. "It's like the chaperones never heard of someone keeping kosher before. I can buy frozen food at a nearby supermarket, but I need to find a microwave that I can use. Also, it's cold. What about you?"

Gracie shrugged. "I haven't really seen much outside of the hotel, but the museums look really nice from here." She gestured to the lawn they were standing on. "And you do know that New York and DC are pretty much the same temperature, right? It's not like we're in Antarctica or something."

"Fair," Raina said, her eyes on something over Gracie's shoulder. Gracie turned to see what had captured Raina's attention and scowled when faced with a smirking Dean.

"What are you doing here?" she demanded.

"What, no greeting?" Dean asked. "I'm offended, Adams, really."

"I repeat, what are you doing here?" Gracie resisted the urge to roll her eyes.

Dean glanced around casually. "I'm enjoying this lovely day," he said pleasantly. Gracie clenched her fists, wondering if he was ignoring her question on purpose.

She huffed. "Fine. Whatever. Now, can you go to your group, please?"

"Ah, but I am in my group."

Gracie's mouth dropped open. "Where's Zara?" she demanded, glancing frantically at her best friend. Her best friend, who was supposed to have charmed the chaperone into letting her join their group.

"In her group," Dean said, nodding across the lawn. "Group Four."

"No," Gracie protested. "Go switch groups with her."

Dean tilted his head to the side, considering the idea. "How do I put this nicely? No." Gracie growled at him. "Easy tiger," he added. "Wouldn't want to kill your museum partner before we even reach the first museum."

Gracie spluttered. "Excuse me? Museum partner?"

"Oh yeah," Dean said, his smirk growing wider. "Everyone else has already paired off. You're stuck with me, Adams."

Gracie crossed her arms. She couldn't believe that she had been so busy arguing with Dean that she hadn't even noticed that her group had been pairing up. Raina shot her an apologetic look from where she was standing with a girl Gracie didn't recognize. "Fine. And it's Gracie."

"I know your name," Dean said impatiently, grabbing her arm. "Now come on, they're going to leave us behind."

Gracie wrenched her arm out of Dean's grasp before storming ahead. "This day is going to be the worst," she mumbled under her breath.

"Hey! Adams! Wait up!" Dean called from behind her. Gracie ignored him, walking faster. "Adams! Adams! Gracie!"

Gracie stopped and turned, cocking her head to the side. "Yes, Dean?" she asked in an overly sweet voice. "Can I help you?"

✯✯✯

Dean hurried to catch up with his…enemy? Girlfriend? He truly had no idea, both what they were and where he stood with her. What was it about Gracie Adams that made her able to get on his nerves every single time? She differed from all the other girls in that way, that was for sure.

"I was beginning to think you were going to leave me behind," he said easily, flashing her his trademark grin. Girls fell for it every time, so why didn't Gracie? His face fell when she turned around and kept walking.

"I was," Gracie said shortly.

"What made you change your mind?" Dean continued, keeping pace with her.

"I haven't."

Okay, so she was going to give him the shortest answers possible. He could work with that.

"Gracie," he said in a sing-song voice. "Let's play a game."

"Let's not."

"Pick a number!" Dean exclaimed, twiddling his fingers. He shot a glance at Gracie, wondering if her curls were as soft as they looked.

"Pi."

"Cute." Dean brightened as a new thought came to him. "Hey Gracie," he said mischievously.

She sighed and turned around. "What, Dean?"

Dean paused for a second. "Would you say I'm a cutie pi?" He barely got the words out before bursting into laughter.

"Dear God," Gracie said out loud. Dean snuck a glance at Gracie, noting the small smile that she couldn't conceal.

"Oh! How about this one?" he said excitedly. "Are you an irrational number? Cause you're a cutie pi."

Gracie blushed. "That wasn't very good," she said hotly.

"I thought it was very *cute*," Dean grinned at her. "Not as cute as me, of course."

Gracie scoffed. "You're very full of yourself."

"You can't deny it," Dean said triumphantly. "You think I'm cute!"

"I think you're very full of yourself," Gracie said, tossing her hair over her shoulder. She walked away, leaving Dean to stare after her for a second before running to catch up.

"But you also think I'm cute, right?" he tried. Gracie shook her head but didn't respond. Dean glanced at her out of the corner of his eye. "Unlike some people, I have no problem admitting when things are cute," he continued. "Like you, for example."

"M-me?" Gracie stammered.

"Yes, you," Dean said casually, wondering why he felt so jumpy. "You're cute. I would admit that any day."

☆☆☆

Gracie blushed furiously, hurrying ahead so Dean couldn't see her face. Dean found her attractive?

"Thanks. Um, you're not so bad looking yourself," she said finally.

"It's okay, Gracie," Dean said seriously. "I know it's hard to admit when someone is incredibly sexy and gorgeous."

"I didn't say that!"

"Course you did."

Gracie opened and then shut her mouth, unable to come up with a good comeback. "Oh look, we're here!"

She hurried through the doors to the museum and into the rotunda, hoping that Dean hadn't noticed her unnaturally high voice. Gracie leaned over to grab one of the pamphlets by the door.

"National Museum of Natural History," she read. She glanced over at Dean, who was reading a pamphlet of his own. "Since we're stuck together all day, I suppose I should ask you where you want to go first."

"How very generous of you," Dean said. "We're right here, so should we look at this elephant first?"

Gracie shrugged, wandering over to the display. "'Elephants in danger,'" she read from the sign. "Dean, did you know that 'your choices make a difference?' And this elephant is thirteen feet tall, that's like two of you."

"Henry."

Gracie looked over at him, puzzled. "Excuse me?"

"The elephant," Dean repeated, nodding over at the display. "His name is Henry."

"Oh." Unable to help herself, Gracie glanced over at Dean again as he leaned over the display.

"He's been here since 1959, staring at all of us," Dean said with a laugh. "Must be boring. I'd hate to watch tourists ogle me all day."

Gracie stepped aside so a flood of young kids in purple t-shirts could point at Henry. "Do you want to keep moving?"

"Sure," Dean said easily, shoving his hands into his pockets. He ambled around the elephant, casting it one last glance before nodding his head at one of the nearby staircases. "Should we see what's up there?"

"Sounds like a plan. I want to go see the gemstones, though."

"Oh, we can head there then," Dean said quickly.

"Are you sure?"

"Course."

"Okay, then."

✯✯✯

Gracie followed Dean into an exhibit, her nose buried in her information pamphlet. "We're in the Harry Winston Gallery, hope to the Hope Diamond," she said distractedly, her eyes scanning the pamphlet.

"You said hope to the Hope Diamond," Dean said.

Gracie glanced up in surprise. "Did I?"

"You did."

"Oh, I meant *home*." Gracie glanced up to see Dean fighting to hide a smile.

*The Gossip Games*

"I know."

Unsure of how to respond, Gracie rushed over to one piece of the display—a giant quartz crystal that was probably taller than her. It was built into the wall, leaving her a clear view of the crystal's every nook and cranny. "Ooh," she breathed, unconsciously reaching out. She looked down, surprised to see a hand on her wrist. Dean gave her an apologetic look.

"No touching," he said, nodding to the sign. Gracie blushed, snatching her hand back and glancing around the room. Glass shields kept visitors from touching the room's smaller treasures, but she would be able to walk around and marvel at the rocks found in France, Asia, Africa, and even Arizona. The room was nearly empty, with only a harried looking mom in the corner trying to keep her three boys from climbing half-glass partitions and touching the bigger rocks.

"Oh, look!" Gracie exclaimed, hurrying to put as much space between her and Dean as possible. "The Hope Diamond. Isn't it stunning?"

She gazed at the necklace in front of her, walking around the glass case in order to examine it from every angle. As a beader, expensive jewelry was one of her favorite things to admire, and the Hope Diamond did not disappoint. It was one of Gracie's favorite pieces, and she had spent a good twenty minutes jumping up and down when this year's fall field trip had been revealed.

"It's pretty," Dean agreed, moving to stand next to her. "How many diamonds do you think are in that necklace?"

"Sixty-one," Gracie replied instantly. "Forty-five in the chain and sixteen around the sapphire."

Dean whistled, eying the necklace appreciatively. "Damn, that's more than my mom's given Zara as an 'I'm-sorry-for-not-being-in-your-life-for-the-past-two-months-let's-pretend-to-do-better-this-month-even-though-nothing-will-change' present."

Gracie laughed. There was a warm feeling in her chest as she took one last glance at the necklace. "Come on, let's go find the Star of Asia. Ooh! And Marie Antoinette's earrings. And the Amethyst Heart Brooch." She bounced excitedly as she led the way out of the exhibit. "And we have to see the Sapphire Butterfly too."

"One piece of jewelry at a time," Dean joked, slipping an arm around her shoulders. Gracie's face reddened as they walked to the next room, but she made no move to remove Dean's arm.

## Chapter Eight

Dean slumped onto the bus seat with a sigh. "After two days of visiting every single museum in DC, I. Am. Done," he declared, digging in his bag for his earbuds. With everyone crowding onto the bus in an attempt to get their favorite seats, he really needed the few moments of relaxation that his music would give him. Jesse sat down next to him, already playing some game on his phone.

"I'm sure you didn't visit *every* museum." Theo rolled his eyes, dropping into the seat in front of Dean and Jesse. He tossed his cousin a pack of chips, and Dean eagerly accepted it.

"Okay fine," Dean allowed. "But Adams dragged me all over the place. That girl does not take breaks!"

Jesse laughed, pausing his game to tease his cousin. "How'd you get stuck with her as a partner anyway?"

Dean winced. "We may have been arguing."

"That should have made the chaperone separate you." Theo frowned.

"We missed the parent person telling us to pair up, so we were stuck with each other." Dean pulled open the bag of chips and shoved one into his mouth.

Jesse raised an eyebrow. "Parent person?"

"Shut up." Dean shoved his cousin, sending Jesse stumbling into the seat across from him.

"Ooh yay, a seat for me," his sister said dryly, sitting down in Jesse's vacated spot.

Gracie stood hesitantly in the aisle. "Um, hi."

"You can sit next to me," Theo offered.

Gracie gave him a shy smile. "Thanks."

Dean turned to Zara. "Not that I don't love you, sister dearest, but what are you doing here?"

Zara looked puzzled, before realization dawned on her face. "Oh yeah. I came here for a reason."

Dean stared at her for a few seconds. "Which was…?" he prompted.

"Christmas!" Zara clapped her hands. "We need to talk Christmas."

Dean groaned. "Must we?"

"Yes," Zara said sternly. "We need to make a decision. People have been asking me and I need an answer for them."

"Uncle Aaron can wait a couple more days," Dean said, crossing his arms. "I'm tired and I want to sleep."

Zara threw her hands up in frustration. "I really need to know, Dean. I don't care what Uncle Asshole wants, but I need to tell Gracie's mom if I'm going or not. It's not fair to her."

"Fine. I'll push off my sleep, which I clearly don't need," Dean said crossly. "Are you happy?"

"I'd be happy if we could decide," Zara shot back.

"Okay, fine. What are our options?"

Zara sighed. "Mom's not coming to school for Christmas. Aunt Becky texted me this morning."

Dean fought to keep the hurt look off of his face. He hadn't believed that his mom would show, but without knowing for sure, there had always been that 1% chance that she'd decide to spend time with her own children. Judging by the worried looks Zara and

Gracie shot him, he didn't do such a great job of hiding his expression. "Fine. So?"

Zara let out a deep breath. "So, are you just going to stay at school then?"

"What are you going to do?" he asked.

"I think I'm going to go home with Gracie. Is that okay?"

"You mean we're going to be separated for Christmas?" Dean frowned.

"Yeah," Zara winced. "But if you're not okay with that or something, I'll just stay at school with you."

"No, no," Dean shook his head. He might not be excited for Christmas at school, but that didn't mean Zara should have a terrible holiday too. "You should go. Have fun at Adams'."

"You can come too, if you'd like," Gracie offered quietly.

Both twins whipped their heads around to stare at her. "You're inviting me?" Dean questioned at the same time Zara exclaimed, "You're inviting him?"

"Thanks," Dean shot his sister an offended look.

"No, I just thought you didn't like him." Zara shook her head. "And you're inviting him to spend Christmas with you?"

Gracie shrugged. "If he doesn't come, you'll spend the entire week moping. And mopey Zara is no fun."

Dean snickered before sobering beneath Zara's glare. "Thanks, Adams. That would be great."

"Good." Zara pulled her sweatshirt hood over her eyes. "Now that's settled, I'm going to go to sleep for the next four hours. Someone call my name when they take attendance but don't wake me up until we're back at Trinity."

☆☆
☆☆

Dean hummed quietly as he tugged on the rope attached to Jesse's bed, his fingers nimbly tying the last knots. Finishing, he took a proud step back to admire his handiwork. Dozens of fake spiders were individually tied to the curtains on Jesse's bed, which had been pulled up the night before. A thick rope at the end of the canopy ran across the ceiling and through the open door. In the doorway, Dean had tied a thin, clear piece of string that, when tugged upon, would release the drapes and send the spiders tumbling down.

While Dean knew they were fake, Jesse, who was completely and totally terrified of spiders, did not. Dean deemed it appropriate payback for the glitter incident, but he would probably throw in a shaving-cream-instead-of-toothpaste level prank to make sure the score was even. "Jesse is going to be so surprised," he said with an evil grin, rubbing his hands together.

"I'm going to be what?" a voice asked from next to him.

"So surprised, Jesse," Dean said distractedly, turning to check on the knots again. "Wait, Jesse?" Dean whipped his head back and forth between the door and his cousin, who was standing not even a foot away. "How did you avoid triggering the door?" he asked, stunned. "It was the perfect prank!"

Jesse snorted. "Please. I can see a string hanging there. I just ducked under it. Easy peasy."

Dean crossed his arms and scowled at his cousin. "You ruined the prank. You were *supposed* to walk into the string."

"And what was going to happen?" Jesse asked, raising an eyebrow. "Honey? Shaving cream? Kool-aid? Glitter?" He peered around the room, a frown on his face. "There's no bucket above the door," Jesse stated, a confused look on his face. "What's the prank?"

Dean smirked, running a hand through his hair. "When will Theo be coming up?" he asked instead, ignoring Jesse's question. "He'll trigger it, but it won't be as much fun."

"I'm right here," Theo said, exiting the bathroom. He rubbed his hair with the towel slung around his neck, before dropping it onto his bed. "I've been here for the past hour, and I'm not dumb enough to fall for whatever prank you're planning."

Dean huffed loudly. "Well, someone's got to trigger it, if neither of you will."

All three boys looked at each other. "Shot not!" they all exclaimed at the same time.

"Okay, this is ridiculous!" Zara's voice carried through the open door, getting louder with each word. "She can't just walk—" Zara ranted as she stormed into the boys' dorm room, ripping the string. Dean and Jesse looked at each other, wide eyed. "—into my life and demand to see me again!" Zara finished, her fists clenching. As the last words left her lips, the curtains rolled down, complete with their new addition of large black spiders. A scream ripped out of Zara so loudly that it was a wonder none of the other students poked their heads in to ask what had happened.

Zara shrieked again, running across the room and barreling into Dean. Dean gasped for breath as his sister accidentally smacked his throat, cutting off his air supply momentarily. He lost his footing, and if it wasn't for the bed behind him, both of them would have tumbled to the floor.

"S-spiders!" Zara screeched, drawing Dean's attention back to the wild-eyed girl clinging to him. She clutched his hoodie, whipping her head around and pointing with a shaky finger. "So many of them!"

Dean sighed, spitting a few strands of her fiery hair out of his mouth. "They're not real," he explained. "They were a prank for Jesse, but someone," he turned to scowl at his cousin, "decided not to fall for it."

Zara shuddered, rolling off of him and crossing her arms tightly across her chest. "So there aren't any spiders?" she asked in a small voice.

Dean shook his head, mimicked by Theo, who had moved to the other side of the room and was leaning against the bathroom door. Jesse, on the other hand, was lying on the floor in tears, failing to compose himself. Dean shot him a scathing look, making sure to accidentally tread on his foot as he rose.

"Dean."

"Yes, Zara, my lovely, gorgeous, smart, talented sister?"

Zara had two angry moods—she would either explode on her target, yelling accusations and releasing her Ashcroft-inherited temper, or she would go silent, stewing in her fury and leaving her opponent wondering if she was even mad at all. It was always best to try and appease her, but if you really angered Zara, nothing would save you from her inevitable revenge.

"*Mother dearest* would like us to spend Christmas with her and her new boyfriend," Zara practically spat out the words.

"That doesn't sound that bad—" Dean started.

"In Brazil. The boyfriend's home country."

Dean blinked. "Does she even speak Portuguese?"

"Nope," Zara said, shaking her head. "And I'd bet you all the diamonds that I'm sure I'm going to get that she thinks they speak Brazilianese."

Dean scoffed. "I'm not taking that bet."

"Yeah, I'd win." Zara shrugged and turned to leave the room, stopping at the door and spinning around to fix him with a piercing glare. "Oh, and Dean? Watch your back."

☆☆☆

Gracie hurried down the hall to the library, juggling five books in her arms. The top book slipped off of her stack and fell to the floor with an audible *thud*, and she groaned, attempting to pick it up without toppling the rest of the books.

"Here," a voice offered, holding out the fallen book.

Gracie took it gratefully, shifting the rest of her books to her left arm. "Thank you," she said, before getting a good look at her helper.

"Hey, it's you!" she said, surprised. "I haven't seen you at all since the last time I bumped into you!"

Blake laughed, smoothing his shirt. "Well, I try not to hang around in empty hallways too often," he teased.

Gracie eyed him before blushing and looking down at her books. Had he seen her staring at him? She hoped not. He looked good in his white button-down and black pants, the basis for every male Trinity uniform. What would he look like with the tie and blazer? She blushed again.

"Are you a junior? Because I didn't see you on the trip we just had."

Blake raised an eyebrow. "Were you looking for me?" he asked, an amused tone in his voice.

Gracie's face was surely tomato red by now. "Maybe a little," she admitted.

"I think I'm worth more than 'maybe a little,'" Blake joked. Gracie laughed, reaching out to smack him gently with the book in her hand. "And to answer your question, you wouldn't have found me on the trip, anyway."

Gracie's brow furrowed. "So, are you a senior?"

"Technically." Blake shrugged. "I'm not a Trinity student."

"Then why are you here?" Gracie asked. She eyed him suspiciously. He *was* wearing part of the uniform, but that didn't really tell her anything. "You didn't break in or anything like that, did you?"

He laughed loudly. "No, I'm not hiding in the kitchen or basement or anything. I'm a staff kid; my school is nearby so I visit a lot. You know, see the school, annoy my dad, all that jazz."

Gracie nodded, waving absently to a girl on the other side of the hall. "Is your dad one of the teachers? And if he works here, then why do you go to another school?" she asked curiously. "You don't have to answer if you don't want to," she added, shuffling her books and pressing them to her chest. "Sorry. I'm just a curious person. I ask a lot of questions."

"I've noticed," Blake said, sending her a grin. "And don't be.

There's a perfectly normal, non-traumatic answer. It was my mom's alma mater, and she insisted I go there both because it was her school and because it has a better engineering program. My dad is *not* a teacher. He would have no idea what to do in a classroom full of kids, so he didn't put up much of a fight when my mom announced she was sending me to her old school."

"You know, that actually makes perfect sense," Gracie agreed. "What does your mom do, if your dad's at one school and you're at another?"

Blake shoved his hands into his pockets. "She spends a lot of time here, but she also travels often. She writes for one of the travel magazines. Like one of the big-name ones, so they're always sending her places."

"And that works for your parents?"

"Strangely, it does," Blake said. "I get the sense that they're really only together because they want this perfect family image." He looked down at his feet. "Sorry, I don't really know why I'm telling you this."

"No, it's fine," Gracie shook her head. "Sometimes it's easiest to talk to total strangers or people you don't know very well."

"Are you telling me that after bumping into each other in the hallways twice, we're not instant BFFs?" Blake gasped, bringing a hand to his chest dramatically. "I'm very offended, Gracie."

"Either way, if you want to talk to me about anything, you can," Gracie offered. "I've been told that I'm a good listener. Well, that could just be because all my friends are all talkers."

"I'm a mix of both," Blake smirked at her. "So, I guess I'll have to bring out *your* talking side to get us even. So Gracie Last-Name, tell me all about your life."

"Well, it's actually Gracie Adams," Gracie said with a laugh. "And my life is pretty basic. Parents divorced when I was younger but are still friendly, so it's not like there's constant arguing and stuff. My dad remarried when I was ten, so I got a stepmom and a brother, and we're all really close now."

"Can I make the assumption that you're one of those kids who's really excited for Christmas break?" Blake asked.

"I actually am!" Gracie exclaimed. "And before you ask, I'm going to my mom's. My dad moved to Pennsylvania so he's still close, but he and Alicia are actually going to Switzerland this year for Christmas, so I'm spending the holidays with my mom."

"Is your brother going to be there too?" Blake asked with a frown. "Or is he going to be alone at your dad's?"

Gracie was confused for a moment, before realizing what Blake meant. "Oh no," she explained. "He's seven years older than me. He's spending it with his wife. They just got married last summer. It was really nice. And Skylar is lovely. So it'll just be me and my mom for Christmas. Oh, and Zara and Dean."

"Zara and Dean?"

Gracie nodded. "Zara's my best friend, and Dean's her twin. I invited her to come since her parents won't be here, and then I invited Dean because I didn't want them to be separated for Christmas," she rambled, before blushing as she realized just how much she had said. "Sorry, I'm going to stop talking now."

"Don't," Blake chuckled. "By Zara and Dean, do you mean Zara and Dean Ashcroft?"

"Yeah, do you know them?" Gracie asked, glancing sideways at Blake.

"I've heard of them," he said vaguely. Gracie frowned, getting the feeling that he was hiding something. She decided not to push it.

"So, what will you be doing for Christmas?" Gracie changed the subject.

"I'll be here, probably," Blake said with a shrug. "My mom will be coming in a couple days before break starts. We've got a family reunion in the area."

"That sounds fun."

"Eh. My cousins don't like me very much, so it'll just be a weekend of me talking to adults about boring things." He perked up slightly. "It's at a nice hotel, though. With a pool."

"Are you a swimmer?" Gracie asked.

Blake nodded. "Yeah, I'm on the swim team. The pool at my school isn't as nice as the one I have at home, so it'll be great to swim in a decent pool for once. Normally, I have to sneak out to one of the local pools." He grimaced.

Gracie laughed uncomfortably. She had never snuck out before, although Zara had tried to convince her to go to a party this summer that would've required missing her midnight curfew. She also wasn't the biggest fan of pools, thanks to a recurring nightmare that starred her jumping off the diving board in her unicorn pajamas. "Yeah." She started walking again, Blake falling in step behind her.

"Where are you headed?" he asked.

Gracie nodded her head at the sign on the wall. "The library. I guess I'll see you around?"

"Yeah, someone's got to keep you from causing accidents in the halls," he teased. "I mean, bumping into defenseless students, dropping books everywhere..." he trailed off, grinning at her.

"Definitely," Gracie giggled. "Have fun at your reunion."

"Oh, I won't, but thanks." Blake sent her another grin before walking away.

Gracie shook her head at his antics before pushing open the library door. Hopefully she'd bump into Blake again soon. He seemed like a fun person.

## Chapter Nine

Dean tapped his foot as he sat in the uncomfortable velvet chair, matching his pace to the grandfather clock ticking directly in his line of sight. Next to him, Zara fidgeted in her identical chair. He glanced over at her, noting her bored expression. He looked back at the clock. Another minute had passed, totaling eight.

"Ahh children, you're both here," Uncle Aaron beamed, walking into his office. He ran a hand over his patchy reddish-gray hair, smiling at them with the trademark Ashcroft hazel eyes. Dean resisted the urge to roll his own. They had been called to the principal's office because where else would they meet? Uncle Aaron sat down in his equally uncomfortable looking chair, opposite the twins. They all stared at each other for a few seconds before Uncle Aaron broke the awkward silence. "So, are my favorite niece and one of my favorite nephews staying at school for Christmas?"

Dean winced. "No, we're not," he replied. Clearly Zara had no interest in the conversation since she was picking at her nails. "We'll be going to Gracie Adams' home."

The principal frowned. "You too?"

"Yes, sir," Dean nodded. "Gracie is Zara's best friend, and she was kind enough to invite us both."

"Yes, of course," Uncle Aaron nodded sharply. "Wouldn't want you two to be separated for the holidays."

Dean pasted a fake grin on his face before he kicked Zara to make sure she was paying attention. His sister jumped in her seat, forcing a smile on her face.

"Well, now that that's settled," Uncle Aaron continued, "I just wanted to remind you both about the family reunion that's taking place this weekend."

"Why aren't Theo and Jesse here then?" Zara asked. "If it's such a big deal that you need to call us into your office to remind us and all."

Uncle Aaron cleared his throat. "Yes, well, I wanted to check with you both about the holidays, and I know that both Jesse and Theodore's parents have spoken to them about the reunion."

"So, because our mom doesn't give a shit about us, you're our stand-in parent," Zara said sarcastically. "Lovely."

"Mind your language, Zara," Uncle Aaron reprimanded.

"Am I wrong?"

Uncle Aaron ignored her, turning to Dean instead. "Dean, I hear you have a new girlfriend," he began. Zara snickered; Dean kicked her again. "I'd like for you to bring her to the reunion."

"Excuse me?" Dean asked, his eyes widening. Did Uncle Aaron mean Adams? Because they certainly weren't dating.

"I would like you to bring her along to the reunion," Uncle Aaron repeated. "It will be nice for the family to get to meet her. If I'm not mistaken, my son said her name was Grace?"

Dean scowled inwardly. Of course, his cousin would be the one snooping and tattling to his dad. "Gracie," he muttered, not wanting to admit that they weren't actually dating and give away the game.

"As in the same Gracie you and Zara are visiting for Christmas?" Uncle Aaron checked, a frown appearing on his face.

"Yes." Dean nodded, rubbing his palms against his pants. "But, um, we hadn't started dating when we agreed to the plans," he lied.

"Does her mother know?"

*The Gossip Games*

"Yes," Dean lied again. "And she has separate rooms for us. Separate floors, in fact. Zara will share with Gracie, and her parents will be home the entire time, so there's nothing to worry about."

"Alright then," Uncle Aaron said with a nod. "Please bring her to the reunion. I would like to meet her, especially since you will be going to her house for the holidays. I'll call her mother and get permission for her to come."

Dean just nodded, not wanting to point out that he had met her before, with Gracie having been a student at Trinity since her freshman year. However, Zara had no such restraint, opening her mouth gleefully. Dean kicked her again to get her to shut up, and after Zara scowled at him, the three occupants of the principal's office sat in silence for a few moments.

Of all places to have awkward conversations, the administration offices were some of Dean's least favorites. Other than a few pictures on the desks, the offices barely had any personality, and Dean always hated uncomfortable meetings with nothing interesting to look at. He glanced at the tree pictures on the walls, but there was nothing exciting about them, and soon his gaze turned back to his uncle.

"Can I bring someone also?" Zara blurted out. Dean groaned, dropping his head into his hands. It was both an open secret and a taboo topic in the family that Zara was bisexual, but certain members of the Ashcroft clan refused to acknowledge it. He had accepted it right away, of course, and he knew that neither Jesse nor Theo had any problems with it. Jesse's dad didn't care. In fact, Dean wasn't sure if he even knew. Both Aunt Eliza and Aunt Lisabeth were supportive of his sister. If anything, they went overboard and showered Zara with all sorts of pride stuff. Pins, jackets, flags, buttons… Zara had a million of them in her closet.

The real problems were Uncle Aaron and Uncle Alex, who, coincidentally, were the president and vice president of Trinity. Uncle Alex refused to believe Zara, saying that she was just going through a phase. Uncle Aaron preferred to ignore Zara completely when she was talking about girls and pretend that she was straight.

Uncle Aaron looked uncomfortable. "If this person you would like to bring is of the opposite gender, you may," he said finally.

Zara scowled, popping her gum loudly. Dean startled, having not realized she had been chewing gum this whole time. "Never mind then," she muttered.

Dean glanced at her out of the corner of his eye before turning his attention back to Uncle Aaron. He knew full well that his sister wasn't dating anyone at the moment and had just been trying to annoy their uncle. "Was there anything else you needed?" he asked politely.

Uncle Aaron looked pleased suddenly, likely from the fact that at least one of his nieces and nephews had manners. That, or they could at least control themselves and not antagonize everyone within a five-mile radius. "No, that was it. The cars leave Friday afternoon, and we will return Sunday evening. You will not be missing any class."

"Sounds good," Dean said. "We'll see you Friday then."

"I will see you then, Dean, Zara." He nodded, effectively dismissing them. Zara didn't need him to tell her twice. She shot out of her chair as fast as humanly possible, leaving Dean to smile apologetically to their uncle before joining her outside the office.

"Let's go," Zara said the minute the door shut behind them. "If we hurry, we can still make the last bus to town. Theo and Jesse are already there, and we've got to stock up for the family playdate."

Dean sighed. "Did you really have to antagonize him like that? You could've been a little nicer, Zar. I know it's not easy, and they can be real assholes sometimes—"

"It's not my—"

"But," Dean continued loudly. "We're about to be stuck with them for a full weekend and I'd rather it not be arguments and fights the whole time. You know I love you. You know that I'm 100 percent on your side. I just don't want another reunion ruined because everyone can't stop fighting."

Zara rolled her eyes. "Yeah, yeah, whatever. I'll be nice when someone is nice to me. Now come on, we're stuck spending the weekend with Voldemort and the Death Uncles. I need proper supplies."

⭐⭐
⭐⭐

Gracie's face brightened as Zara and Dean joined her outside the strip mall. She hugged her best friend quickly. Jesse and Theo had arrived a few minutes ago and waited with her, but she didn't know them very well and it had been awkward.

"Good, you're finally here," Jesse said impatiently. "What took so long?"

Dean winced. "The talk with Uncle Aaron took a little longer than expected."

Gracie glanced at him curiously, before stepping forward. "So, where are we going?" she asked.

"We're going to split up," Zara answered. "Oh, and Gracie?"

"Yeah?"

Zara glanced at her brother before turning back to Gracie. "Dean has something to tell you," she blurted.

"Thanks, sis," Dean said sarcastically. He turned to Gracie. "Apparently Annalisse and Juliet are so talented that even the school administration thinks that we're dating. Even Principal Ashcroft."

"Okay," Gracie said slowly. "Does it matter? You're free to tell him the truth, of course."

Dean smirked at her and shook his head. "Yes, but he also knows that we're going to your house for Christmas. Now he wants you to come with us to our family reunion this weekend."

"Oh, I almost forgot about that!" Jesse exclaimed.

Theo rolled his eyes. "Seriously? How could you forget? We've been getting nonstop texts from our parents for the past month! We came here to buy supplies! I sent you a reminder text this morning!"

"Like I open any of them," Jesse scoffed, sticking his hands in his pockets. "And besides, you know I only come here for the waffles. The waffle store is pretty damn good and the Trinity waffles *suck*."

"As I was saying," Dean said loudly. "Adams, our dear old Uncle Principal has officially ordered you to attend the yearly Ashcroft family reunion."

Gracie bit her lip, glancing between the cousins. Theo was thrusting his phone in Jesse's face, while both Zara and Dean looked at her expectantly. Did she really want to play Dean's girlfriend for an entire weekend? *Could* she pretend for an entire weekend?

"Well, I guess I can't really say no to Principal Ashcroft," she said finally. "And a weekend away from school would be nice. I've done all my work for the next week and a half, and it's not a test day on Monday, so I guess it's fine. I just have to let my mom know. But why are we *here*?" Gracie gestured to the strip mall.

Dean's eyes gleamed. "We have a bit of a family tradition," he said.

"Yeah, because our asshole cousin is going to be there as well, so we try to avoid him as much as possible," Zara piped up.

"I was telling the story." Dean scowled at her.

"Well, you were taking forever."

"Enough," Gracie interrupted. "I get the point. So, are we splitting up or sticking together?"

"Splitting up," Theo said firmly. He glanced sideways. "I'll take the supermarket," he said before hurrying off abruptly.

"Weird," Dean muttered, staring after him. "Normally he takes the candy store." He shook his head before turning back to the rest of the group. "I'll take the candy store then," he offered.

"I'll go to the Mini-Mart," Jesse said.

"And that leaves Gracie and me with the Dollar Store," Zara said with a nod. She grabbed Gracie's wrist and began tugging her away from the two boys. "We'll see you later!" Zara called over her shoulder, almost stumbling on a crack in the sidewalk.

Gracie followed her friend into the Dollar Store. "Where are we going?"

"Candy aisle," Zara said impatiently, turning to her left. Gracie followed her into one of the aisles, glancing at the different candies.

"What are we getting?" she asked, running her fingers over a bag of gummy fish.

Zara grinned. "Jelly beans."

"Okay," Gracie said slowly. "Just jelly beans? Or can I get something else as well?"

Zara shrugged. "You can get whatever you'd like," she responded. "But I'm just getting jelly beans."

Gracie nodded, wandering down the aisle as Zara grabbed a shopping cart. She cast a wary glance at the number of jelly bean bags Zara was shoving into the cart before grabbing a box of chocolate for herself. As Zara gathered the entire Dollar Store jelly bean supply, she walked through the aisles, checking out anything that looked remotely interesting. Gracie grabbed a couple of art supplies off a nearby shelf, cradling them in her arms as she walked back to Zara.

Her jaw dropped as she saw her best friend's cart, eying the piles of jelly beans, candy bars, and bags of Hershey's chocolates that Zara had tossed inside. "Are you buying out the store or something?"

"Yes," Zara said seriously.

Gracie shook her head. "Why do you need so much candy anyway?"

Zara winked at her as she pushed the cart to the checkout counter. "You'll see. Pass me your stuff?"

Gracie placed her items in the cart, knowing better than to argue with Zara about paying. The redhead would end up insisting that she should pay since she was dragging Gracie along to the reunion. Even if it wasn't true, Zara would likely get her way, so Gracie didn't even bother to try.

While Zara paid, Gracie drifted away to check out the items on display. A grin split her face when she came to the checkout counter next to Zara's, where a bunch of random items were hanging. Gracie reached out and ran a finger over a couple of the jeweled mirrors, taking one off the shelf and flipping it over.

"Hi there, are you ready to check out?" someone asked.

Gracie spun around, a surprised look on her face, to see a Dollar Store worker smiling at her from behind the checkout desk. "Excuse me?"

The employee nodded at her. "The mirror?"

Gracie looked down at her hand, where she was still clutching the mirror. On one hand, it would make a cute gift. On the other hand, she didn't know if she was going to be giving a gift to the person she had in mind.

"Sure," she said with a shrug. "I might as well. It's not that expensive." She dug into her shoulder bag, pulling out a five. "This should cover it," she said, taking the bag offered to her. "Thank you, have a nice day."

Zara turned to her, toting three bags in each hand. "Ready to go?"

"Yeah," Gracie said with a nod. "Are we meeting up with the boys?"

"No, we're going back." Zara shook her head. "Dean texted. He, Jesse, and Theo took the bus already."

☆☆
☆☆

The first thing Dean noticed when he, Jesse, and Theo exited the shuttle was the abnormal number of students clustered on the lawn.

"What's everyone doing here?" Dean questioned.

Jesse shrugged his shoulders. "No clue," he responded, handing Theo his shopping bags. Striding over to a group of freshmen girls, he flashed them a grin, returning a couple seconds later with a piece of paper in hand and a smirk on his face.

"What is this?" Dean asked, his neck craned to see what Jesse was holding out. He shifted his own bags and snatched the paper from Jesse's hand. "Who took this? Where did this come from?" Dean glared down at the paper.

"It's a picture," Theo said, confused.

"Yes," Dean spat out. "Of me. And Adams. Asleep! When was this taken?"

Theo leaned over to look at the picture again. "From the looks of it, it was taken on the bus."

Dean thought back to the bus ride to DC. "Oh yeah. Adams sat next to me because Zara was snoring or whatever, and we fell asleep on each other. Somebody must have taken a picture of us."

"Who would do that?" Jesse wondered.

Dean turned to him grimly before gesturing to the lawn. "The two girls who are handing out the pictures." He watched as Annalisse and Juliet ran around outside the school, handing out papers to every person they passed.

"What's going on?" Zara asked, appearing behind the three boys.

Jesse yelped. "Don't scare me like that!"

Zara grinned at him, clearly amused. "No promises. Anyway, what's going on?"

"Somebody took a picture of me and Adams and made a ton of copies," Dean said sharply, thrusting the picture at Zara. Dropping her bags on the grass, Zara took the picture from his hand, Gracie peering over her shoulder to see.

"Oh hey, that came out nicely!" Gracie exclaimed.

All four Ashcrofts spun around to look at her. "What do you know about this?" Dean asked suspiciously.

Gracie gave him a sweet smile. "I don't know, Dean, is there something you'd like to confess?"

Dean gnashed his teeth, sending her a fierce glare. Did she somehow orchestrate this? He'd never thought her to be that devious, but she had surprised him in the past couple of weeks. "No," he spat out.

"Well, in that case, I know nothing," Gracie declared, walking past him and into the school. Dean hurried to catch up to her.

"Was it you?" he asked.

"Was what me?"

"The pictures," Dean insisted. "How did you take them? I know it was you."

Gracie shrugged smugly. "Maybe it was. Maybe it wasn't."

"Come on, you can tell me," Dean continued. "I'm not going to tell anyone. If anything, it'd be more believable if it was me who did it. No one would believe that straight-A, teacher's pet, goody two-shoes Gracie Adams spread those pictures around the entire school."

"Hypothetically, somebody may have seen you sleeping and faked being asleep and then let the people in the seat in front of them know we were asleep."

Dean glanced at her admiringly. "That's pretty impressive, Gracie," he admitted.

"So I'm Gracie now?"

Dean shrugged. "You've earned it," he conceded.

## Chapter Ten

What does one call a hotel that looks like it was carved out of a movie about Ancient Greece? Complete with marble pillars, three fountains that were overflowing with a sparkling gold liquid, and a diamond encrusted sign proclaiming it to be the Olympus Hotel, it was one of the most stunning things Gracie had ever seen.

She climbed out of the van, her mouth dropping open at the unobstructed view of the hotel. It had been gorgeous through the van windows, but there was something different about staring at it from only a few feet away. "Okay, I knew your family was rich, but this is ridiculous."

Zara barely gave the hotel a second glance as she strode down the red carpet. Yes, there was a literal red carpet. Gracie was beginning to think the thirty-minute car ride had taken them all the way to Hollywood. She glanced down at the red and white squares pathway under the carpet, glad that they were smooth granite and didn't have a star etched in each one. They were still in New York, but Gracie had never seen a part of New York like this before.

"This is nothing," Zara said dismissively, snapping her fingers.

Someone in a fancy uniform rushed over and began collecting their bags. "You should have seen the hotel in Paris."

Gracie shook her head in awe as she followed her friend into the building. "Hey, where did the boys go?" she asked, glancing around the lobby. It was just as mesmerizing as the outside. Gracie was tempted to spend all weekend just petting the soft-looking walls.

"Who knows?" Zara shrugged, heading to the front desk. She slid her ID out of her leopard-print shoulder bag, handing it and a twenty to the desk clerk. Gracie joined her, still unable to tear her eyes away from the elegant decor.

"We're right here," Dean said from behind Zara, sliding out from behind a marble pillar and causing her to jump.

"Don't do that!" Zara exclaimed, hitting his chest with every word. "God, will you ever learn?"

Dean laughed, turning to Gracie. "We ran into my aunt and uncle outside," he answered her earlier question. "Jesse and Theo are still stuck talking."

Gracie nodded, stepping a little closer to him as Zara moved to get something else out of her purse. "Makes sense. So, where are we going now?"

"Our rooms. Then we'll probably chill until it's time to eat. There's not much of a set schedule for these things outside of meals."

Zara turned around, a handful of keycards in her fist. "We're right next door to each other," she reported.

"Good." Dean grinned. "That'll make it easier."

"Voldemort's opposite us girls." Zara groaned.

"That'll make it much harder," Dean corrected himself.

Gracie frowned, looking between the twins. "Who's Voldemort?"

"Our evil cousin," Zara told her seriously.

"Okay," Gracie drew the word out. "How evil are we talking?"

"Super evil," Dean said. "You'll meet him either at dinner tonight or hopefully tomorrow, but I would stay far, far away."

"I'll keep that in mind."

"Zara! If you don't get out of that bathroom, I *will* leave without you!" Gracie yelled, banging on the door. She crossed her arms as she stomped back to the really comfortable bed, sitting down with a huff.

"I'll be out in a minute," Zara called. "Relax. We have time."

Gracie sighed. She didn't really want to go down to dinner without Zara, since it wasn't her family and she didn't know most of the adults. On the other hand, she definitely didn't want to be late. Gracie stood up and moved to the mirror, giving herself one last look.

The Ashcrofts had a strict dress code of *formal*, so both girls had dolled up for the family dinner. Zara had sequestered herself in the bathroom, short black dress half on as she applied an obscene amount of eyeliner. Gracie had taken the simpler route, applying basic makeup before shrugging into a lavender dress she'd gotten at Macy's this summer. The dress cinched at her waist and fell down to her knees, the three-quarter sleeves perfect for the cool December air.

"Zara!"

"I'm almost out!"

Gracie made a face at the bathroom door, before frowning as a knock echoed through the room. Who could that be? She had thought they were meeting everyone downstairs.

"Hi," Dean said when she opened the door.

"Hi," Gracie responded. "Um, what are you doing here?"

Dean's face got a little redder. "Well, I know how long Z takes to get ready, so I figured I would walk you down, seeing as we're supposed to be dating." He stared at some point behind her.

Gracie ran her eyes up and down Dean's body. She had read somewhere that all boys looked hotter in a suit but hadn't believed it until now. It was hard to tear her eyes away from how the silky navy material hugged his body. "Should we go?" she prompted when neither of them made to move.

"Yes!" Dean exclaimed, hurriedly stepping out of the doorway.

Gracie stifled a laugh as she followed him. The elevator was just down the hall, and the two walked side by side, careful not to touch each other. Gracie was very conscious of Dean next to her, and judging from the looks he kept shooting her, he felt the same.

Suddenly, Dean stiffened, and he let out a groan. "Uncle Aaron approaching," he muttered to Gracie.

☆☆☆

Dean glanced around wildly, reaching out to jab the elevator button multiple times. "Come on, faster," he hissed, pressing it again. He shot Gracie a look, hoping to convey his panic, but her face stayed blank.

Dean pressed the button again, wondering if there was any way to get out of the impending uncomfortable conversation. He glanced at Gracie again, his eyes taking in how her curled hair barely brushed her shoulders, and how her lips looked even more glossy than usual.

He froze as an idea came to him. It would both keep Uncle Aaron away and pay Gracie back for the picture prank. Without thinking it through any further, Dean spun around, pressed Gracie against the wall, and kissed her.

This kiss was their most passionate so far, Gracie's hand finding his hair instantly. Dean slipped an arm around her waist, pulling her closer. He heard a strangled cough coming from down the hall. Grinning, he nipped at Gracie's bottom lip, opening her mouth to him.

"I leave you alone for two minutes and this happens?" Zara's voice rang out. Dean kissed Gracie for a second longer before breaking away and forcing himself to take a step back before he kissed her again.

"Hello, Zar," he said casually, wiping his mouth with the back of his hand. He made a mental note to find a tissue to clean the lip gloss off. "You look nice." His sister was dressed in one of her endless black dresses, this one a fancy material that shimmered in the hallway light. Dean couldn't claim to be a fashion expert, but he could tell that his sister had definitely put in effort for tonight.

Zara's red curls danced as she pushed past them to press the elevator button. "I know. Now let's go."

Dean let his gaze linger on Gracie as she followed Zara into the elevator, which somehow opened almost instantly after Zara pressed the button. Out of the corner of his eye, he saw Uncle Aaron hurry to make the elevator, carefully avoiding his and Gracie's eyes.

"Hello, Uncle Aaron," he said pleasantly. "How was your drive?"

"Very nice, thank you," his uncle muttered. "Zara. Ms. Adams."

Both girls murmured hello, and Dean took the opportunity to slip his arms around Gracie and tug her against his chest. He couldn't see her face from his position, knowing Gracie, her entire face was red. Zara looked at them curiously, but Dean only hugged Gracie tighter.

---

Dinner with the Ashcrofts was nothing but entertaining. Zara and Dean's mother wouldn't be arriving until tomorrow, and Zara had gleefully proclaimed that "Voldemort" would be too, but everyone else was there. In her seat between Zara and Dean, Gracie stayed quiet and enjoyed her fancy meat and potato dish as the rest of the table started arguing.

Dean nudged her. "Sorry about them all," he said in a whisper, gesturing to where his aunts were comparing something on their phones. His uncles were talking loudly about school business, and Zara and Jesse were blatantly hitting each other. Theo, opposite Zara, had his eyes glued to something under the table and was ignoring everyone else. "This isn't normal."

"You mean your aunts and uncles don't normally argue about

who has the most money?" Gracie exclaimed with a fake gasp, careful to keep her tone low as well.

Dean shrugged. "Well, that's pretty normal between Theo and Jesse's parents," he said, pointing out each couple. Gracie stared at Jesse's dad, who looked shockingly similar to both Theo and Dean.

"What about your mom?" Gracie asked curiously. "When she arrives tomorrow, I mean. Where does she fall in?"

"Oh, she'll compare clothes with Jesse's parents or argue about the school with the uncles," Dean said. "And by argue, I mean protest whenever they try to get her to show a little responsibility. Theo's mom and Aunt Becky—Principal Ashcroft's wife—are the good ones; they usually keep to themselves and get as drunk as possible. But my mom jumps right into the arguments. Well, half the time they're about her and how she's not doing anything with her life."

Gracie nodded silently. "Zara's told me a bit about her."

"So you know she's not really in our lives," Dean said, glancing at her.

"Yeah, that was the gist of Zara's hour-long rants." Gracie chuckled slightly.

"Oh, I've been on the receiving end of those way too many times," he said with a laugh, before sobering up. "When you meet her tomorrow, I'd just like to apologize in advance for anything she says or does."

"You don't have to do that," Gracie reassured him.

"Still," Dean insisted. "She's probably going to say some stuff. Just...don't take any of it personally, okay? It won't be as bad as it usually is because she's around other people, but don't take any of it to heart."

"I won't."

Dean nodded, picking up his fork again. After a few bites, he turned back to Gracie. "Hey, want to get out of here?"

Gracie bit her lip. "Where would we go?"

Dean grinned at her. "Anywhere we want," he said, holding out a hand.

Gracie glanced between Dean and her half-eaten plate of food. "Why not?" she said with a sigh, taking his hand. "Anything's got to be better than this."

Dean stood up, tugging Gracie out of her chair. "Come on, let's go walk along the beach."

Gracie's mouth fell open. "There's a beach!?" she exclaimed. "How fancy *is* this hotel?"

"Pretty fancy," Dean replied. "We Ashcrofts are great swimmers, so the uncles always make sure to book a place with at least three pools. This one just happens to have a beach too." He nodded towards the exit. "It's back out this way."

✯ ✯
✯

"No way." Gracie laughed, stumbling down the hotel hall. She wrapped her arms around Dean, barely able to keep her shaking shoulders upright. Thanks to a private party and a mean-looking security guard, they hadn't made it to the beach, but there had been a really comfy couch nearby that was perfect for listening to music with Dean's earbuds and trading childhood stories. She hadn't even noticed that three hours had passed, until the playlist they were listening to ended and Dean checked the time.

Dean grinned proudly. "Way," he said, leaning around her to slide the keycard into the reader. Gracie swung the door open, detangling herself and taking her card from Dean's hand.

"I can't believe that you guys had a chalk fight on the beach in onesies." She shook her head.

"You told her that?" Zara asked, appearing in the doorway.

"Um, yeah," Dean said, glancing at his sister. "Are we doing the thing tonight?"

Zara shrugged. "Might as well. We'll certainly need it tomorrow."

Gracie whipped her head between the two siblings. "What are you talking about?" she asked suspiciously. "It's not, like, illegal or anything, right?"

Zara laughed. "No, it's not." She turned back to Dean and ordered, "You go get Jesse and Theo." Dean saluted before running out of the room.

"Zara, what's going on?" Gracie asked with a sigh.

Zara gestured to one of the beds. "Take a seat. You're about to witness one of the Ashcroft family traditions."

Gracie acquiesced, scooting herself to lean against the headboard. She hugged a pillow to her chest, watching as Zara dug through her suitcase.

"Oh, put on pajamas," Zara said, poking her head up. "Just put on a bra or something since the boys are coming."

Gracie nodded, slipping off of the bed and grabbing her pajamas from her suitcase. She changed into the tank top and shorts, keeping her bra on like Zara had directed. "Where are the makeup wipes?" she called through the bathroom door.

"On the table out here!"

Gracie nodded, opening the bathroom door. She quickly wiped off her makeup and crawled back onto the bed, making herself comfortable again. "When will the boys get here?" she asked Zara, who was currently placing bags on the other bed.

Zara grinned. "Any minute," she said as a knock sounded on the door. Zara made a shooing motion and, grumbling, Gracie got up to open the door.

Jesse pushed past her into the room, making a beeline for the candy. "Hey, Grace," he called over his shoulder.

Gracie sighed. "It's Gracie," she said wearily.

Theo shot her a smile. "Ignore my less charming cousin."

Gracie nodded at him, turning to greet the last member of their group. "Hello again, Dean," she teased. "I see you couldn't stay away for long."

"Ahh, yes." Dean cleared his throat. "My dear Gracie, 'I miss you like the sun misses the flowers, like the sun misses the flowers in the depths of winter, instead of beauty to direct its light to, the heart hardens like the frozen world which your absence has banished me to.'"

Gracie stared at him, stunned. Did he just quote Shakespeare to her? Gracie blushed. "T-that's very i-impressive," she stammered. Dean grinned at her, and Gracie realized they were still standing in the doorway. "Come in," she offered, thankful that her voice seemed to be working again.

Gracie followed Dean into the room, blinking when she saw what Zara, Jesse, and Theo had done. Someone had covered every inch of both beds with plastic bowls, the kind her mom bought in bulk from the supermarket. Assorted bags and containers of jelly beans littered the room and were currently being opened and dumped into even more plastic bowls.

"What are you doing?"

"We are separating jelly beans," Jesse said excitedly. "As in rainbow color. Like a pride flag! Or a packet of colored pencils. Or, or, those little troll people whose hair you brush and then have them act out Marvel movies and kill-slash-dump-red-food-coloring-on each other!"

Gracie stared at him for a second, having gotten lost somewhere around the colored pencil. "Okay, I have a question," she began. "Do you even know what you're saying? Like, do you know how ridiculous that sounds?"

"No, I 100% know it's ridiculous," Jesse said cheerfully, a playful twinkle in his eye. "Most of the time."

"Do you—"

"No, I don't think before I talk."

Gracie nodded. "Glad to have that cleared up." Still slightly confused, but accepting that Jesse was simply a unique human, she turned around. "How can I help, Zar?"

Zara pointed to the dresser. "You can start by dumping the jelly beans into the bowls."

"What if I want to sort them from the bag?" Dean called from the other side of the room.

Zara huffed. "You can do that too, Dean. You know that, considering you ask the same question *every* reunion."

Gracie laughed, picking up a bag. She quickly pulled it open and spilled the jelly beans into a dish before moving over to the bed and sorting the candy into their appropriate bowls. "What if I don't know which bowl it belongs to?" she asked.

Theo tossed her a container, which Gracie barely caught. It had images and a list of the flavors on the back. "Use this. If you're still not sure, it goes over there." He nodded to the nightstand, where three small beans sat.

Gracie nodded, picking up a blue bean. She deduced it was blueberry flavored and placed it in the right bowl. "So what happens after they're all sorted?" she asked curiously.

"We eat them," Jesse piped up. "We each like different flavors, so we take the ones that we like."

"Yeah, I like the lemon and apple ones," Theo said. "Zara will dump the red ones into a bowl and eat them randomly, and for some reason," he said, making a face, "Jesse likes the orange ones."

"And I like the berry blue flavor," Dean cut him off.

"Gracie likes the marshmallow and vanilla ones," Zara said absently, sorting beans on the floor.

"I do," Gracie confirmed.

"That's perfect then." Theo nodded.

"What do you do with the leftovers?" Gracie asked curiously.

All four Ashcrofts grinned at her. "Pranks," they all said in unison.

Gracie winced. "I feel bad for your victims," she said dryly.

"Last year we covered Uncle Asshole's floor with them."

"The year before that, we used hot glue to stick them to his suitcases in a certain phallic shape."

Gracie laughed, going back to her sorting. When she had finished the bag, determining the last bean to be a green apple, she looked up. "How did this start?" she asked the quiet room. "Like, did you just go somewhere and decide to buy a ton of jelly beans on a whim?"

"By a ton, you mean every single jelly bean in the area," Jesse said smugly.

Gracie ignored him, turning to Dean. "Our grandmother used to bring jelly beans along to the reunions," Dean explained. "She would use treats to keep us quiet when we were bored. We would hide in a corner of the room and divvy up the jelly beans by our favorite colors. Our grandmother loved lighthearted pranks, so one year, when the reunion happened over her birthday, we bought out the nearby stores and filled her entire room with jelly beans while everyone else was at dinner. Of course, we had to clean them up after," he said with a laugh. "But she loved it."

"Aww, that's so cute," Gracie sighed happily. "Will I get to meet your grandmother tomorrow?"

Dean swallowed, looking down at the beans in his lap. Gracie glanced around the room, noting Zara's sharp intake of breath and Jesse's and Theo's morose faces. Had she said something she shouldn't have?

"She passed away when we were twelve," Zara cut in sharply.

Gracie's eyes widened. "I'm so sorry."

"It's okay," Dean said, his expression casual once more. Gracie studied him closely. Had she imagined that upset look? "Anyway, we do this every year now to honor her."

"Was her favorite candy jelly beans?" Gracie asked cautiously.

"Yeah, she loved them," Theo said with a smile. "When we sorted them, she used to have us take out one of every flavor for her. She ate every one."

"Even the banana ones?" Gracie asked, making a face.

"Even the banana ones."

## Chapter Eleven

"Today will be a lot more casual," Zara explained, sitting down in front of the mirror. "Wear a casual dress but not too fancy, something that you wouldn't mind getting dirty if we go to the beach. We've had some epic sand fights there."

Gracie stared at her, still half asleep after Zara had dragged her out of bed five minutes ago. "I don't have a casual dress," she said after a minute, having taken her that long to comprehend what Zara had said.

"Oh, that's okay, you can borrow one of mine. I brought extras."

"*You* brought extra dresses?"

Zara scowled at her. "Yes, me. I may not like my relatives, but I'm not going to show up to a formal event wearing a t-shirt. "

"What about your mom?"

Zara scoffed. "My mom doesn't care what I wear. Even if she does, she has no say in my clothes."

Gracie nodded, taking the dress Zara offered to her. "Why did you pack short sleeves?" she asked, holding the dress up against her body.

"Why not?"

"Because it's November and it's cold outside? Never mind. I'll just wear my jean jacket."

⭐⭐⭐

"You're not supposed to wear it like that," were the first words out of Dean's mouth when he saw Gracie that morning. She was standing outside the dining room, fidgeting with her dress. Dean hurried out of the elevator and over to her.

She frowned. "Wear what?"

Dean blushed, wondering if he shouldn't have said anything. Years of knowing Zara had taught him that it was never a good idea to comment on a woman's outfit unless you were complimenting her. "Um, the dress."

Gracie glanced down at her outfit, wobbling slightly in her three-inch heels. "How is it supposed to be worn?"

Dean gestured to her body. "May I?" he asked, stepping closer. Gracie nodded, and Dean reached out to pull the string. "You're supposed to tie it in the front," he explained. "Not the back."

Gracie let out a small chuckle. "How do you know this? Zara didn't mention that to me. It's her dress, by the way."

"I know." Dean nodded. "It's from Mom. It's one of the better ones she's sent. I was there when Zara opened it and threw it across the room," he said with a frown on his face. "So I know what it's supposed to look like."

Gracie gasped. "She did this on purpose!"

"Who?"

"Zara! When I asked for a dress, she gave me this one even though she had a ton of others in styles that I normally wear." Gracie motioned to the light blue striped dress. "I prefer flowers over stripes or polka dots."

Dean finished tying the bow, remembering something Zara had told him. "Your mom also likes flowers, right?"

"How do you know that?" Gracie asked.

Dean ran a hand through his hair. "Zara told me," he said after a minute, shoving his hands in his pockets and ambling forward a few steps. He didn't think he could get out his next words without blushing if he was staring at her. "I asked her for something your mom likes so I could bring it. For the holidays, I mean. It's very kind of her to have us over for the entire time."

"Oh, don't you know?" Gracie asked. "We're sending you back to school on the 27$^{th}$."

Dean spun around to face her, a panicked expression plain on his face. She was kidding, right? He voiced the question out loud.

"Yes, I'm kidding," Gracie said with a laugh.

Dean pressed a hand to his chest, feeling his heart beating faster than usual. "That was evil, Gracie Adams," he declared. "I need to sit down now." He migrated towards one of the lobby couches, motioning for Gracie to sit down next to him. He didn't really care whether they were sitting or standing, but he noticed that Gracie looked uncomfortable in her heels.

"Just call me Satan," she teased.

Dean looked at her, mock horror on his face. "You *are* Satan," he proclaimed. "The evilest of all evil!"

"Is that even a word?" Gracie laughed. She took the offered seat, one hand reaching down to rub her left ankle.

"Hey, you're the smart one, you tell me."

Gracie shrugged, before turning to glance around the lobby. Dean followed her gaze. If he was being honest, it wasn't the most impressive hotel he'd stayed in. But Gracie seemed to like it, and to him, that was what mattered.

"It's funny, because outside of my clothes, I'm not a big flower person. My mom loves the ground stuff—flowers, gardening, trees. I prefer the sky. Rainbows, clouds, the sun…"

"Understandable," Dean said with a nod. "The sun is pretty impressive. Not as impressive as me, of course."

Gracie shoved him lightly. "You are very full of yourself," she remarked.

Dean leaned in closer, and said in a mock whisper, "It's an Ashcroft thing."

"You know, I have no trouble believing that." Gracie shook her head.

Dean laughed. They fell into a comfortable silence, watching guests pass through the lobby. "We should go to breakfast," he said after a few minutes, noticing Zara walk into the dining area. "They'll be expecting us."

"Right." Gracie nodded. "I'll be meeting your cousin and mom, right?"

"Oh yeah," Dean said casually. "Evil cousin and absent mom. Great pair."

"I've met your mom before," Gracie offered. "Briefly. It was at the end of freshman year; she came to pick you guys up. We said hello while Zara ran around looking for her stuff."

"So you met her the time she was bribed to go pick up her own children," he said dryly.

Gracie gasped. "She was bribed?"

"Yeah, she was going to stay in Europe." Dean rolled his eyes. He looked at Gracie seriously. "Zara doesn't know. She still thinks it was our mom's choice. Please don't tell her."

"I won't," Gracie promised.

"Thank you," Dean said quietly.

"Does that happen often?"

Dean shrugged. "Once in a while," he said. "Really, the only time of year we're guaranteed to see her is at this family reunion. Uncle Aaron controls the family finances, and she knows unless she shows up, she doesn't get her year's allowance."

Gracie whistled. "I'm sorry," she said, reaching out to squeeze his shoulder. "You guys deserve so much better."

"It's okay." Dean shrugged again. "There's nothing we can do. Zara and I have each other. That's all we need."

"Well, you're going to have the Christmas of your lives at our house," Gracie said determinedly.

Dean laughed. "I can't wait. It's just you and your mom, right?"

"Yeah, she's amazing," Gracie said proudly. "Just wait. By the end of the break, she'll have adopted you both as her children. She's met Zara a couple of times, and sometimes I wonder which of us is her actual daughter."

"Zara writes to her," Dean realized. "She was sending letters last year, but never told me who they were to. And the cookies. Was that your mom as well?"

Gracie nodded. "Yeah, she bakes a lot. Expect to be well fed."

"I can't wait," Dean repeated. He cleared his throat. "We should probably stop stalling and go in now."

Gracie laughed nervously. "Probably."

"You don't want to, do you?"

Gracie shook her head furiously. "No. I'm scared."

"You'll be fine," Dean reassured her. He reached down and grabbed her hand, holding it for confidence. "Come on, let's go. I need my morning hot chocolate to be ready to face everyone."

☆☆☆

Gracie pushed open the door to the breakfast room, clutching Dean's hand a little tighter. She was still a little shocked that he had taken her hand in the first place but figured that since everyone assumed them to be a couple, he was just putting on a show. Either way, she was grateful for the constant reassurance that he was next to her.

She scanned the long table, seeing all the adults scattered throughout the seats. Jesse was with a dark-haired boy at the coffee station, but from the color of his hair, it wasn't Theo.

"Where's Theo?" Dean asked, having come to the same conclusion she did.

Gracie shrugged. "No clue. Who's that with Jesse?"

Dean's jaw clenched. "That's Voldemort," he informed her.

"He looks familiar," Gracie commented.

"Come meet my mother," Dean said abruptly, leading her to the far end of the table where a woman was picking at a plate of fruit. Gracie admired the woman's blue dress and elegant curls, a dark red that reminded her of Zara.

"Hello, Mom."

"Dean!" the woman looked up and beamed, the smile a bit too bright for her face. She raised her voice slightly, and Gracie noticed Principal Ashcroft glancing over from the other end of the table. "How lovely to see you, darling. It's been so long!"

Dean smiled, but Gracie could tell that it was fake. "Yes, it has," he said, sitting down and motioning for Gracie to take the seat next to him.

"And who is this lovely lady? Wearing the dress I sent. I see at least one person at this school has some taste," Zara and Dean's mom continued, brushing an invisible speck of dust off her heavily made-up face. "I'm not surprised Zara gave it away. She's never been able to appreciate good clothing."

"I'm Gracie Adams. Nice to meet you," Gracie offered, hoping to cut off any further remarks. She barely contained her surprise at the ease with which Ms. Ashcroft delivered snide comments.

"Ahh yes, Gracie, my children speak about you all the time," their mom said with a faint smile, before turning her gaze away and taking a bite of her fruit.

Gracie turned to Dean, raising her eyebrows at him before grabbing the spoon for the eggs. "Really?"

"No," Dean snorted. "We don't really tell her anything." He lowered his voice. "She just likes to give off the impression that she knows everything."

Gracie nodded. "Got it."

"Sorry I'm late," Zara said, plopping down in the chair opposite Dean. She reached across the table to grab his fork and stab a bite of Gracie's eggs. "Mother. Brother. Best friend."

Ms. Ashcroft coughed delicately, looking disapprovingly at her daughter. "Zara, darling, how is school going? Have you brought up that math grade yet?"

Zara gave her a fake smile. "Just great."

Her mother waited, but Zara volunteered no more information. "How about you, Gracie?" she said breezily. "Aaron tells me you're in honors classes. You *must* tell me what it's like. My own children never tell me anything, so I have absolutely no idea."

Zara dropped Dean's fork abruptly, and Gracie could see her clenching her fist. Next to her, Dean tensed. Reaching under the table, Gracie grasped his hand tightly. "It's going well," Gracie said politely. "A lot of work, Ms. Ashcroft."

"Oh, call me Alexandra," she said. "Ms. Ashcroft makes me feel like I'm back in high school again! Why, it was only a couple of years ago!"

Gracie stifled a laugh. From their brief conversation, Alexandra didn't seem as bad as her children had made her out to be. Alexandra attempted to ask about Zara and Dean's lives, but once the basic questions had been asked, she quickly lost interest. Sure, there had been a bunch of snide comments, but from Zara and Dean's stories, Gracie had been expecting so much worse.

"So, do you have plans with my nephews today?" Alexandra asked.

"Yes, we'll be hanging out later," Gracie answered when no one else made a move to.

"Sounds fun," someone behind her said. "What am I crashing?"

"Nothing," Zara spat, glaring furiously at a point behind Gracie's ear.

Gracie spun around, her eyes widening when she recognized the person standing in front of her, holding a plate of eggs and bacon. The boy looked just as surprised to see her, but his full lips quickly stretched into a smile. He was dressed nicely in an untucked green button down, but if it were blue, Gracie would have had trouble distinguishing between him and Dean if she had seen the duo from across the room. "Blake?"

*The Gossip Games*

"You know him?" Zara and Dean asked in unison.

Gracie glanced at them both before turning her attention back to Blake. "Yeah, we've run into each other a couple of times at Trinity. What are you doing here?" she addressed the question to him.

"This is my family reunion," Blake said, gesturing to the room. He walked around the table and sat down next to Zara, who scooted her chair away.

"No way," Gracie breathed. "I didn't know that *you* were Zara and Dean's cousin!"

"Yeah, it's not exactly something I advertise," Blake said casually.

Dean coughed. "You two are friends?" he asked incredulously.

"Yeah, Blake's cool," Gracie said. She shook her head. "I can't believe that *he's* your cousin." The twins had told her about their evil cousin, but she had trouble with the fact that said cousin was Blake, the charming boy who hung out in the halls.

Zara scowled. "Well, believe it, accept it, and stay far, far away."

"This was fun," Blake said sarcastically, shoving his full plate forward. "But I've got to jet. We should hang out later, Gracie," he tossed over his shoulder, four pairs of eyes watching him go.

Zara turned to Gracie. "Why didn't you tell me that Hallway Guy was my cousin?" she exclaimed.

"Why didn't you tell me your cousin was Hallway Guy?" Gracie retorted.

"Well, I didn't know his name," Zara pointed out. "Believe me, if I had known, I would have told you everything. In fact, I really should tell you everything. Then you can see that you don't want to be friends with Blake."

Gracie winced. "I'm not sure I want to know," she mumbled under her breath. Gracie cleared her throat and turned to Alexandra. "It was nice to meet you," she said politely, before standing. "I'm going to run back to the room real quick," she told Zara and waved to everyone before leaving.

Dean collapsed into bed that night, tired from the day's events. Zara had dragged him, Gracie, Jesse, and Theo—who had eventually shown up—all over the nearby town. Based on how much his feet hurt, they had visited every store at least twice.

Jesse groaned from the other bed. "I'm tired," he whined.

Dean laughed hoarsely. "Go to sleep then."

"I'm not *that* tired." Dean couldn't see him, but he knew Jesse was rolling his eyes.

"Hey, I'm stepping out to take a call," Theo said, poking his head out of the bathroom. Groaning to himself, Dean slid off the bed and went to brush his teeth. When he came out a couple minutes later, Theo was gone, and Jesse was snoring in the other bed.

Since none of the cousins had wanted to share a room with Blake, they had drawn straws to decide who would get a bed to themself. Jesse had tried to argue, but after the field trip, Theo and Dean had outvoted him. Dean had drawn the short straw and happily claimed the bed closest to the window, leaving Theo to grumble about sharing a bed with Jesse, who moved just as much as Zara did. However, Dean had barely seen Theo at all. The dark-haired boy would come in late and be gone in the morning without Dean ever noticing.

Dean climbed back into his bed, drawing the covers up to his chin.

When he drifted into consciousness again, Dean realized he was freezing. "Ugh, go away," he mumbled, swiping at what he assumed to be Jesse dumping ice on him again. His fingers hit nothing, so Dean opened his eyes, taking in the quiet room. He scanned the room again, realizing that the window was open and blowing cold air into the room. How had he not noticed that earlier? Dean padded to the window and pulled both the panel and curtains shut, glancing at the clock on his way back to bed.

Dean tossed and turned in bed until the clock struck three before resigning himself to the fact that he wouldn't be getting a full night's sleep. He pulled himself out of bed and grabbed his laptop before returning to sit cross-legged on the blanket. He glanced absentmindedly around the room, noting only one person asleep in the other bed.

"Where are you, Theo?" he muttered to himself, flipping the laptop open. Dean checked his email quickly, sending most of his unread box to junk. He opened his text messages, intent on sending Gracie a text asking her for more details about Christmas. He could just ask her tomorrow, but he would probably forget, so Dean figured he would just send her a quick text.

Speaking of Gracie, he also had to plan proper revenge for the picture. Dean's mind traveled through a variety of different ideas, ranging from mild revenge to utter humiliation. The door creaked open as he vetoed an idea involving shoes and shaving cream, and Theo slunk into the room.

Dean cleared his throat. "Just where do you think you're going, mister?" he said in a perfect imitation of his uncle.

Theo paled before relaxing as he realized it was just Dean. "Nowhere?" he offered.

Dean scoffed. "Not good enough, Theo. It's three in the morning!"

"I know, I know," Theo sighed. "I just lost track of time, okay? Don't tell anyone, please."

"Where were you?" Dean asked suspiciously. He eyed his cousin. Theo was definitely hiding something. He had been acting off since the jelly bean collection trip, and if Dean thought about it when it wasn't three am, he would probably be able to come up with a whole list of times Theo had disappeared or acted weird.

Theo looked away. "I just had to make a phone call."

"Fine," Dean said slowly. Since it was Theo, he probably wasn't doing anything illegal, so he decided to let the matter drop. "I won't tell anyone, but I want your help with something."

A look of resignation appeared on Theo's face. "Deal."

## Chapter Twelve

"Freedom!" Zara sang, jumping out of the car and throwing her arms open. She spun around, grinning at the Trinity building. Her next moves included a Rockettes-worthy kick and a little shimmy before she pretended to kiss the brick walls. "Freedom! Freedom!"

Gracie laughed at her friend from where she was standing on the sidewalk. They had taken two cars back from the reunion, and Gracie and Dean's car had arrived a few minutes before the other. "It wasn't that bad," she said, stretching her arms above her head. She yawned, pulling her earbuds out of her ears and tucking them into her bag. Her nap in the car had been nice, but she was more than ready to get back to dealing with the constant stress of tests and homework.

Zara scoffed. "Maybe for you. But *I*, on the other hand, had to deal with the constant nagging and 'oh Zara, when are you going to get a boyfriend?'" she mocked her family. "'Don't you own anything that's not black or doesn't have a leopard print?'"

"Okay, I see your point," Gracie agreed.

Dean joined them, a duffel bag slung over his shoulder. "What point?"

"That your family sucks," Gracie deadpanned.

"Fact," Dean nodded seriously. "Or at least some of them do."

Zara coughed, "Blake," but Gracie ignored her.

"I'm going to get my books and then go to the library," Gracie said. "I have some books I want to read, and an essay due in a few weeks that I can start."

"No," Zara whined. "Just come play with me!"

Gracie laughed. "Remind me how old you are again?"

"I'll go with you to the library," Dean jumped in, cutting Zara's snarky remark off.

"You?" Gracie asked, surprised.

Dean shrugged. "I go every once in a while. I do study, you know."

Zara snorted. "When hell freezes over, maybe."

Dean looked insulted. "I'm just going to go. Are you coming with me, Gracie?"

Gracie glanced between the twins before nodding. "Can you take my bag to my room for me, Zar?" she said, before hurrying to catch up with Dean. She offered him an apologetic smile. "Sorry about back there."

"You didn't do anything," Dean reassured her. "Besides, Zara's my twin sister. I'm pretty used to her by now."

"I would hope so," Gracie joked. She sobered up again. "But you shouldn't have to put up with it. There's nothing wrong with the library."

Dean shrugged. "We grew up very privileged. Zara's used to that. I hate to say it but growing up with no active parents and a ton of money didn't teach her the value of hard work. She still believes that she can do pretty much anything she wants."

"That's not a bad thing," Gracie said cautiously.

"No, it's not," Dean rushed to add. "It's great to have dreams. But you can't just expect everything to be handed to you on a silver platter. You have to work for it. If you put in hard work and dedication, you can do anything you want." He offered her a soft smile. "You've probably noticed, but Jesse and Zara are similar. And I'm not just talking about their looks. So are Theo and I. But while Zara was roping Jesse into playing games with her, Theo and I were sneaking around the house, listening in on the adults' conversations and having serious discussions. Zara was spared the harsh reality, and everyday I'm grateful for that. No child should have that burden."

"But you do," Gracie said. The words hung heavily in the air.

Dean looked at her. "Yeah."

They walked in silence for a minute, arms barely touching. It wasn't a long walk from the entryway to the library, but both Dean and Gracie were content to slowly stroll through the corridors.

"How bad was it?" Gracie asked, breaking the silence.

"Not that bad," Dean said honestly. "There are tons of bigger problems in the world. But to my eight, nine-year-old self, it was everything. You have to understand, our mother abandoned us when we were younger. We stayed at Theo's for a bit before our grandmother took us in. My grandfather passed away before we were born, so she was basically raising the two of us on her own. But then she got sick and couldn't watch two exuberant children full time. Z and I were shuttled off to whichever aunt and uncle had the least plans that week."

"I'm sorry," Gracie said quietly.

Dean smiled sadly. "It's okay. It was a while ago."

Gracie glanced over at him. "I've been wondering something, but I didn't really want to ask Zara since she'd—"

"You want to know about Blake, and you want the facts rather than an entire rant," Dean finished.

Gracie shrugged. "I was going to say it in a nicer way, but essentially, yeah."

"It was a long time ago," Dean said slowly. "Well, it started then anyway. We never got along as children, really. Blake was always a bit of a spoiled brat and loved showing off his new toys. But as we grew older, and after our grandmother died, he got cruel. He would tell Zara things, and it really affected her."

"What things?" Gracie asked softly. "C-can I ask? You don't have to answer."

"I'll answer," Dean said after a minute. "It's not really my story to tell, so I won't go into detail. But he tried to convince Zara that nobody wanted her, that everyone in her life either abandoned her or died. She spent months following me everywhere after that." He let out a small chuckle. "Even to the bathroom. She had to sit right outside, and I had to talk to her the entire time. He was also the one that told our uncles that she was queer. He overheard her telling me, and everyone in the family knew within a few hours. She didn't get to come out or even understand her sexuality herself. Blake took that from her."

Gracie covered her mouth with her hands, tears welling in her eyes. Zara had never mentioned how she came out, and Gracie hadn't pressed. Gracie had figured it hadn't gone well, but this? She wished she could go back in time and give little-Zara a hug.

Dean looked at Gracie solemnly. "Look, I didn't want to bring it up at the reunion because it's not really my story to tell, but I know you care about Zara. Please don't tell her you know; it's a really touchy subject with her. It's affected all of us, really. I don't want you to base your opinions on Blake because of something that happened to us in the past, so can we just pretend this conversation never happened?"

"If that's what you want," Gracie said hesitantly.

"Yeah."

Gracie swallowed, unsure of what to say next. If Dean didn't want to bring the conversation up again, then she would put it out of her mind entirely. They spent the rest of the short walk to the library in silence.

"See you later, Gracie," Dean said after they passed through the doors.

Surprised, Gracie turned around, only to find him already gone. Shaking her head, she made her way to her usual desk, before realizing that she had left her bag with Zara. "Stupid," she muttered, smacking herself on the forehead. She looked around helplessly, but without her notebooks, she wasn't sure what work she had to do.

After a few seconds of panicking, Gracie decided to find Dean and ask him what work he had. They were in the same math and history classes, so if he had homework in those classes, she would as well. Nodding to herself, Gracie set out on her quest.

Dean was sitting at one of the tables in the back, his head bent low as he flipped pages of a textbook. Gracie was about to go over and tap him on the shoulder before she stopped herself.

Dean had kissed her without warning at the hotel. It was only fair that she repaid the favor. Smirking, Gracie walked over and spun Dean's chair around, quickly kissing him.

It only took a few seconds for her to realize that the kiss wasn't as good as it normally was. She had little to compare it to, but Dean was definitely a better kisser than the last guy she had kissed. Today, however, it was like Dean wasn't even trying. The kiss seemed hesitant, as if he wasn't sure what he was doing. He kissed back after a few seconds, but it wasn't as passionate as it normally was.

Also, Dean wasn't touching her hair. He *always* threaded his fingers through her hair.

Gracie broke the kiss, staring wide-eyed at Theo's shocked face. "You're not Dean!" she sputtered.

Theo laughed nervously. "Um, no."

"I'm so sorry," Gracie blurted. "You look just like him from the back, and I thought you were him."

Theo shrugged. "It's a common misconception," he said casually.

"But...I kissed you!"

"You kissed me," Theo agreed. He stared at her for a second.

"Well, you kissed back," Gracie pointed out. She felt like smacking herself but figured that if she had already gone this far, she might as well dig the hole deeper. "You know what? I'm just going to go." She crossed her arms and hurried out of the library.

As soon as she was outside the doors, Gracie hit herself. "Stupid,

stupid, stupid!" she hissed. "Why couldn't you check to see if it was Theo or Dean? They look so much alike!"

A freshman passing by gave her a weird look, but Gracie ignored him. She felt so ridiculous, having kissed the wrong Ashcroft. Would Theo tell Dean? They weren't *actually* dating, so did it even matter? She could kiss whoever she liked. Dean was a better kisser than Theo, though. Gracie blushed.

Did she like kissing Dean?

Okay, she liked kissing Dean. But that didn't mean that she liked him.

He could be spiteful and rude and got her into trouble.

He was also caring and smart and a great brother.

And he was a damn good kisser.

★
★ ★

Dean looked up from his spot on the bed as Theo rushed into the dorm room, his hands moving wildly. "What's up?" he asked, stretching his legs and standing up. He had been sitting in that spot for hours since he had returned from the library, so it was good to be moving again.

Theo's eyes were wide. "I've just spent the past couple of hours hiding in the library."

"Okay," Dean said slowly. He inspected his cousin, who was breathing raggedly. "Is this an SCT conversation?"

Theo considered the question for a moment before nodding. Dean motioned towards his bed, before getting up and locking the door. He checked the bathroom, but Jesse wasn't hiding in there, so he returned to the bed and sat opposite Theo.

Theo looked down at his hands. "I—" he began, before stopping.

Dean waited patiently. "You can say whatever you want," he said quietly. "I won't judge you. Take your time."

Theo nodded, taking a deep breath. He laughed shakily. "I don't really know what I'm doing. Like, is this really happening?"

Dean raised his hands in a shrugging movement. "I don't know what you're talking about, so I can't give you a straight answer," he answered honestly. "But if you want to tell me, then I'm here to listen. If you don't want to tell me, then we can sit here like this all night."

They sat in silence for a few minutes, Dean trying not to make it look like he was staring at Theo picking at his hands.

"I think I'm gay," Theo said suddenly.

Dean glanced at him. "You think?"

Theo just looked back down at his hands. "I don't know," he said quietly. "But I met these guys recently, and there was one that I liked a lot, you know? I thought it was just friendship, but it was different from you or Jes. And then a girl kissed me earlier, and I didn't really feel anything."

Dean brightened. "Was it Gracie?" He shook his head. "Never mind. Not important right now. So you think that you're gay because you're not attracted to a pretty girl and you had feelings for a boy?"

"I think so." Theo bit his lip. "Like, I don't know for sure. It's not like I've kissed a boy or anything. But I've never had a crush on a girl before, so I don't know what that's like either."

"Do you want to kiss a boy?" Dean asked quietly.

"I wouldn't...be opposed to it."

Dean nodded. "Okay, then."

"I've been trying to find out more. I even took those stupid Buzzfeed quizzes, and I reached out to a few people online. That's what I was so busy with at the reunion. One of the people I spoke to is in a different time zone. And that time at the strip mall, the boy was at the supermarket. I just wanted to spend time with him, you know?

"I also don't know what to tell my parents," Theo continued. "Like, I know you, Zar, and Jes would be fine, but my dad will never accept it. You know how old school the Ashcroft men are, and my dad's the worst of them all. My mom will probably be okay with it, but she always does what my dad says."

Dean winced. He knew firsthand how his uncles could be. "Maybe it'll be different," he offered. "Since you're his son and all." He waited for Theo to respond, but the dark-haired boy said nothing. "What do you want to do now?" Dean asked.

Theo thought for a moment. "I don't know."

"Do you want to tell someone else?"

Theo shrugged again. "I don't know."

"Do you want to find out for sure?" Dean tried.

"I think so," Theo whispered.

"Okay," Dean nodded. "Then we will."

"How?" Theo asked, lifting his head up. "In this school?"

Dean gave his cousin his trademark smirk. "Leave it to me."

☆☆
☆

"You said Gracie was pretty," Theo said. He had returned to his own bed, and Dean had unlocked the door.

Dean glanced over at him. "No, I didn't."

"Yes, you did," Theo countered loudly, ignoring Dean's protests. "But putting how you find Gracie pretty aside, why did you want me to do my hair your way and sit in the library?"

"For Gracie to kiss you," Dean said patiently. "I knew she wouldn't be able to pass up the chance for revenge, not after what happened at the hotel."

Theo sat up. "What happened at the hotel?" he asked suspiciously.

"I may have kissed her in front of Uncle Aaron," Dean said reluctantly. "And then spent the elevator ride hugging her right in front of him."

Theo snorted. "Uncle Aaron, the hater of PDA?"

"The very same," Dean agreed.

"So she was trying to catch you off guard. But you expected that, and even planned for it. You rigged it. She played right into your hands."

"Oh yes," Dean said, rubbing his hands together with a satisfied look on his face. "Gracie Adams is about to realize that if she messes with an Ashcroft, she's going to get revenged upon, or something."

"Great comeback," Theo said sarcastically.

Jesse threw the door open, catching both boys' attention. "You two left me to deal with Zara alone, you know that?" he complained. "Like, I love her and all, but she is unbearable when she's annoyed about something. Uncle Aaron was in our car and just decided he had to give us a talk about the proper type of person to date, and ugh!" he exclaimed, throwing his hands in the air. "You two missed it in the other car, and Gracie was asleep, but Zara and I had to spend an hour listening to a lecture on who we should date!"

Dean exchanged a sly look with Theo. "Like Raina?" he said innocently.

Jesse looked confused for a moment before he scowled at his cousin. "Shut up."

"Why didn't you invite her to the reunion?" Dean asked.

"I said shut up!" Jesse glared at his cousin before storming into the bathroom and slamming the door.

Theo winced. "I think you went a bit too far there, Dean."

"Yeah," Dean grimaced, glancing at the bathroom door. "But I've teased him all the time before. Why'd he get so upset about this?"

Theo shrugged, lying back down. "Who knows?"

Dean let his head rest against the wall. "Who knows?" he echoed his cousin, sighing loudly. "I just can't wait for this whole day to be over. Like, it wasn't bad. It was just so mentally exhausting. I had to watch Gracie be buddy-buddy with fucking Blake all morning and pretend I didn't want to tear her away from him every second. She's my girlfriend, not his."

"*Fake* girlfriend," Theo pointed out.

Dean blinked at him. "Yeah, but still. She was all over him." He scowled. "She's supposed to be all over *me*."

Theo laughed. "You're just jealous because Gracie spent her time talking to Blake and not you."

"I am not," Dean said testily. He crossed his arms. "And then Zara makes 'love is love' comments throughout the entire day, but only when our uncles are around. Does she have to antagonize them every three seconds? And to top it all off, Mom basically ignored us the entire day. Just booked a facial, as if she saw us all the time and was using this trip as an excuse to get a break from us. Sundays are supposed to be fun!"

"Tomorrow will be better," Theo offered. "Your mom's already jetted off to Spain, and you can ignore Uncle Aaron and my dad as much as you'd like. Now that the reunion's over, we can happily avoid our family members. Well, you can. I've still got weekly dinners with my dad."

Dean shrugged, lying down. "I hope so. Oh, and I've already got an idea for how you can get that kiss," he said absently.

Jesse burst out of the bathroom. "Kiss? Who's Theo kissing?" he demanded, apparently not mad anymore.

Theo shot Dean a look. "I'm going to sleep," he snapped.

Dean looked at him apologetically, but Theo had already rolled over, the covers pulled over his face. "Me too," he said when Jesse turned his attention to him.

Pouting, Jesse went to his own bed, pulling his pajama shirt on as he climbed under the covers. Dean turned over, mashing his face into the pillow. Despite his unease at how the conversation with his cousins ended, it hadn't been such a bad day. He had gotten his revenge on Gracie, after all, and that always put him in a good mood. Dean fell asleep with a smile on his face, imagining the look on Gracie's face when she realized she was kissing the wrong Ashcroft.

## Chapter Thirteen

Surprisingly, Gracie didn't bring it up the next day, and Dean experienced a morning as boring as mornings could get. He woke up, went to classes, and teased Gracie during breakfast and lunch. Simple, everyday routine. Dean hadn't realized it, but he was used to seeing her every day at his lunch table, sitting next to him and taking delicate bites of her food. She would savor each piece, and Dean found it oddly endearing. More than once, Theo or Jesse would nudge him, and he'd realize that his fork had paused halfway to his mouth because he was too busy staring at Gracie.

Theo swallowed hard next to him, drawing Dean's attention back to the present. Dean held an arm out, stopping his cousin from going down the stairs. "Are you sure you want to do this?" he asked carefully.

Theo nodded, his face pale. "I have to. I need to know," he said, a determined look on his face.

Dean breathed out, lowering his arm. "Okay."

The two cousins followed the steps to the common room, waving and high fiving everyone in sight before settling down with a group of boys and girls in the corner. Dean held up the bottle he had grabbed with a grin.

"Who's ready to play?"

Hands reached for the bottle, but Dean lifted it out of reach. He set it down in the middle of the circle.

"Are you sure you should play?" Nicole asked with a frown.

Dean shot her a quick glance, unsure of what she was talking about. "Why?" he asked.

She stared at him incredulously. "You. Have. A. Girlfriend."

"Oh yeah," Dean said casually. "But Gracie doesn't mind. She knows it's just a game."

Juliet vibrated excitedly from her spot in the circle. "I'll go first!" she squealed, reaching out to spin the bottle.

Dean eyed the room, spotting his sister and Gracie almost instantly as Juliet leaned across the circle to kiss a senior. The duo sat in the corner—Zara working on homework and his kinda-girlfriend reading a book.

Could Gracie even be called his girlfriend if they weren't dating for real? Dean knew that fake relationships were a thing, but somehow the term "fake girlfriend" didn't seem right for Gracie. Besides, it wasn't like he wanted her to be his real girlfriend anyway. They were just pretending, and it would all come down to who gave up the charade first.

Dean wouldn't break, though. He was more than capable of keeping up with Gracie's mild attempts to get him to admit that they weren't actually dating.

"Dean, what do you think?" someone asked. Dean turned his attention back to the game, seeing eight faces staring expectantly at him.

"Um, what's the question?"

Theo nodded to the bottle. "It was Oliver's turn to spin, and it landed on Liam," he said.

Dean tilted his head to the side. "It's only a game," he offered. Oliver shrugged, leaning forward and kissing Liam on the cheek.

"No fair," one of the other boys in the circle complained.

"Hey, a kiss is a kiss," Oliver said with a smirk. "You're just jealous you didn't think of it."

Dean rolled his eyes. He wasn't the blond's biggest fan. "How about from now they need to be actual kisses?" he suggested.

"Fine, but you have to take a turn then," Oliver bargained. Dean sighed, casting a glance back at the corner. Gracie had disappeared, but Zara was still there.

"Fine. Just give me the bottle," he said. Dean spun the bottle, watching as it landed on Annalisse. "Yay," he said weakly. Someone snorted from behind him, and he whirled around. "Gracie!" Dean exclaimed gleefully. "You're here! Great, now let's go!"

"Oh, not a chance," Gracie said, settling down in between him and Annalisse. "It's your turn, isn't it?" Dean nodded reluctantly. "So then go."

Dean closed his eyes briefly before looking at the bottle again. He blinked twice. Whereas the bottle had been on Annalisse before, it was now on Gracie. "You sly girl," he muttered admiringly. In sitting between him and Annalisse, she had forced the other girl to move out of the bottle's path.

Grinning, Dean leaned forward and pecked Gracie on the lips.

"Come on, you can do better than that!" Oliver called out.

Dean turned back to Gracie hesitantly, not sure if she would be okay with him kissing her in public or not. A couple of days ago, he wouldn't have hesitated, but something made him seek her approval today. Gracie rolled her eyes, shooting her hands out to grab a fistful of Dean's shirt, tugging him closer and pressing her lips to his. Dean lost himself in the kiss instantly, wrapping his arms around Gracie.

"Okay, long enough!" Oliver called, but Dean ignored him. "Okay, *long enough!*" he screeched. Dean and Gracie broke apart, the former glaring at Oliver.

Gracie shot a smirk at him. "You're just jealous you didn't think of doing that," she said nonchalantly, before flouncing off to rejoin Zara.

Dean stared after Gracie, unable to tear his gaze away.

*The Gossip Games*

Theo began to laugh. "It's always the ones you least expect."

"Hey, can I play?" a boy Dean vaguely recognized from one of his classes asked. Theo nodded, telling two people to move over and make room.

"My turn!" Annalisse exclaimed, snatching the bottle. She spun and landed on the new boy. "Freddy!' she squealed. Freddy looked uncomfortable with her attention, but dutifully kissed her for a few seconds.

"Is it my turn?" he asked.

Dean nodded. "Yeah, that's how it goes."

When the bottle landed on Theo, the entire group went wild. Dean grinned inwardly, happy that his plan had worked.

"He won't do it," Oliver said spitefully. "He'll just chicken out or do it for all of half a second."

Dean smirked, knowing that this entire game had been orchestrated just for Theo to kiss a boy. Oliver's snarky comments were just a happy surprise, as they gave Theo an opportunity to have a real kiss with no one questioning him about it afterward. "Wanna bet?"

"Fine," Oliver said crossly. "What are we betting?"

Dean tapped a finger against his chin. "Run around the school in your underwear," he bargained.

Oliver's face paled a little. "Now? It's raining!" He gestured sharply in the window's direction.

"Think you're gonna lose?" Dean asked, raising an eyebrow.

"Never," Oliver declared. "You're on."

It was Theo's turn to smirk at the newly confident boy. "Get ready to strip, Ollie," he said, before leaning forwards and connecting his lips with Freddy's. Theo pulled the shorter boy closer, fingers tangling in his hair as they kissed passionately. Oliver's face got redder every second the kiss lasted.

When they finally broke apart, Oliver's face was bright red as he stared at the mussed Theo. "Wh-w-I-but," he stammered. "It's raining!"

Theo crooked a finger at him, a wide grin on his face. "Deal's a deal, Ollie," he said casually.

Oliver fumed. "Don't call me that," he muttered, before yanking his sweatshirt over his head.

Dean smirked as Oliver stripped before wandering away to where Gracie and Zara were sitting in the corner. Now that Theo had his chance, Dean had lost interest in the game, deciding to bother his sister instead.

✯✯✯

"Damn, that's hot," Zara whispered, nudging Gracie. Gracie looked up to see two boys kissing during the spin the bottle game. "Is that...Dean?" she asked hesitantly.

Zara's eyes grew wide as the two boys broke apart. "No, that's Theo," she replied, before her mouth dropped again. "Wait, Theo? It would make so much more sense for it to be Dean."

"You called?" Dean asked, appearing suddenly.

"Gah!" Zara exclaimed, pressing a hand to her chest. "Don't do that!"

Dean grinned. "Were you talking about me?" he cooed, pinching his sister's cheek.

Zara batted his hand away. "No, we weren't," she said grumpily. "You're not important enough to talk about."

Dean opened his mouth to respond, but Gracie changed the subject before it escalated into a full-blown argument. "Question," she said loudly. "Why is that guy over there taking off his clothes?"

Dean smirked. "He lost a bet," he said smugly. "So now he has to run outside in his boxers."

"Classic," Zara snorted. "After years of falling for that, you do it to other people."

"I do not fall for that!" Dean exclaimed, his cheeks reddening.

Gracie laughed, wishing she could have seen that—but just Zara getting one over Dean; she had no interest in seeing Dean mostly naked.

Why did her brain put images of Dean naked into her mind?

"Gracie," someone said, and Gracie snapped out of her daydream to see that Zara was staring at her impatiently.

"Sorry, repeat the question?"

Zara held up her phone. "Classes are being canceled for three days," she reported. "There was a leak in the chemistry lab or something and it spread to half of the school. Nothing's wrong, but they need to call in some plumbers and people who can check that it hasn't spread to the pipes. We either have to go home for a few days, or they'll put us up in a hotel. But Theo's parents have a small house nearby for when his mom comes, so we're going to stay there. Do you want to come?"

Gracie glanced warily at Dean, wondering if she really wanted to spend three days in close quarters with him. "Who else is coming?" she asked.

Zara's face brightened. "Theo and Jesse, of course, and I'm going to ask Nicole and Raina. And assuming Raina's coming, Aunt Eliza's going to run to the store and buy food that she can eat. She's also going to make the microwave kosher, so Raina can have hot food."

Gracie looked around the common room, noting the grins and cheers as people read the text message from the school. "Maybe check with Raina first. I think she might need to do that herself. But it sounds like a plan," she replied. "I'll check with my mom, but she'll probably say yes. When are we leaving?"

"Tomorrow morning," Zara replied. "So go pack a bag."

"Please, I haven't even unpacked my bag from this weekend." Gracie snorted. "It's literally been one day!"

Zara shrugged. "Hey, I'm not complaining about days off of school."

"True," Gracie agreed, snapping her book shut and tucking it under her arm. She pulled out her phone and texted her mom, smiling when she received an affirmative text almost instantly. "My mom said yes. I'll go pack now. If Raina and Nicole are there, I'll send them down to you."

"I'll let Theo and Jesse know," Dean offered.

Zara nodded, making shooing motions with her hands. Gracie watched as Dean darted over to the spin the bottle game, pulling his cousin aside and whispering something in his ear. Theo must have nodded or something, because both boys stood, waved to the group, and made their way to the stairs.

"Gracie," Zara said, bringing her attention back to her friend. "I'll stay down here for a few minutes. You go on up."

✯
✯ ✯

"What's going on here?" Gracie demanded. She stared at her two friends, but neither Nicole nor Raina met her eyes.

"Nothing," Raina muttered finally. She turned away from glaring at the other girl and walked to her bed, grabbing her brush and yanking it through her hair.

Nicole snorted loudly. "Nothing, my ass," she said, pushing past Gracie and slamming the bathroom door. Gracie let her go, knowing that the best way to help Nicole right now was to give her space.

"What's going on?" Gracie asked softly, sitting down gingerly next to Raina.

Raina shrugged, crossing her arms as she attempted to hide the tears coming out of her eyes. "Nicole was throwing her relationship with Jesse into my face," she said quietly, wiping her face. Another tear dripped down her face, and Gracie handed her a tissue from the box on the nightstand.

"What relationship?" Gracie asked, confused.

Raina shrugged again, her hair falling over her shoulders. "All about how she knows him better than I ever will, how I'm not his type," she listed. "I just don't get why she doesn't like me. Have I done something?" She looked at Gracie helplessly. "Okay, maybe I

## The Gossip Games

wasn't as friendly as I could have been, but I was polite. I didn't tell her she meant nothing to someone that she likes!"

Gracie inhaled sharply. "She said that?"

Raina nodded tearfully. "I don't know what to do," she cried, dropping her head into her hands. "Nicole's going to tell Jesse, I know it. And then he'll never speak to me again!"

"What if Nicole's wrong?" Gracie asked tentatively, putting an arm around her friend. "Maybe she doesn't know Jesse as well as she thinks."

Raina sniffled. "It's not worth the risk to find out. I'd rather keep this crush a secret for however long it lasts than possibly risk him never speaking to me again. I can't handle that. He's my friend. We sit together in Math and pass notes during English. We study together after school and go outside for snack picnics; he only brings foods I can eat, and I don't think I could lose that," she sobbed.

Gracie's eyes widened. She hadn't known that Raina and Jesse were that close, but apparently while she had been fighting with Dean, they had become friends. "It's going to be okay," she said soothingly.

Nicole exited the bathroom and pointedly walked to her own bed, grabbing a bottle of water without as much as glancing toward the other half of the room. Gracie sighed, squeezing Raina's hand before standing up and heading to her own bed to begin her nightly routine.

Just as she had tied the string on her pajama pants, Zara walked in, oblivious to the tension in the room.

"Oh, you found them!" she beamed at Gracie. "Awesome!" Zara spun around in a circle. "Guess who's going on a two-day break from school in a little cottage!" she sang.

"You are," Raina said listlessly. Nicole scowled.

Zara stopped dancing, her arms dropping to hang by her sides. "No, silly, we are!" she said, waving her hands to indicate all four people in the room. "Surprise! We're leaving tomorrow morning," she said excitedly. "And I've got the boys on board, so it's going to be super fun! You just have to check with your parents." Zara stopped smiling and glanced around the room. "Why aren't you guys happy?" she asked, frowning.

"Yay," Raina said dully, before climbing into her bed and closing the curtains. Zara turned to Nicole, but the dark-haired girl just copied the motion.

"What's going on?" Zara whispered, coming closer to Gracie.

Gracie shrugged as she packed some of her jewelry making supplies into her overnight bag. She glanced at her friend out of the corner of her eye, before checking that Raina and Nicole were out of earshot. "They got into a fight," she related quietly. "But don't bring it up. They're being very touchy about it. Just give Nicole space tomorrow and keep Raina distracted enough so she won't start crying again. Keep them both away from Jesse."

Zara frowned. "I had them sharing a room," she said. "I guess I can't do that now?"

"Probably not the best idea," Gracie agreed.

Zara sighed. "Well, these next few days are going to be fun."

## Chapter Fourteen

"This is a cottage?" Gracie exclaimed, her mouth dropping open as she stared at the large home in front of her. She gazed in admiration at the assorted flowers and plants that surrounded the lawn, but which seemed trivial compared to the house itself. The cottage was made out of white marble with a smattering of windows lining the front. Four columns lined the large porch, as if guarding the steps that led up to the white door. The door itself was as immaculate as the rest of the house, with not a single scratch or dirt mark in sight. Gracie glanced down at her feet self-consciously, not wanting to trek any mud into the house. "This is larger than my house!"

Zara glanced over from where she was climbing out of the car. "Oh yeah, cute, isn't it?"

"Here you go, Miss Zara," the Ashcrofts' driver chimed in, handing the girl two matching suitcases. "Your uncle would like me to remind you that he is trusting you to stay here without an adult, and that you should behave responsibly. Everything you need is already inside and there is money on the counter to buy food if it is needed. If you need anything, you can call me. I'll be back to pick you up in a few days." The driver nodded once before getting in the car and driving away.

Gracie shook her head in amazement, carrying her own duffel bag into the house; Raina fell in step beside her, peering around the elegantly decorated rooms. They passed through a formal living room and a spacious family room, complete with three cozy couches and a wide-screen TV, before ending up in a small room that appeared to have no other purpose than to lead to the upstairs.

"This is amazing," Gracie breathed.

"I know, right," Jesse agreed, appearing behind them.

Raina let out a small yelp. "You scared me!" she exclaimed.

"Sorry," Jesse said. "Want me to take your bag up?"

"Sure." Raina gratefully handed him her bag. "Where are the rooms?"

"This way," Jesse said, grabbing Raina's hand in his free one and leading her up the stairs.

Gracie tried to conceal her small smile as Dean strolled into the room, hands in his pockets. "Hey, Dean," she said.

"Hey, Gracie," he greeted her. "What's up?"

"Nothing much," she said with a shrug. "Just waiting a couple of minutes before going upstairs. Raina and Jesse just went up."

Dean nodded in understanding. "Want to see something cool?" he offered. Gracie hesitated for a second before nodding. "Great," he said. Dean motioned to a door, holding it open for Gracie. With a slight blush, she passed through, glancing at the black and white diamond tiles under her feet before taking in the entire room. Her jaw dropped at the state-of-the-art kitchen that she was standing in. Each appliance appeared brand new, all of them a shiny silver that gave the kitchen a sleek and modern feel.

"So this is the kitchen."

Gracie pretended to gasp. "Really? I thought it was your bedroom!"

"Oh, I see where you want to be right now," Dean said playfully.

All of a sudden, the pearl backsplash was extremely interesting. A lot more interesting than thinking about Dean in his bed or *her* in Dean's bed...

"Is this what you wanted to show me?" Gracie asked quickly, banishing all thoughts of Dean's bed from her mind.

"Nope. Right this way, please. The kitchen leads to a back staircase." He pointed, walking over to another door and pushing it open. Gracie followed him, curiously glancing at the narrow staircase. It gave off fairytale-princess-in-a-tower vibes, and Gracie had the immediate urge to sing her favorite Tangled song. But if Gracie was the princess, would that make Dean her prince?

"Does this go somewhere?" she asked.

Dean put a finger to his lips and winked, taking the steps two at a time. Gracie laughed, a fluttery feeling in her stomach. She pushed it down and focused her attention on Dean again. The brunette was pulling a key out of his pocket before inserting it into the door. He motioned for Gracie to enter ahead of him.

The first thing that Gracie noticed was that the room was pretty small, and that it was very blue. The walls and soft carpet were blue, the beanbags in the corner were blue, and a variety of blue snacks lay on a small table.

Dean smiled at those. "They must have known I was coming," he said with a laugh, striding over and picking up a packet of blue sour sticks.

"Who?" Gracie asked curiously.

"My aunt and Delia, who cleans the house bi-weekly. Sometimes my aunt will tell Delia to buy me snacks and leave them up here," he explained. "If snacks are in the kitchen, they're fair game and are usually gone within a day."

Gracie headed straight for the bookshelf, running her hands over the many titles. "You read fantasy novels?" she asked in surprise.

Dean gave an embarrassed shrug. "Sometimes."

Gracie grinned widely. "Me too. I love them," she said, pulling a copy of *The Cruel Prince* off the bookshelf. She leafed through the pages, breathing in the classic book smell. "Where are we?" she asked, turning to Dean.

Dean stuck his hands in his pockets. "It's my safe room," he explained. "When Uncle Alex started working at Trinity, Aunt Eliza bought this house to be closer to him when she's in town. Zara and I would spend breaks here, and at some point, Aunt Eliza made each of us our own special rooms."

"Where's Zara's?" Gracie asked curiously.

"I don't know." Dean shrugged. "The only person who knows where they are is Aunt Eliza. Oh, and Delia, of course. She has a spare key. Wait, no, actually, that's a lie," he added. "I'm pretty sure Jesse knows where Zara's is."

"And you took me here?" Her eyes locked onto Dean's. "Why?"

Dean looked away first, staring at his feet. "I don't know," he mumbled. "I…I just wanted to."

"Thanks," Gracie said. "I'm very honored." She took off her sweatshirt, suddenly feeling very warm. "Can I stay here and read?"

☆☆☆

Dean nodded at her, still turning her earlier question over in his head. He hadn't lied. He really didn't know why he had brought her here. She had been standing there, glancing around the house, and next thing Dean knew, he was leading her up the stairs. It was the same back at the library. He *never* talked about Blake, not if he could help it. Blake had nearly destroyed his sister, and after that, they had never referred to him by name again. But he'd told Gracie, and even after pondering the conversation over in his head, Dean still had no idea why.

He wandered over to the window, pulling the drapes open.

"We should probably get back," he said after a few minutes of staring at the sunshine.

Gracie looked up from her book and blinked. "Do we have to?" she asked with an adorable pout.

"Sadly," Dean said. "I know. I'd love to spend all day up here, but we've got to make an appearance at some point."

"Aww," Gracie said with a sigh.

Dean took a closer look at how she was sitting. "Why are you sitting in the corner? I've got very comfortable bean bags. Personally tested," he added, making her laugh.

Gracie shrugged, standing and stretching. "I just like them. Whenever I'm upset, or sad, or want to hide away from the world, I go sit in a corner."

"They're your comfort place." Dean nodded understandingly.

Gracie's eyes widened. "Yeah! I never had a name for it before, but yeah, pretty much."

"This is mine," Dean said, motioning to the room. "It's my favorite place to be."

"I figured." She placed the book she had been reading back on the shelf before following Dean to the door.

"You can come back," he offered as they descended the stairs. "I'm here most of the time. So just knock if you want to come in. Like, you don't have to," he blurted. "But if you want to."

Gracie smiled. "I want to," she reassured him.

"Good." Dean tried to think of something else to say, but he couldn't find the right words. "I'm glad I showed you," he said finally, stopping at the bottom of the stairs so he could peer into the kitchen and make sure that no one was around.

"Should we go upstairs?" Gracie suggested. "I think everyone else is already there." She gasped, a horrified look on her face before she abruptly darted away.

Dean hurried after her, grabbing their bags as they passed through the entryway. "Wh-why are we running?" he panted, following her up the staircase. Normally Dean wouldn't even break a sweat running up and down the stairs, but the two heavy duffel bags he was carrying took a toll on him.

Gracie spun around once she reached the landing. "Nicole and Raina currently cannot be in the same room without arguing, Zara will be no help, and Jesse will unknowingly egg them on," she summed up, before dashing through the only open doorway.

Dean went into the opposite room, placing his bag down before doing the same in the room that Zara and Gracie were supposed to share. He figured there would be last-minute room changes, but they weren't his problem.

"—so Raina and I will take the other one, and Zara and Nicole can share this room," Gracie was saying when he entered the room. Dean's eyes widened at the sight. Nicole and Raina were standing on opposite sides of the room, Nicole's all black ensemble a stark contrast to Raina's striped dress. Random things lay scattered around the floor, making him think that a bag had been dumped. Jesse cowered in the corner next to Zara, who was examining her nails. Theo was noticeably absent.

"So…is everything all settled?" Dean asked tentatively. He glanced around the room, checking that nothing had been broken or ruined.

Gracie turned and gave him a small smile. "We're all good. Would you mind showing me and Raina to our room?"

"Of course," Dean said, motioning for the girls to follow him.

✯✯✯

"*Avengers.*"
"*Clueless.*"
"*Spider-Man.*"
"*Clueless.*"
"*Black Panther.*"
"*Clueless!*"

"Does anyone else get a say in the movie vote?" an irritated Theo called out.

Zara and Jesse spun around to glare at him. "NO!"

"Fine, fine," he grumbled, settling back down on the couch.

Gracie shifted her eyes to the boy sitting next to her. Dean was being unusually quiet this evening. "Do you have an opinion?" she asked.

Dean shrugged and joked, "I mean, I'd rather watch Marvel, but Jes clearly has his heart set on Alicia Silverstone."

"Gimme the movie!" Zara screeched, launching herself onto Jesse's back and hitting him repeatedly in her attempts to grab the remote.

"Oh. My. God." Nicole groaned loudly. "Somebody just fucking pick a movie."

"Clueless!" Jesse yelled as he yanked Zara's hair.

Dean shook his head sadly. "Why are my sister and cousin literal toddlers?"

"This is why I'm your favorite," Theo called from across the room.

"What if I have a movie suggestion?" Raina spoke up.

"No," Nicole said immediately.

"How about a musical?" Gracie suggested.

Theo perked up instantly. "Yes!"

Dean nudged Gracie as everyone else began arguing again. "Hey, I'm going to get some snacks. They'll be at this for a while."

"Okay," Gracie replied and closed her eyes. She squirmed around on the couch, making herself comfortable.

Dean hesitated. "Do you want to come?"

"Me?" Gracie opened her eyes to meet his, a surprised expression on her face.

"Don't be so surprised. It's not like I'm proposing marriage," Dean teased, nudging her arm. "But I *do* have an unlimited credit card. So if you'd like a shot-gun wedding, I can get us to Vegas in a matter of hours."

Gracie laughed and accepted his offered hand. He seemed almost nervous, which she found oddly endearing. "As tempting as that sounds, my mom would kill me if I got married without her. So as long as the snacks aren't in Vegas, I'll go with you."

✩✩✩

"Stop," Gracie panted, unable to keep herself from throwing her head back.

Dean paused from where he was kissing his way down her neck. "We don't have to," he breathed, before his lips found hers again.

Gracie moaned into Dean's mouth, tightening her grip on his neck. He raked his teeth across her bottom lip, grinning wolfishly when she tilted her head up so her gaze could meet his.

"Ugh, they're at it again in the kitchen!" Jesse called out. Gracie separated from Dean quickly enough to see the look of disgust on Jesse's face before he disappeared back into the other room.

"Told you we needed to stop," Gracie said, unable to stop a small smile from crossing her lips.

Dean swept down and stole another kiss, which she happily gave. "We really need to get back," he whispered against her lips.

Gracie closed her eyes. "Do we really?"

He chuckled. "Changed your tune quickly, huh? I told you marriages always start with a kiss, Vegas Girl."

Gracie huffed and pulled away, running her fingers through her hair. It was always a mess after Dean had gotten his hands into it, and this whole "Vegas marriage" had gotten him even more worked up tonight. They'd barely made it into the kitchen before he had pressed her against the wall and kissed her senseless. "You're braiding my hair," she informed him.

Dean sighed. "You're lucky I used to braid Zara's hair all the time," he said, grabbing her hand. He began to make his way to the door.

"Wait, Dean," Gracie said suddenly, remembering the reason they had come into the kitchen. She pulled her hand out of his grip, pointing toward the island. "The popcorn."

Dean shook his head in amusement. He reached over and ripped open the store-bought bag, dumping the popcorn into a plastic bowl. Checking the bag to see if it had kosher certification, he also grabbed a pack of unopened pretzels for Raina. "Come on, let's go get ridiculed by our friends."

Gracie followed him through the maze of rooms until they reached the den. Their friends were lounging on the leather couches and Dean took a seat at the end. Gracie sat down on the floor in front of him, impatiently motioning to her hair. Sighing, Dean picked up the strands as the movie began to play.

Zara and Jesse argued over the movie for a further twenty minutes before finally agreeing on *Airplane*. It was a comedy—not Gracie's preferred genre—but she sat quietly as Dean braided her hair. When he finished, she handed him a hair tie from around her wrist before joining him on the couch.

It had been a long day, and Gracie struggled to keep her eyes open. She moved onto the couch and leaned against Dean, feeling him shift to wrap an arm around her.

Dean had been very intimate today, she realized. Physically, he had pulled her into a heated kiss when they were in the kitchen, and now they were cuddling on a couch. There was no one around that they needed to keep up the fake dating appearance for. Not to mention earlier, when he had shown her his secret room. Nobody knew about it, not even his twin sister, and Dean had shown *her*.

Gracie knew they weren't actually dating, but either Dean was putting on a show all the time or something was off. She didn't mind the attention. If anything, she enjoyed it. It was nice having someone pay attention to her and hang on her every word. And the physical benefits were nice too, she thought, snuggling closer to Dean. His hand was running up and down her arm, and Gracie shivered slightly from the feel of his fingers against her skin.

He looked down at her, a worried expression on his face. "Are you cold?"

Gracie shook her head. "I'm good," she assured him.

Dean pulled her closer before turning his attention back to the movie. Gracie's thoughts drifted off again, going back to her little competition with Dean.

She had gotten one over Dean with the picture of them sleeping, but Dean had kissed her in front of the principal. She wasn't sure if that counted or not, but Principal Ashcroft had refused to meet her or Dean's eyes for the rest of the reunion. On the positive side, it got one of Dean's relatives off their back, leaving them with one less person who could possibly discover their ruse. There were seven people who knew what was going on, and Gracie didn't plan to let an eighth know, so she was glad that the reunion was over.

Although, she wasn't sure whether she preferred being in a public hotel or private cabin with Dean. Their friends might be around now, but come tomorrow, they'd all disappear into their rooms or to the nearby town. Depending on if Dean went with them, they could possibly be alone in the house.

Gracie's eyes fluttered open, seeing everyone still devoted to the movie. She closed them again, intent on keeping them shut for only a minute or two.

☆☆☆

"Is she asleep?" Zara asked.

"Shhh!" Dean hissed, bringing a finger to his lips. He glanced down at the girl who was curled into his side. "Yes, she's asleep."

"Not surprised." His twin shook her head.

"I'm going to go take a shower," Raina announced, standing up. She raised her arms over her head. "Ow, why does everything hurt?" She winced, before making her way to the steps.

Nicole snorted but a glare from Zara kept her quiet. "I'm going to turn in as well."

"I'll go up with you," Jesse said with a yawn.

Theo leaned forwards and grabbed the remote, pressing pause on the credits. "I'll put the bowl in the sink," he offered, swapping the remote for the empty popcorn bowl.

Zara glanced at Dean and Gracie before standing with a slow smirk on her face. "Well, I'm off to bed," she declared. "Have fun with sleeping Gracie." She hurried off before Dean could object. Dean sighed, wondering the best way to carry Gracie to her room. He eased her to lean against the couch, leaving his hands free.

"Noooo," Gracie whined quietly as he turned her, making it easier for him to pick her up. "Sleepy time. No moving."

Dean laughed quietly. "Come on, Gracie," he said, amused by her childish pout. "You can sleep in your bed."

"Stop being so nice," Gracie replied sleepily, her eyelids drooping. She struggled to get them open again, poking him in the arm. "Why are you so adorable? I'm not supposed to like you."

"I am adorable, aren't I?" he grinned down at her, shifting her weight in his arms. He wondered where she had gotten the impression she wasn't supposed to like him before deciding that he could ask her or Zara tomorrow. "Let's not make this a habit, Gracie."

"But I like cuddling," the brunette mumbled, clutching him tighter. "You're warm and cuddly. Can we cuddle?"

"Sure," Dean promised. "If you remember this conversation tomorrow, we can cuddle."

"Yay," Gracie said drowsily. She grabbed a fistful of his sweatshirt before her eyes closed again.

Dean looked down at her fondly, carrying Gracie into her room and gently setting her on the bed. He pulled the blanket over her shoulders before turning to leave. As Dean reached the door, his phone dinged, and he took it out to read the text. Before putting his phone back in his pocket, Dean snapped a quick picture of the sleeping Gracie. He could use it as revenge for the picture she had orchestrated. Dean quietly closed the door, a smile appearing on his face.

"Sweet dreams, Gracie," he said, walking back to his own room. "Enjoy them while they last."

## Chapter Fifteen

The first thing Gracie noticed when she woke was that she was in a bed. She blinked, sitting up and rubbing her eyes. Raina was sleeping across the room, almost directly under the open curtains. Gracie yawned, stretching her arms above her head as she rose and padded across the hall.

How had she ended up in a bed? Had someone carried her there? The last thing Gracie remembered was falling asleep on Dean.

The bathroom door was closed, and Gracie knocked lightly. She could go upstairs to the second bathroom, but Gracie wasn't sure if there was a shower there or not.

"One minute," Jesse's voice called out.

Gracie took a step back, leaning against the wall. She hoped there were towels in the bathroom. She hadn't showered last night and, as someone who usually washed her hair each evening, Gracie felt gross.

Jesse exited the bathroom with a towel slung around his neck. He nodded at Gracie as he made his way back to his room, his wet hair dripping.

Gracie showered quickly and nearly ran back to her room. She had forgotten to bring a change of clothes and definitely didn't want to run into the boys while she was only wearing a towel. After pulling on a pair of jeans and a yellow top from her bag, Gracie headed downstairs.

"Good morning," Jesse said cheerfully from his spot at the island. He was scarfing down a plate of eggs, as if they were too hot to chew properly.

Nicole huffed. "Save some for the rest of us, will you?"

Gracie turned to the third person in the room. "Did you make this?" she asked, gesturing to the plates of eggs and bacon on the table. Someone had set out water and glasses, and there was an untouched bowl of fruit as well.

"Yup," Dean grinned proudly. "And there's toast in the toaster too."

Gracie glanced toward the counter before turning her attention back to the food on the table. "It looks good."

"It tastes *great*." Dean winked. He walked closer and wrapped his arms around her, eliciting a surprised gasp.

"What are you doing?" Gracie asked nervously, tilting her head up so she could see Dean. Gracie fought to hide her blush as he grinned and hugged her tighter. Warmth shot through her body.

"Come on, Gracie, I thought you were smart," he teased. "What's it called when one person wraps their arms around another person?"

"Strangling," she offered.

Dean laughed. "Ah, Gracie," he said with a sigh as he released her. He reached around her and grabbed two plates, handing one over. "Violence isn't always the right way to go, you know."

"Only ninety-nine percent of the time, right?" she said slyly, picking up the serving fork.

Dean looked surprised before a pleased expression spread across his face. "Exactly," he agreed.

✭✭
✭

"It's so nice outside," Raina said with a sigh, leaning back in her lounge chair. "I mean, it's still cold, but the sun is shining and there are still leaves on the trees. I wish it was like this all the time."

Zara smirked from where she was sitting next to Gracie. "It is gorgeous, isn't it?"

Dean laughed. "Z, you didn't make it nice outside. That happened on its own."

"Shows what you know," Zara tossed back flippantly.

Dean ignored his sister, his gaze resting on Theo's treehouse. It was nothing more than a wooden platform and a roof—built after they had begged for one to play in as children. He eyed the distance between the ground and the platform, before taking a running leap and pulling himself easily up to the wooden floor.

"Ha! Top that, Zara!" he exclaimed, thrusting his fists into the air.

"Fine." Zara rolled her eyes dramatically, heaving herself out of her chair. She walked over to the treehouse, using a couple of smaller branches on the tree to ascend with equal ease.

Dean frowned. "Hey, that's cheating."

"There weren't any rules."

Dean nodded in acknowledgement and turned back to the circle of lawn chairs. "Theo? Raina? Gracie?"

Gracie shook her head furiously. "No, thank you."

Theo chuckled as he rose, getting a running start before leaping onto the platform. He stood triumphantly, pushing his hair out of his eyes. "Easy peasy," he said smugly, dropping to the ground again. "I'm going inside and see what food we have for later."

"Raina?" Dean checked. "Want to join the cool kids?"

Raina looked at the shed hesitantly. "I'll pass."

Dean shrugged. "Your loss."

Raina stood. "I'm going to see if Theo needs any help," she said before leaving.

Zara sighed once Raina had gone inside. "Thanks a lot, Dean," she groused, hopping down from the treehouse. "I've got to go in and stop her from thinking about Nicole and Jesse."

Dean winced. Nicole and Jesse had left directly after breakfast, intent on heading to the nearby shopping strip. He and Gracie had been the only other ones awake and had unsuccessfully tried to talk them into waiting for everyone else to wake up. Raina's face had crumpled when she heard, and Zara had made it her personal mission to take Raina's mind off of Jesse. Dean glanced at Gracie. She sat in one of the wicker chairs, eyes closed and head tilted towards the sun.

"Hey, Adams."

"Shh." Her eyes stayed shut. "I'm relaxing."

"But I'm bored. Entertain me."

"You really are a small child, aren't you? Go bother one of your cousins."

"But I'd rather talk to you, my lovely fiancé."

Gracie's eyes popped open. She leveled a fierce glare at him. "We are *not* engaged."

"You mean you don't want to go to Vegas with me?"

"I swear, Dean, if you say one more word," Gracie said threateningly, waving a finger at him.

"Okay, fine! I won't bring it up again."

"*Thank you.*"

Dean managed to keep his mouth shut for a few minutes, but something about Gracie lying a few feet away from him made him want to continue their conversation. He admired the relaxed way she draped a hand over her eyes, ignoring both him and the bright sun. Rolling his shoulders, Dean prepared to jump down from the treehouse.

"Please be careful," Gracie called out.

Dean paused, one hand on the tree trunk he was using to brace himself. "Be careful…"

"Jumping down. Don't hurt yourself."

"Aww, Gracie, do you care about me?" he teased.

Gracie scoffed. "No, I'd just rather not spend my vacation with you in the emergency room."

Despite her answer, Dean beamed. She may not be willing to admit it, but she *did* feel something for him. "Don't worry, Gracie. I'll be careful, *and* I'll make you admit that you care about me."

Without waiting for a response, Dean leapt off the platform, landing neatly on the ground. He glanced over at Gracie, hoping for some sort of reaction, but she had gone back to ignoring him.

"Gracie," he whined, pouting like a child. He stuck out his bottom lip, a pleased feeling spreading through his body when she laughed.

"You're not going to let me sunbathe, are you?" she asked with a chuckle.

"I think you should talk to me instead," Dean responded. He dragged a chair over next to hers and sat, crossing his legs and looking at her expectantly. Contrary to Dean, who had dressed in a hoodie, Gracie was wearing a floaty yellow off-the-shoulder top with her jeans. It was one of those wrap-around shirts that his sister liked to wear, only Zara's never had ruffles or a thin yellow tie that dangled above her belly button. Gracie leaned forward in her chair, the gold star pendant she always wore swinging just below her throat.

"Why exactly do you want me to talk to you, Dean?"

"Because I'm bored."

Gracie cocked her head, hugging herself. "That's not a very good reason."

"Yes, but—" he paused, looking closely at Gracie's body. "Are you cold?"

"A little, but it's fine." Gracie shrugged.

Dean ignored her, instantly pulling his hoodie over his head and handing it over. His t-shirt rode up, and he thought he caught a glimpse of a blush on Gracie's face as he tugged it back down.

"No, it's fine," she protested, trying to give his hoodie back. "I'll be fine."

"Gracie." He fixed her with a stern look. "Your shirt has no shoulders. You're cold. Wear the hoodie."

"That's the style," Gracie argued, but she took the hoodie anyway. "It's a cold shoulder shirt."

"Key word being *cold*."

Gracie laughed, adjusting her hair and the hood. "Fair."

Dean smiled smugly as she settled in the chair once more, wearing his hoodie. It looked better on her than it did on him, and part of Dean never wanted the hoodie back. The other half did, because Gracie was wearing it, and whenever she gave it back, it would smell like the addicting fruity scent that always let him know when the feisty girl was around.

"Now will you talk to me? I gave you a hoodie."

Gracie sighed, but he caught a small smile crossing her lips. "Fine. What would you like to know about me?"

Dean considered her question. He was going to her house for the holidays, but he didn't know what type of holiday person she was. Zara acted like a five-year-old with too much sugar, and while Dean also loved Christmas, he was able to tone down his excitement and behave appropriately for his age. "What's your favorite part of Christmas?"

Gracie tilted her head to the side. "I like the day after Christmas," she declared. "In my town, they have a small street fair, so we can have more Christmas. As a kid, it was like there were three parts to Christmas. There was Christmas Eve, Christmas Day, and then the fair."

"Are we going to go?" Dean asked.

Gracie nodded, her eyes crinkling with happiness. "Of course. We always go."

"What do they have there?"

"There's a small ice rink, as well as stands selling hot chocolate and cookies. You can buy scarves and hats, you can decorate ornaments for a giant tree, and there are a ton of crafts for kids. Everything is Christmas themed, and it's all very vintage-like. There aren't any bouncy castles or anything like that."

"What's your mom like?" he asked.

"She's great," Gracie replied. "She works at a bakery so everything she cooks or bakes is amazing. She gets to bring home leftovers sometimes, so we'll have a ton of good food. And there's always extra, which is great if we want a midnight snack."

"Yum," Dean said, leaning back in his chair lazily. "Now I'm hungry," he complained. "Ugh, when will Jesse and Nicole get back with lunch?"

Gracie shrugged. "No clue, but we can go look for a nearby restaurant."

Dean considered this. He was hungry, but he wanted to make sure Gracie was all good. "Are you hungry?"

"A little," she admitted.

"Then let's go," Dean said decisively. He picked up one of the chairs and began carrying it to the deck as Gracie ran into the house, presumably to tell Zara they were leaving. She returned a few minutes later, still wearing Dean's hoodie but with her hair now in a ponytail.

Dean bent down and tied his shoe before standing again. "The stores are all pretty close to us, which is nice. If we walk down the block for a few minutes, we'll hit the light. We'll make a left there, walk straight for two blocks, and then we'll reach that shopping strip that Jes and Nicole went to. They've got pretty much everything there," Dean explained as they headed out.

"That's pretty neat. It's nice that everything's so close."

"Yeah, it's awesome. We got a lot of freedom when we were younger." He pointed out their surroundings as they passed the light and walked down a residential street. "One of Theo's childhood friends lives here. And if you go down that way, which we're not, you'll hit the park."

Gracie peered down the street. "Nice."

"Now, here's the main street. It's got a couple convenience stores, supermarkets, restaurants, and even a toy store. We used to love going there when we were kids and picking out toys. My aunt hated it because we'd always end up breaking whatever we bought within a day."

Gracie laughed, her head swiveling to take everything in. "My mom would've happily taken me to the toy store anytime I asked. She would've been thrilled by anything that would pull my nose out of a book."

"So is your mom one of those strict moms or is she really relaxed?" Dean asked as they passed a small bookstore. Gracie's eyes drifted to the books, and Dean made a mental note to stop there on their way back. It was a quiet day, with no one else walking outside. There were a few cars parked along the sidewalk, and through the window, Dean could see their owners in the bookstore. Since they were open, he would happily take Gracie there and buy her all the books she wanted.

"She's pretty relaxed," Gracie answered. "Obviously, she has rules and all, but she lets me make my own decisions for the most part."

"Like your decision to bring the boy you're supposedly dating home?"

Gracie winced. "Yeah, she doesn't know that part."

"Gracie Adams, are you keeping things from your mom?" Dean teased her.

Gracie blushed and protested, "Not all things. And besides, worry about yourself. I'm bringing a boy home to meet my mom. You should be the scared one."

"Don't worry, I'll woo your mom," Dean declared confidently.

Gracie made a noise of amusement. "Woo?"

"Yes, woo," Dean said indignantly. "It's a real word, you know."

"I know."

"In fact, I will woo the whole world." Dean arched an eyebrow as if daring her to contradict him.

"Good luck with that." Gracie chuckled.

## The Gossip Games

Dean stopped suddenly, pointing to a shop they had just passed. "Restaurant!" he said excitedly. "Food!"

"It looks good." Gracie nodded approvingly, holding the door open for Dean. Walking inside, she glanced around at the brick walls and cozy decor. Lopsided armchairs lined the walls, and black wicker tables were in seemingly random places around the room. As Gracie watched, a customer picked up one of the tables, moving it in front of one of the chairs. The restaurant gave off a homey feel, with the delicious smell of rich tomato sauce. Gracie inhaled deeply, letting out a happy sigh as they approached the counter.

"Menu?" Dean offered her, picking one up from the stack right next to the register.

"Thanks." Gracie flipped the menu open, her eyes scanning the list of food quickly. As much as she loved pizza, it wasn't what she wanted right now. "I think I'm in a pasta mood today."

Dean hummed. "That sounds really good. They have great pasta here."

"Should we get anything for Zara and Raina?" Gracie asked. She glanced behind the counter, nodding approvingly when she noticed the certificate that declared the place as kosher.

"Let's get food for them before we leave," Dean decided. "We can get it to-go and take it back to the house. We can eat here, though. I'm hungry and the house involves walking."

Gracie laughed. "Hello," she said to the employee at the counter, "can I please get a small mac and cheese? To stay, please."

"I'll take two slices of mushroom pizza," Dean chimed in, placing his menu on the counter. "And fries." He turned to Gracie. "Do you want a drink?"

Gracie turned to look at the drink freezer. "Chocolate milk, please," she requested.

Dean nodded. "A chocolate milk and Fanta as well, please," he told the cashier.

"Will that be all?" she asked.

"For now, yes," Dean replied. "We'll order to-go once we're finished eating."

"That'll be 22.95," she told him. Dean pulled out his credit card, amid Gracie's protests.

"I can pay for my own food," she argued.

"You can," Dean agreed. "But you're not."

Gracie sighed in resignation. "Fine, but I'm paying next time."

"Deal," Dean said. He had no intention of ever letting her pay.

## Chapter Sixteen

"So you're saying that one year for Easter, you and Jesse covered an *entire house* in pink wallpaper?" Gracie asked incredulously. She leaned against one of the porch banisters, crossing her arms over her chest.

Dean nodded proudly. "Well, some of it was purple."

Gracie laughed. "How did you even do that? Actually, how were you not caught doing that?" she corrected herself.

Dean shrugged. "My aunt and uncle were never home. It was the nanny's night off, so I guess she figured it was okay to leave three fourteen-year-olds alone in a giant house with no supervision…" his voice trailed off. "Yeah, now that I think about it, that's actually a terrible idea."

"Really?" Gracie asked sarcastically. She pushed the door open, holding it so Dean could step inside.

"Thanks," he said, shoving his hands in his pockets as he walked inside. The paper bag slid down his arm a little, and Gracie only barely resisted the urge to fix it.

"It's so quiet," Gracie said in a hushed voice. "Where do you think everyone is?"

"We're in the den," Theo called out. "Also, we can hear you."

Dean nodded toward the kitchen. "I'm going to put this in the fridge," he said, lifting the bag.

Gracie nodded, before heading to join the others in the den. "When did you get back?" she asked Jesse and Nicole.

"About half an hour ago," Nicole said nonchalantly. "Where did you go?"

"Dean and I went to find food," she replied. "You weren't here, and we were hungry."

"Did you bring back some?" Zara asked eagerly.

Jesse turned to stare at her. "We just made you lunch. How are you hungry again?"

"I," Theo said loudly. "*I* made you lunch." Thankfully, Jesse ignored him.

"Dean's putting it in the fridge," Gracie told her friend.

"I'll go with you," Raina said quickly as Zara stood up. She practically dashed out of the room, and Gracie turned to Nicole.

"I didn't do anything," Nicole was quick to protest.

Gracie snorted. Somehow, she didn't believe that.

"Anyone want to play a game?" Dean asked as he joined them in the den, sitting down on a couch.

Theo brightened. "I vote Taboo."

"I vote no," Nicole retorted. She crossed her legs and pulled out her phone, pointedly turning her back on the rest of the group.

"I'm in," Gracie added.

Dean grinned triumphantly. "That's three to one. Jes, go grab the box. It's under the TV."

Jesse nodded, standing. He retrieved the Taboo box quickly and set about taking the cards out and placing them in a neat stack. "What teams are we doing?"

"Ashcrofts against everyone," Zara suggested. Gracie jumped, having not realized Zara had returned.

"That's not fair," Raina protested, but everyone else had already separated into two teams.

"I think it's a great idea," Nicole said loudly.

Gracie glanced between her two friends. Had something happened while she and Dean were out? She stole a second look at Nicole, who had suddenly taken a great interest in the game, laughing as Jesse fiddled with the hourglass.

Theo picked up the card stack, and Nicole moved to peer over his shoulder. "Go," she said, flipping the hourglass.

Theo squinted at the card. "You use this to go places," he said slowly. "You can go up and down, and it moves with technology."

"Escalator, moving stairs, hover lift, elevator," Dean rattled off instantly.

Theo tossed the card to the floor. "Female character at the most *special* place on earth."

"Minnie Mouse!" Zara called out from her spot on the floor.

"Twi—"

"Lullaby," Jesse said promptly.

Gracie's jaw dropped, and she glanced at Raina, who looked similarly astonished. "Y-you..." she sputtered. "How often do you play this?"

Theo just grinned and kept going. By the time Nicole had called time, Team Ashcroft had eight cards in their pile. Dean was grinning smugly as he handed the stack of cards to Nicole.

"I think the Ashcrofts need to be split up," Raina declared, grinning as she flicked a strand of Zara's hair. "It's only fair."

"Life isn't fair, Raina," Nicole said bitterly. "Suck it up and deal with it."

Jesse looked stunned, glancing between Nicole and a hurt looking Raina. "Nic, that was a bit out of line," he said cautiously.

Nicole shrugged. "It's true, is it not?"

"Raina was teasing," Gracie said gently. "It's just a game, Nicole."

"Oh, so when I say something, it's just a game, but when Raina says something, you all take it seriously?" Nicole shot back. She crossed her arms over her chest, a defensive expression settling on her face.

"Um, you're the only one who's taking it seriously," Gracie pointed out uneasily.

"Well, what do you know, Gracie?" Nicole exclaimed. "You're never around to play any games, so don't talk!"

"Nicole!" Zara said in surprise, standing up and moving to Gracie's side. "Calm down. Gracie didn't do anything to you."

Gracie winced. Telling Nicole to calm down was never a good idea. "Nic—"

"Don't 'Nicole' me!" Nicole said furiously. "I'm sick and tired of you and everyone else always taking Raina's side. I'm gone for two months and you replaced me, Gracie. I thought we were closer than that, but you're just like everyone else in this fucking school."

Gracie swallowed, Nicole's words cutting her deeply. "We didn't replace you," she tried to protest, but Nicole wasn't having it.

"I come back and it's all about Raina—Raina did this, Raina did that!" Nicole threw her hands in the air. "Raina's all over Jesse, Raina has a crush on him and therefore you all take her side, Raina —" she paused, ignoring Raina's eyes filling up with tears and Gracie's shocked expression, "Raina is so much better, and we always have to take her goddamn side. Don't act like you don't do it! *You* spoke to her yesterday, *you're* the one rooming with her right now, it's always *you!*"

"Okay," Jesse interrupted, grabbing Nicole's arm tightly. "Nicole, we're taking a walk."

"No, I'm not," Nicole growled, attempting to wrestle her arm from Jesse's grip.

"Yes, you are," Jesse said firmly, half-leading and half-dragging her from the room.

Gracie stared after them, wondering how a simple game of Taboo had turned so sour. A shaky sob left Raina's mouth before the blonde ran out of the room, her hands covering her face. Zara cursed under her breath before running after their friend.

"I'm going to make sure that everything's okay," Theo said awkwardly, before hurrying out of the room too.

Gracie turned to Dean, her eyes blurring with tears. She wrapped her arms around herself, trying to calm her shaking limbs. "How could she say that?" she whispered.

Dean approached her, holding out a hand. Gracie looked down, pretending she didn't see him. "It's not your fault," he said softly. "You didn't do anything. Nicole's upset and taking it out on everyone."

Gracie bit back a sob, not wanting to cry in front of Dean. "I-I'm going to go," she muttered, before running out of the room. She turned corners blindly, not even knowing where she was going.

She ended up in a small room that she'd never been to before. It could've been fully furnished or nearly empty, and Gracie wouldn't have noticed. The only thing that caught her eye was the large couch in the middle of the room. She sank onto it, before burying her face in her knees and beginning to cry.

How could Nicole say stuff like that? If she wasn't in the common room or wherever everyone else was playing games, it was because Gracie was working hard in order to stay at the school. She didn't have rich parents like everyone else did. She was there on a scholarship. If she didn't have great grades, she could get kicked out. So, of course, Gracie had to study a lot in order to stay at Trinity with all of her friends. Nicole had never complained about Gracie's absences before, so why was she starting now? Had this been festering in her mind this whole time? Or was she merely grasping at straws as she tried to hurt the nearest person?

Gracie and Zara hadn't replaced Nicole with Raina. Nicole hadn't been there at the beginning of the year, and when Raina had been assigned to their dorm, they hadn't wanted to spend the year at odds with their new roommate. Gracie considered Raina to be one of her closest friends, even though they had only known each other for a few months. Nicole was also one of her closest friends. It wasn't like she could only have a specific number of friends.

If Gracie took Raina's side, it was because Raina was right. She wasn't going to side with someone just because she liked them better.

And she was only rooming with Raina because Nicole and Raina couldn't be in a room together for longer than five minutes! It wasn't that she liked Raina better. Gracie had just been trying to separate the two girls, and she had been standing closer to Raina. That was why she had chosen the blonde, it had nothing to do with preferring one girl over the other.

"Gracie?" Dean's voice interrupted her tears. She glanced up just in time to see him stepping into the room. He kicked the door shut with his foot, folding his arms across his chest. "Are you okay?"

Gracie shrugged, swallowing the lump in her throat. She didn't try to talk, knowing that if she did, she would probably break down in tears again.

"Can I sit next to you?" he asked.

Gracie considered this for a second, before nodding.

"How are you doing?" he asked, still standing by the door. He ran a hand through his hair, a worried expression on his face.

"'kay," Gracie mumbled. She tilted her head so her hair fell over her face, hiding her tear-stained cheeks and puffy eyes.

"Well, you're not in a corner, so I think I'm good," Dean teased, sitting down next to her on the couch.

Despite herself, Gracie smiled. Dean had remembered, even if she had only mentioned her safe place briefly.

"What's going through your head right now?"

"I don't know," Gracie answered honestly.

Dean nodded. "That's fair."

Gracie peeked at him through her hair. He was sitting at the edge of the couch, as if he were afraid of a crying teenage girl. The thought made her giggle.

"You good?" Dean asked cautiously.

Gracie giggled again before swallowing. "Yeah. I'm good. You can come closer, you know."

"Okey dokey." He scooted closer. Gracie untucked her knees to sit properly, her leg brushing against Dean's as she leaned against one of the couch's pillows.

"Where's Nicole?" Gracie asked. "And everyone else?"

Dean paused for a second. "Last time I saw her, she was storming to her room. I don't know where Jesse disappeared to, but Raina and Theo went for a walk and Zara's probably in her secret room."

"Raina and Theo?" Gracie raised her eyebrows.

Dean shrugged. "He was the only person left, but Raina's not his type. Besides, she likes Jesse. Theo respects the bro code too much to go for a girl that likes his cousin."

Gracie winced. "Yeah. I think the whole house knows that now."

"Jesse," Dean said, realization dawning on his face. It may have been evident to everyone else, but his cousin was extremely oblivious. "Jesse knows."

"No shit, Sherlock," Gracie muttered, before snapping her head around to look at Dean. "I'm sorry, I didn't mean to insult you."

"You didn't," Dean said. "It's been a long day. I've also never heard you curse before."

Gracie blushed. "Yeah, well, I don't do it often," she admitted. "My mom was pretty big on proper language growing up, so all of my exposure to curse words and anything rated higher than PG comes from Zara."

"My sister certainly has a talent for going against adults," Dean said with a chuckle. "Nicole was really out of line, Gracie. I hope you know that."

Gracie swallowed. "Yeah. I do."

"I'm really sorry. She shouldn't have said that. Any of it."

"I know," Gracie said, shaking her head. "It's just...she knows why I work hard, and she's never said anything against it before, so why start now?"

"She was just looking for anything she could use to start an argument," Dean theorized.

"And Raina," Gracie said, biting her lip. "She completely crushed Raina. As in, she took Raina's heart, bared it for the world to see, and then stomped on it and crushed it."

"If it's any consolation, we think Jesse likes her back," Dean admitted.

"I hope so," Gracie said quietly. "Because if he doesn't and it gets all awkward between them, it's going to drive a wedge between everyone. Raina and Nicole aren't likely to talk to each other again, and I have no idea what it's going to be like between the two of them and Jesse."

Dean let out a breath. "It's not going to be pretty," he stated. "Nicole's of the opinion that since Jesse is her best friend, he can't spend that much time with other girls. Especially Raina, who Jesse took to instantly and has basically spent the past two months with. She feels threatened, and so Nicole lashes out."

Gracie looked at him in surprise, having not realized how perceptive he was. "Did you pick up on all that in the past couple of days?"

Dean gave her a small shrug. "More or less. Jesse mentioned the situation once or twice and I've known Nicole for a while, so I just made a couple of guesses and hoped that they were right and I wasn't saying bullshit."

"You weren't."

"Good," Dean said with a grin. "Because that was a pretty damn impressive speech, and I'm not going to let it get ruined by the truth."

Gracie laughed and joked, "Sorry, Dean, but you're actually one hundred percent wrong. They're fighting over some hair tie they both wanted, not a boy."

"Please," Dean rolled his eyes. "If you're going to lie, you have to make it believable. Nicole? Wear a hair tie? She's a clip person through and through."

Gracie studied his face as he spoke. She *really* hadn't realized how perceptive he was. "Do you think we should make sure that everyone's okay, and that, you know, everyone's alive up there?"

"Yeah," Dean agreed. He stood from the couch, offering her a hand. Gracie took it gratefully, almost flying across the room as he pulled her up. "And Gracie," Dean began as she reached the door.

Gracie turned around, one hand at the doorknob. "Yeah?"

"I get that you want everything to be okay between everyone, but some things might not be fixable," he said carefully. "Obviously try, but I don't want you getting hurt because they're being ridiculous. You've done nothing wrong here, and you don't deserve to be yelled at. It's not your fault, and it's not your fight either. It might be best to step back and let the two of them argue it out."

Gracie blinked at him. "I really don't know what to say to that. Like, I know," she said with a sigh. "But I just don't want to see two of my close friends fighting. It may not be my fight, but I'm affected by it. I live in the same dorm as them, for goodness' sake. I have to wake up in the morning and deal with this, whenever I'm in the dorm I have to deal with this, and at night when I'm getting ready for bed, if they're still arguing and Zara or I don't stop them, we're not getting any sleep."

"I get that," Dean said. "But remember you're not in the wrong here. You may be affected by it, and you may have to get in the middle of Raina and Nicole a lot, but that doesn't make it your fight."

"I know," Gracie said, smiling warmly at him. "Thank you for caring."

"Of course. You're my sister's best friend. If you got caught in the crossfire, I'd have to deal with all of Z's bitching."

## Chapter Seventeen

Dean found himself in his secret room the next day, sitting on a beanbag and watching a movie on his laptop. The villain was just about to die when the door creaked open and Gracie poked her head in.

"Hey, can I come in?" she asked hesitantly.

"Of course," Dean jumped up. "You want anything to eat? Drink? Read?"

Gracie laughed, holding up a book. "I'm just here to read," she said, dragging a beanbag over to a corner and sitting down.

Dean sat down as well, but he couldn't focus on the movie anymore. "Is everyone upstairs?" he asked. Last time he was in the kitchen, the only people who had come downstairs all day were Gracie and Theo.

Gracie sighed. "Zara's still missing, but if you say that she's in her secret room, then I'm not that worried. Raina and Nicole are in their rooms, Theo's watching TV, and I think Jesse went for a run."

"That's not as bad as I thought," Dean said, rolling out his shoulders. He stood and grabbed a package of sour sticks from the small coffee table next to him. "Want one?" he offered.

She shook her head before closing her book and stretching her arms.

"Want to play a game?" he asked when Gracie made no move to open her book again.

Gracie glanced at him. "What game?"

"Truth or dare?" Dean suggested.

"Okay," Gracie said, biting her lip. "I pick Truth."

"What's your favorite color?" Dean asked, going for a simple question. He knew it was the most cliché question there was, but he still wanted to know the answer.

"Either jade or pale yellow," Gracie replied promptly. "Truth or dare?"

"Truth."

"What's *your* favorite color?"

"Dark blue," Dean answered confidently. He reached out to grab another sour stick, shoving the whole thing into his mouth. "Are we just playing Truth or Truth now?"

Gracie laughed, her shoulder-length hair falling across her face as she made herself comfortable in the beanbag. "Guess so. Your turn."

"Favorite chocolate?"

"Dove dark chocolate. Hoodies or zip-ups?"

"Hoodies, all the way. If you could travel anywhere in the world for a day, where would you go?"

"Italy," Gracie said after thinking for a minute. "One of my favorite books is set there, and I've always wanted to visit." She shrugged, a small blush spreading across her face. "You know, act out the book and all that."

"So you're looking for romance in Italy," Dean deduced.

Gracie's blush grew. "Yeah, basically."

Dean debated what to ask her next. It was too cruel to ask her to name her greatest fear, and he wanted to stay away from questions about friends. "What's your favorite book?" Dean finally said.

Gracie gasped. "That is an evil question!" she declared. "You can't make me pick!"

"Alright," Dean chuckled. "Fair. I see your point. I get to ask another question then." He thought for a minute. "When did you realize you were in love with me?"

✩✩
✩

Gracie's mouth dropped open. Had Dean really just said what she thought he said? "I'm not...in love with you," she said slowly. "You know that, right? It's all a ruse, a joke. I'm not actually in love with you. I don't even like you or think of you that way."

Dean raised his eyebrows, and Gracie thought over what she had said, wincing inwardly. "Are you sure?" he asked.

"Yes, I'm sure!" Gracie declared, unable to stop herself. "You're my best friend's brother. That's it. I'm not madly in love with you like the whole school thinks. You know that. You're the one who started this whole thing."

Gracie covered her face with her hands, wondering if she could take back everything that had just spewed out of her mouth. Of course, she thought of Dean *that way*. How could she not? His gorgeous face and tousled hair distracted her every couple of seconds, and the years he had spent swimming had made Gracie steal a couple of glances at his body as well.

She wasn't in love with him, that was for sure. She definitely didn't want to run off to Vegas with him, even though she blushed every time she thought of what had happened in the kitchen. But she was kind of...slightly...maybe...attracted to him. Physically, of course. Gracie didn't *like-like* Dean; that would be absurd. Dean was Zara's brother, and Zara was her best friend, and Dean only thought of her as Zara's best friend, so it was completely fair of her to only think of him as Zara's brother.

Gracie cringed inwardly. As much as she only wanted to think of Dean as Zara's brother, he had become her friend in the past couple of weeks. She had thought that spending time together and hanging out made her and Dean friends, but apparently she was wrong, because yesterday he'd said that he only thought of her as Zara's best friend.

"Relax," Dean was saying when Gracie turned her attention back to reality. "I'm just messing with you, Gracie. I know you're not *actually* in love with me or anything like that."

Gracie laughed a little too loudly. "No, of course not. That would be ridiculous," she declared. "Insane, crazy, absolutely preposterous." She continued to laugh nervously, her voice getting slightly higher with each word. "Absurd, ludicrous—"

"Synonym overload!" Dean said loudly, and Gracie stopped speaking.

She stared at him. "How did you know that?"

Zara had discovered early in their freshman year that when Gracie was nervous, she had a habit of listing synonyms to various words. It had continued on for a couple of months before Zara had eventually come up with a code phrase. If Gracie heard the code phrase, it would let her know that she was listing synonyms again, and she would stop. Most of the time, Gracie didn't even realize she was doing it, so it helped to have someone to keep her in check.

But since Gracie had stopped speaking in synonyms at some point during her first semester of sophomore year, she hadn't thought it was important enough to mention it to Dean.

Dean avoided her eyes, a sheepish expression crossing his face. "Zara...kind of told me."

"She what?" Gracie asked, stunned. She stood furiously, three seconds away from running out of the room and confronting her best friend. Gracie had sworn Zara to confidence on the matter, and Zara had promised never to tell a single soul. They had even made a pinky promise on it!

"She doesn't even remember doing it," Dean said quickly. "It was during a party after finals freshman year. Zara was drunk, and I was taking her up to her dorm. She asked where you were and before I could stop her, I was getting a ton of random facts about you. Also, on a completely unrelated note, do your pajamas still have Minnie Mouse on them?"

"No," Gracie lied, blushing furiously. She made a mental note to burn both the pajamas and Zara as soon as possible.

"I haven't told anyone," Dean said seriously. "I promise. I wouldn't. I'm not like that."

"I know," Gracie said quietly. "Thank you. For not telling anyone, that is. And for stopping me."

"Course," Dean replied. They stood in silence for a few minutes before Dean spoke again. "We should be getting back now…"

Gracie glanced in surprise at the clock. "Oh wow, it's late!" she exclaimed. "The car will be here at seven. We need to go find everyone and pack. Can you track down Jesse and Theo? I'll text Zara and get Raina and Nicole, assuming they're both still in their rooms."

"I can do that," Dean assured her.

"Great," Gracie said, smiling shakily under the weight of Dean's intense gaze. "You're staring at me."

Dean jumped. "Oh. Sorry."

"It's fine."

"I'm going to go now," Dean blurted out before rushing from the room.

Gracie stared after him for a second, wondering if she would ever figure him out. She decided that the matter wasn't worth pondering over before leaving the room herself, taking care to lock the door behind her.

☆
☆ ☆

The car ride back to Trinity was spent entirely in silence. Dean had sat in the back, in between Jesse and Nicole. Raina, in the front seat, had kept her gaze on the road the entire time. When they had finally parked, Jesse had practically run out of the car. By the time Dean and Theo made it to their dorm, their cousin had already been moping on his bed.

Dean exchanged an exasperated glance with Theo before both cousins made their way to join Jesse on his bed.

"How are you doing?" Theo asked.

Jesse laughed bitterly. "Perfectly fine. Just dandy. It's been a stupendous day."

Dean winced. It was worse than he thought, apparently, if Jesse was spitting out big words with every sentence. "Have you spoken to Raina?"

"I spoke to Nic," Jesse said, ignoring the question. He shook his head again. "She was way over the line and she knows it. She's going to apologize."

"To who?" Dean pressed. "Because there's more than one person in that room who deserves an apology."

"I know!" Jesse exclaimed. "But Nicole is one of the most stubborn people I've ever met, and it was hard enough convincing her to apologize to Gracie."

"You don't think we know that?" Theo shot back, his normally calm voice now angry. "Jesse, I know better than anyone else why Nicole hates apologizing so much. She fucking turned up on my—" he cut himself off, shooting a look toward Dean.

"I'm going to go to the bathroom," Dean said quickly, realizing that Theo needed to talk to Jesse alone. He had never been privy to all of Nicole's secrets, nor had he been close with her as a child like Zara, Jesse, and Theo had been.

His aunts and uncles had asked him before whether he was okay with the dark-haired girl coming over so often, seeing as he often played by himself or read a book when Nicole was over. Dean had assured them he was fine and that he and Nicole got along perfectly well. They just hadn't clicked like she had with his cousins. As they grew older, Theo spent more time reading with Dean, while the other three played together. Nicole had stopped coming around during middle school, but at some point during their freshman year, she had reappeared with no explanation.

Dean took awhile to brush his teeth, making faces in the mirror until a decent amount of time had passed. Then he turned the handle on the door, stomping loudly so that Theo and Jesse would know that he was coming. Sure enough, they stopped talking once Dean entered the room and rejoined them on the bed.

"So," he said slowly. "What'd I miss?"

"Headfirst into a political abyss," Theo said absentmindedly. "Nicole's going to apologize to Gracie for shouting at her, even though she really should say that to Zara and Raina as well."

"She's never going to apologize to Raina," Jesse argued. "She won't. I know it."

"We all know it," Dean said. "I suppose this is the best we're going to get."

Jesse shrugged. "They just need to work it out on their own."

Dean shot a glance at his cousin. "And…what about the other thing Nicole said?" he asked delicately.

"There is no other thing," Jesse said, his pink cheeks betraying his otherwise blank face. "I'm going to bed. I'll talk to Nic in the morning."

✯✯✯

"Hi," Nicole said quietly, pushing open the drapes around Gracie's bed.

Gracie glanced up from the book she was flipping through. "Hey," she replied, equally quiet.

Nicole fiddled with her thumbs, unusually nervous. She was already dressed in pajamas, a black t-shirt and checkered pants. "Can I sit down?"

Seeing as she was already standing by the bed, it wasn't a request, but Gracie nodded. Neither girl spoke for a few minutes.

"I was wrong," Nicole said out loud. "I should not have yelled at you. I was out of line, and I was upset. I said some things I did not mean."

Gracie turned to face her friend. It didn't escape her notice that Nicole was speaking more formally than she normally would—a clear sign that the dark-haired girl was out of her element. "Then why'd you say them?" she asked, letting some of her hurt seep into her voice.

"I don't know." Nicole stared down at her lap. "I was upset and angry. What I said, Gracie, I didn't—I don't mean it. I know that you work really hard and that you *do* spend time with us. I just wanted you to stop defending Raina."

"Saying hurtful things wasn't the way to go," Gracie told her friend. "Why didn't you just talk to me? We could've avoided this whole thing."

Nicole shrugged. "I'm not very good at talking to people. Jesse's one of the few people I can actually talk to, and I guess I just got really upset when he stopped talking to me and started spending all of his time with Raina. He's my best friend, and it felt like he was replacing me."

"Did you tell him this?" Gracie asked gently.

"I did," Nicole said, her eyes now focused on the ceiling. "We talked for a bit. We're probably still going to talk more, but he said I should talk to you first."

"And what about Raina?" Gracie asked cautiously.

"Jesse and I agreed it was best for me to have some space from her," Nicole said slowly. "And maybe just some space in general. I've asked the administration if they can move me into another dorm. It's not that I don't love being with you and Zara," she added quickly, "but six people in this dorm is too much. It was meant for four or five, not six teenage girls who clash far too often. Especially when you toss in Annalisse and Juliet. They're loud enough for four people."

"Do you think this will help?"

"I think the chance to be on my own and make some new friends will," Nicole said. "I guess I came back and expected that everything would be exactly the same, you know? But Raina came, and now Jesse spends all of his time with Raina, and whether you admit it or not, you're spending a ton of time with Dean. And Zara disappears too…"

Gracie looked up in surprise. "She does?"

"Yeah," Nicole nodded. "She's gone most afternoons. I don't know where she goes, and I've never asked."

Gracie frowned to herself, having never realized this before. Had she really been spending so much time with Dean that she hadn't even noticed Zara disappearing?

She sighed, scooting closer to Nicole. "Do you think we can all get through this?"

"I can't promise that Raina and I will be BFFs or some other crap," Nicole said. "But I'll try. I won't start fights or argue with her anymore, and I'm going to work on my temper. Jesse, he said he'd help me with that."

"That's a good idea," Gracie said with a nod. She leaned closer to her friend, resting her head on Nicole's shoulder. Gracie looked up just in time to see a smirk on Nicole's face.

"Bet you wish it was Dean instead of me," the taller girl teased.

Gracie laughed and reached for her pillow, hitting Nicole's shoulder. Everything wouldn't be okay overnight, but if Nicole was willing to try, Gracie had hope for the future.

## Chapter Eighteen

Dean had never seen the common room as quiet as it was the morning after he, his family, and Gracie returned from their mini-break. Two girls whispered together in a corner and a boy sat reading by the fire, but otherwise, the room was empty.

Dean made himself comfortable in a chair and pulled out a book, but he had barely gotten to the second page before the book was yanked out of his hands.

"Did you hear?" Zara demanded eagerly, a gleam in her eyes.

Dean had no idea what she was talking about, so he just shook his head. Zara plopped down next to him on the chair, forcing Dean to squish to one side. The chair was not meant for two teenagers to sit on, but as Zara wriggled around to get comfortable, it was clear that she wasn't leaving.

"There was no gas leak," Zara said in a hushed voice. "It was all a ruse. Someone was stealing chemicals from the school labs. And there wasn't a pattern or specific thing that could be created with them. There were some that were completely random, like someone just went in and grabbed a bunch of random stuff off the shelf. The teachers have no idea what they were taken for."

Dean's eyes widened. "Where did you hear this?" he asked. "Do they know who did it?"

Zara shook her head grimly. "No. Annalisse told me this morning. She and Juliet eavesdropped on a couple of the teachers talking about it. They were trying to keep it a secret from us, but, well, that never ends well."

Dean snorted. Juliet and Annalisse might not be very bright, but their one talent was spreading gossip around the school in under an hour. Dean sat up straighter, an idea occurring to him, but he pushed it aside for now and continued asking Zara about the theft.

"They don't know anything else," Zara said. "And I've tried finding Uncle Aaron, but no one's around. It wasn't like a break in or anything—nothing was broken—but they know they weren't used for a lesson or something because the cameras went offline for an hour. Once they were back up, the chemicals were gone."

"Damn." Dean whistled. "The parents are going to have a field day with this one."

"I don't know that they're saying anything," Zara said with a shrug. "After all, they didn't tell us. Who knows what Uncle Aaron's going to do."

"So they canceled classes for two days just so they could figure out who did it," Dean summed up. "But they didn't. Also, why did they let people leave if that was their intention?"

"They checked bags extensively," Zara said. "And only select people."

Dean frowned. "They didn't do that to us."

"Ashcroft," Zara reminded him. "They can't really touch us."

Dean shrugged uncomfortably. "Still, it doesn't really show fairness. Just because our ancestor founded this place and our uncle is the principal, we shouldn't be getting special treatment."

"Oh, lighten up," Zara said with a sigh. "Listen, enjoy it while you can." She glanced back at the steps. "I'm supposed to be waking Gracie up now. I'll see you at breakfast."

Dean waved as his sister disappeared up the stairs, not bothering to tell her he'd already eaten. He'd see her later, but when he did, she'd have far bigger things to worry about than Dean skipping breakfast.

✦✦
✦

Gracie tapped her foot impatiently as she sat in her chemistry class, her eyes fixed on a stack of papers on the teacher's desk. Dr. Jameson had promised to give back their tests a couple days ago, but due to the gas leak, she'd pushed it off until today.

Gracie twirled a strand of her hair in her fingers, unable to focus on the class' material. Tests were given back at the end of the period, and it was always an agonizing forty minutes. They had taken the test a few weeks ago, and she had been in agony waiting for them to be returned. Next to her, Zara was glued to her phone, which she was hiding behind her backpack. She didn't look worried about her grade at all.

"Okay!" Dr. Jameson announced finally, clapping her hands together. "We can stop there for today. Don't forget that we have a lab tomorrow where we *will* use what we have learned today, so please come prepared with the material." She picked up the pile of tests, glancing at the one on top. "Ms. Raleigh."

Gracie frowned, looking around the classroom. Had someone switched into the class without her noticing? She didn't remember anyone with the last name "Raleigh" in the class.

"Ms. Raleigh?" Dr. Jameson repeated, this time mostly to herself. Gracie's chemistry teacher looked down at the tests again before her eyes widened in surprise. "Oh no, I took the freshman biology tests by mistake!"

Zara glanced up from her phone. "What's happening?" she whispered to Gracie.

"Ms. Adams," Dr. Jameson said. "Would you mind running down to Lab C for me and grabbing the pile of tests? They should be in one of the desk drawers. Actually, while you're there, I need a couple of extra lab beakers for my next period. Would you mind grabbing those as well?" She quickly scrawled something on a piece of paper, holding it out.

"Of course," Gracie said, her face brightening up as she hopped off the stool. Quickly, she grabbed the pass and she darted out of the classroom. The faster she ran, the faster she would get to the lab and back, and the faster she could get her test grade.

Gracie was so busy thinking that she barely even noticed where she was going until she ran into a hard body, looking up to meet Blake's sparkling eyes.

"We really have to stop meeting like this." The boy laughed.

Gracie laughed too. "Sorry, I'd love to chat, but I have to go," she said apologetically before hurrying off again.

"Where are you headed?" Blake called after her.

"Chemistry lab!" Gracie yelled over her shoulder.

A second later, he had caught up to her. "I figured I'd come and keep you company," Blake said, matching her stride. "I've got nothing better to do, and I enjoy hanging out with you."

Gracie tried not to, but she blushed a little. "I'm just picking up some tests," she said nonchalantly. "Nothing interesting, but you're welcome to tag along if you'd like."

Blake slung the bag he was holding over his shoulder so he could keep up with her more easily. "Sounds interesting to me," he said, shooting her a grin.

Gracie turned the corner, coming to a stop outside of the chemistry labs. A burly adult was standing in the hall, hands stuffed in his belt loops as he scanned the surrounding area. Another guard stood at the end of the hall, by the door that led to the science teachers' offices. "What's with all the security?" she whispered to Blake.

"My dad told me it's because of the gas leak," Blake explained. "They want to make sure it can't happen again."

"Wasn't it an accident?" Gracie asked.

"They're not so sure," Blake said in a low voice.

Gracie straightened as they approached the unfamiliar man

outside of Lab C. "Hi, I'm here to pick up something for Dr. Jameson. Are we allowed inside?"

"What do you need?" the man grunted.

"Chemistry tests and beakers," Gracie replied promptly. She handed over the pass Dr. Jameson had given her.

The man studied it for a second before unlocking the door and waving them inside. Gracie made a move for the desk, opening the top drawer to find a stack of papers.

"I can get the beakers," Blake offered. "Are they in that closet?" he motioned to a door in the back of the room.

"Yes, thank you," Gracie said gratefully. She turned back to the man guarding the door, giving him her most polite smile. "Excuse me? Would you mind unlocking the closet for us? We need to get beakers."

The guard nodded. Without a word, he walked over to unlock the door before returning to his original position in the doorway. Blake headed inside, and Gracie returned her attention to the tests. She checked the page on top to confirm that it was her class' before she balanced the papers in her arms.

"Blake? Did you find them?" she called.

Gracie heard a bit of shuffling from the closet before Blake reappeared, beakers in hand. "Got them!" he said cheerfully. "A little tricky to find, but no match for me." He winked.

Gracie grinned back as they exited the classroom. "Thank you for your help," she said. "Want to walk me back to my class?"

"Sure," Blake agreed, readjusting the beakers in his hands. They walked silently through the halls, Blake focused on holding all the beakers and Gracie preoccupied with her thoughts. She was struggling to reconcile the Blake that Dean had told her about and the Blake that she knew. Her Blake was nice, polite, and fun to chat with, but she barely knew him. Even so, he seemed like a completely different person from the one that Zara and Dean had described.

"Good luck," he said once they had reached the classroom, nodding toward the papers.

"Thanks again," Gracie repeated as he transferred the beakers to her arms. She caught one last glimpse of him as he walked away, hands in his pockets, whistling softly. She walked inside and handed everything to Dr. Jameson, who began passing out tests immediately.

"What took you so long?" Zara whispered as soon as Gracie sat back down. Zara's name got called then, so Gracie waited for her friend to come back before responding.

"The beakers were hard to find," she said vaguely, not wanting to admit that she was with Blake and have Zara go off on another rant about how her cousin was evil. From what Dean had told her, it was justified, but not for the first time Gracie wondered if Zara's method of coping with Blake's betrayal was healthy. Gracie's mom had always been a firm believer that bottling things up and staying angry was never the way to go.

When Gracie's name was called, she escaped to the front, returning to her desk with a wide grin on her face and a ninety-eight on the paper.

"Told you, you would do it," Zara said smugly. "Did I ever doubt you?"

"No, but I certainly doubted myself," Gracie said, suddenly feeling very relieved. She quickly packed up her books. "Come on, let's go back to the common room. My mom sent me some chocolate and I'm in a mood to celebrate."

"Ooh, I love chocolate. And remember the chem leak? Well, Annalisse told me…"

✯✯✯

"How dare you!" someone yelled, causing Gracie to look up from her book and blink at what was surely another arguing couple. Zara had left a while ago, and since then, Gracie's reading had been interrupted three times. Couples had passed through the common room, arguing with raised voices that were extremely

# The Gossip Games

distracting when all Gracie wanted to do was finish her current chapter. But an even bigger distraction was the boy standing in front of her, his hands on his hips.

"I'm sorry?" Gracie asked in confusion.

"How could you?" Dean continued yelling. "I trusted you! And him! My own *cousin*, Gracie. How could you?"

Gracie laughed nervously. "Dean, I don't know what you're talking about. *Stop yelling*," she hissed, trying not to draw the attention of the packed common room.

It didn't work, though, considering that Dean's voice was loud enough to draw the entire school. "You kissed my cousin!" Dean shouted, his voice rising with each word. "He told me all about that day in the library, so don't try to talk your way out of this. You kissed him, and you enjoyed it!"

"Well, he certainly kissed me back!" Gracie shot back at him, throwing her book on the couch and jumping to her feet. She had no idea why Dean was confronting her about this now, in the middle of the common room, but she would be damned if she let him walk out as the angel in all of this. "And why should it matter to you?"

It was Dean's turn to look puzzled, and Gracie's inner self grinned triumphantly. "W-why should it matter to me?" he sputtered. "I'm your boyfriend! You kissed another boy! You kissed my cousin, for god's sake!"

"And if I recall correctly, we were on a break," Gracie said smugly, wondering how in the world she'd come up with that in all of three seconds. "So technically, I did nothing wrong. If anything, you should be asking Theo why he was kissing a girl he thought you were dating, because *I* didn't tell anyone about our break, did you?"

Dean growled angrily, his hands curling into fists. Gracie took a step closer and Dean backed up until they were in the middle of the common room. "It was a break that you initiated," Dean said. "I wanted nothing to do with it, so I'm sorry for caring when my girlfriend and my cousin kiss. Because it was your idea to take a break."

"Well, you agreed to the break, and I thought I was kissing you!"

Gracie shouted. "It's not my fault you two look exactly alike! I stopped the kiss as soon as I realized, why didn't Theo?"

Dean glanced around the common room wildly, before snapping his head around to glare at Gracie. Gracie took her own scan of the room and found Theo hiding behind a group of sophomore girls but decided not to call him out.

"Oh, so now it's my fault for having a cousin who looks exactly like me?"

"No, it's your fault for having a cousin with no self-control!" Gracie mentally winced at the insult to Theo. "Like cousin, like cousin, they say."

"What's that supposed to mean?" Dean demanded furiously, taking a step closer.

"I don't know!" Gracie threw her hands up in the air. Dean's eyes darkened, and Gracie realized they were standing mere inches apart. This time, Gracie was certain she initiated the kiss, but within seconds, both she and Dean had their hands roving over the other's body. Gracie wrapped a hand around the tie Dean wore and tugged him closer; he responded by pulling the hair tie out of her hair.

Gracie barely registered the sound of someone coughing before a loud whistle pierced through the room, and she shoved Dean away. He stumbled back a few steps, rubbing his mouth. His eyes were filled with an emotion Gracie didn't recognize, but it was intoxicating. Even though Gracie wanted nothing more than to kiss him again, she reluctantly tore her eyes away.

Zara shook her head, glaring at her best friend and brother. "Ugh, I can't take this anymore! I swear, you guys are getting worse by the day. I leave you alone for one minute and you two are already all over each other. Gah! Just make up your mind already. Dating, not dating; break, no break. I can't do this anymore!" Zara stormed off, spurring a whole new round of whispers as she headed for the steps.

Gracie's face flamed instantly. She made a run for the door with Dean on her heels. She knew that leaving the room with Dean would only further the rumors, but Gracie found she couldn't care less as she wrenched the door leading out of the common room open and furiously stalked down the hallway. She turned a corner and paused, letting out a ragged breath. The footsteps behind her stopped, but Dean stayed silent and let her breathe.

"So...you want to help get revenge on Zara?" Dean asked after a minute.

Gracie made a huffing noise, crossing her arms over her chest. "I want to know what she was thinking, egging everything on like that. I mean, we were doing just fine on our own."

"Yeah," Dean agreed. "Although, what exactly were we doing?"

"I don't know," Gracie confessed with a small laugh.

"And if I asked you to kiss me again..." Dean said softly, taking a step closer and backing Gracie against the stone wall. "Would you know then?"

Gracie's gaze flickered to his lips before returning to his eyes. "I don't know," she breathed, struck by how much she wanted him to kiss her.

Dean smirked before pulling away. "Okay," he said casually, walking away as if nothing had happened.

Gracie stood there for a moment, frozen in place, before shaking her head and running after Dean. She caught his arm, spinning him around. For a second, the two faced each other in silence.

"You owe me a kiss," Gracie said finally, leaning forward and lifting her chin to brush her lips against his. The first kiss was soft and gentle, barely a touch of lips. Dean made an impatient noise and kissed her again, this time more heated. Gracie's eyes fluttered closed as her mouth opened for him, their tongues fighting for dominance. When he broke the kiss, panting, all Gracie could do was stare.

Dean's hair was completely messed up after their kiss in the common room. He was missing his blazer and his tie was so loose it could've slipped off. His lips seemed pinker than they normally were, but no less kissable. Gracie moved forward without thinking, and continued kissing Dean in the middle of the school hallway.

## Chapter Nineteen

The next week was Christmas break, and Dean happily welcomed the reprieve from schoolwork. The day they were leaving, he finished packing his duffel before dragging it down to the car Uncle Aaron had ordered. He'd never been to Gracie's house before, and he was curious to see where she lived. The car ride was only an hour and a half, and even though Zara had immediately claimed the front seat, Dean didn't mind sitting in the back at all. It meant an hour and a half of sitting next to Gracie, exchanging exasperated smiles every so often as Zara rambled on and on. He was almost sad when the car rolled to a stop, parking directly in front of a chalk-covered driveway.

Gracie leaned forward, waving her hand to catch the driver's attention. "It's the next house over."

The second time, Dean didn't wait for confirmation before exiting the car. His left leg had fallen asleep twenty minutes ago, and it was a little uncomfortable as he limped around to the trunk. After opening the trunk, Dean heaved his suitcase onto the sidewalk and slid some of the other bags onto his arms. With his hands full, he headed down the stone walkway.

The neighborhood was filled with medium-sized brick houses,

and Gracie's home was no exception. Her door was bright red and wide open, and he could see the silhouette of a middle-aged woman standing inside as Gracie and Zara ran to hug her. Dean glanced around, noting a group of kids playing next door as he dragged both his and Zara's suitcases up to the front door, precariously balancing the gift he had bought for Gracie's mom on top of one of the sleek black bags.

"Hello! You must be Dean," the woman said with a warm smile as he entered the house. From the brown waves around her shoulders to the dimples in her cheeks when she grinned, Dean knew instantly that this was Gracie's mother. She looked to be around the same age as his own mom, but unlike Alexandra, Gracie's mom's only adornment was a dusting of flour on her cheek.

Dean smiled back politely and handed her the large bunch of colorful flowers. With his hands now free, he detangled himself from Zara's Christmas present and a bag of clothes Gracie was bringing home, dropping them both on the floor. "Yes, it's nice to meet you, ma'am. This is for you."

"Aww, you're so polite!" Gracie's mother gushed. "Why is my own daughter never that polite?" There was a twinkle in her eye as she turned to look at Gracie.

"Mom, stop bothering Dean." Gracie rolled her eyes. She took a step back, leaning against the pale yellow wall.

Leaving the suitcases on the floor for a moment, Dean's eyes traveled across the open entryway. A set of gleaming wooden steps were directly in front of him, bisecting two arched doorways. On his left, he could see the cluttered kitchen, already bubbling and popping with the sounds of dinner cooking. A glance to the right showed a small living room, complete with wall-to-wall bookshelves and a fully decorated Christmas tree. The house itself was overflowing with heat, warmth immediately seeping through Dean's body. He shrugged out of his coat, placing it on the coat rack next to the door.

"Come on, I'll show you to your room." Gracie motioned to him and grasped Zara by the wrist before practically tugging his sister up the steps.

Dean smiled again at Gracie's mother before picking up the bags and following Gracie and Zara upstairs.

"You'll be staying with me," Gracie was saying when he joined them. She turned around to face Dean, gesturing to another door. "This is yours."

"Thank you," Dean said, handing Zara her bag. He pushed open the door to his room, which was decorated in various shades of blue and white. "Nice colors," he told Gracie.

She flashed him a grin. "I thought you'd appreciate them."

"I do," he said sincerely. Dean walked into the room and set his bag down on the bed before rejoining the girls in the hall. "Do we get to see your room?" he asked.

Gracie and Zara exchanged a look before Gracie shrugged, opening the door to her room. Gracie's room was decorated just as tastefully as the guest room, only in shades of yellow. Fairy lights were strung all across the ceiling, and silver stripes accented the pale yellow walls. Zara plopped down on the yellow and white bed, hugging one of Gracie's toddler-sized teddy bears to her chest.

Dean tore his eyes away from the room, turning to Gracie. "So what do we do first? Unpack? Go somewhere? Food?"

"There's food downstairs if you're hungry," Gracie said, nodding toward the door. "I didn't really have anything planned for today. We'll start decorating tomorrow, but feel free to unpack if you want."

A buzzing interrupted Dean's reply, and he pulled his phone out to see a text from Theo. "I'm going to step outside for a moment," he said, wondering why his phone was blowing up with a million exclamation marks. Dean headed downstairs, asking Gracie's mom if it was okay for him to step outside for a minute. He didn't want to worry her on his first day there, and she happily agreed, telling him to unlock the door and come back whenever. Dean flipped the lock easily, pulling the door shut behind him as directed. He didn't want to stand in the middle of the sidewalk on a call, so he started walking down the block before pressing the call button.

"Dean, I don't know what to do," Theo said instantly, picking up before the phone had even rung once.

"And I have no clue what you're talking about," Dean said, an amused tone in his voice. "Calm down, take a deep breath, and start from the beginning."

Dean could hear Theo breathe through the phone. "Mom, dad, and I are at the school house for Christmas, but Mom invited family friends for company."

Dean's eyebrows rose. "That's new."

"It's new to me too," Theo agreed. "And it's *not good*. Not good at all."

"Why isn't it good?" Dean frowned into the phone as he turned a corner.

"Because my mom's friends have kids!" Theo exclaimed. Dean could just imagine him throwing his hands up in frustration. "One of them is our age, and he's really, really cute."

Dean laughed, shaking his head. He should have known that this was over a boy, as both he and Zara had the exact same reaction when they had gotten their first crush. They had sent a message to the group chat with more exclamation marks than necessary, but Dean figured that since he was the only one who knew Theo's secret that wouldn't be happening this time.

"Aww," he teased. "Theo's got a crush."

Theo growled. "This isn't funny!" he exclaimed. "What do I do? How do I act? Do I say something? Make a move?"

Dean shook his head, forgetting that Theo couldn't see him. He could spend all day joking with Theo about this boy, but it would only take a second for his uncle to break Theo's heart. He had been there for Zara when she had been outed, and he'd seen firsthand how cruel his family members could be. "You can't, Theo. I don't care how attractive this guy is. You're both under the same roof as your parents, as your dad. You can't do anything unless you want your dad to know that you're gay."

"And I want to prolong that revelation as much as possible," Theo's voice took on a defeated tone.

"Act normal. Be yourself," Dean advised his cousin. "And whatever you do, don't make a move on him. There's a chance that everything you do will be reported back to Aunt Eliza and Uncle Alex. He could be another Blake, for all you know. You need to keep this under wraps until you're ready to come out to your dad, and you need to be more comfortable with yourself first before that happens. Look, if you want, I'll come back to your house and take you to a gay bar or something—"

"We're seventeen," Theo cut in.

"—and you can figure everything out there," Dean continued loudly, as if Theo had never interrupted. He lowered his voice when a woman walking in front of her house shot him an odd look. "But you're not ready to come out now. I know you aren't. I'm not saying that I don't want you to come out, or that I don't support you or anything because I absolutely do," Dean added hastily. "I'm saying that as your cousin, I'm telling you not to do something that you're going to regret in the future."

Theo was silent for a minute before he sighed. "When did you get so good at giving advice?"

Dean laughed. "I have a teenage twin sister, Theo. Nobody gets through *that* without learning how to give crush advice."

"And what about Gracie?"

"What about her?" Dean asked, a slightly defensive tone entering his voice.

"Nothing, man," Theo said. "But it's odd how someone so good at dealing with other people's crushes can't seem to recognize his own."

Dean frowned into the phone. "What are you talking about? Does Gracie have a crush on me?"

"Oh, I'm not talking about Gracie," Theo said gleefully. "But I wouldn't want to deprive you of your fun, so I'll let you figure it out."

"What are you—" Dean began, but Theo had already hung up. Dean stared down at the phone for a minute before shaking his head and sliding the phone back into his pocket. He quickly glanced around at the street signs before turning around and heading back the way he had come.

He didn't have a crush on Gracie.

Did he?

★★
★★

"So I was thinking," Dean said abruptly.

Gracie turned from where she had been examining the bookshelf in the kitchen, mentally cataloging all the new cookbooks her mom had bought in the past few months. "Should I be worried?"

"Very funny," Dean said dryly. "But I was thinking that we call a truce for this week."

Gracie blinked at him. It was the logical solution, and she didn't particularly want her mom finding out about whatever it was she had going on with Dean. "Sounds fair," she responded.

"Okay," Dean said slowly. "Well, that was it."

★★
★★

The next day Gracie stumbled into the dark attic, her fingers fumbling blindly against the wall. The bulb above the staircase had gone out, and she had been forced to ascend in darkness. Hopefully, the attic itself would have a working light.

Gracie's hand found the switch, and she quickly flipped it up, sighing in relief as light filled the room. She glanced up and froze, her eyes narrowing as she registered who exactly was standing in front of her, hand three inches away from the light switch.

"What are you doing here?" she demanded, shutting the door behind her.

Dean raised his hands in surrender, his black t-shirt somehow becoming even more fitted with the move. "Nothing. Seriously. I was sent up here to get some stuff."

"Doesn't sound like nothing," Gracie muttered, but she ignored him in favor of pushing past cardboard boxes to make her way across the room.

"What are you here for?" Dean asked lightly. A crashing noise as he bumped into a box alerted Gracie to his position, and she purposefully refused to turn around and look at him.

"My mom asked me to find the extra tinsel," she answered after a moment.

"That's funny," Dean said, and Gracie definitely didn't turn around to see the frown she knew was on his face. "Because Zara sent me up here to find some more tinsel."

Gracie dropped the box she was holding. "Why would they both ask us to find tinsel? Especially my mom; she hates tinsel. Says it always gets everywhere and it's a pain to clean up after Christmas." Gracie let out a chuckle. "Well, she doesn't use those words exactly, but I try not to repeat her words in the company of children."

"Hey, we had a truce," Dean mock complained. "You can't call me a child."

Gracie shrugged. "Sorry, force of habit."

"It's okay, wouldn't expect a child like you to understand," Dean said playfully. Gracie laughed. A surprised look flitted over his face, but Dean covered it up quickly.

"Zara's not a big fan of tinsel either," Dean said after a minute, once they had both returned to searching the boxes. "Especially when it comes from dusty places like this. She starts sneezing around dust."

"Do you?" Gracie asked, looking up from her current box. It

contained an army of plastic dolls she had played with as a kid, but no tinsel.

"Do I what? Hate tinsel?"

"Start sneezing around dust."

"Oh that," Dean replied. He set his box down and leaned against the wall, crossing his arms. "Not me. Zara's got all the sneezing stuff—sneezing around dust, sneezing in winter, sneezing outdoors. There's a bit of a list." He chuckled. "Theo's got it too, but Jesse and I are good."

"You four are really close." Gracie stacked a box of old cooking supplies on top of the dolls.

Dean shrugged. "Yeah, well, we're family. And we've kind of had to stick together."

Gracie moved her gaze away but couldn't keep from sneaking one last glance at Dean. He rarely wore t-shirts at school, and he had never worn one that molded this perfectly to his body. She quickly focused on the box in front of her—the last one in the stack she had been looking at.

"Tinsel!" she cried triumphantly, holding up a glittery blue strand.

"Nice work, Adams," Dean said with an approving nod, walking over and giving her a high five. "Yep, that's definitely tinsel."

"What did you think it was, confetti?" Gracie teased, pointedly ignoring her hand, which was still tingling.

"Of course not," Dean said seriously. "I was educated on the art of confetti when I was thirteen. If anything, I thought they were streamers."

"This sounds like a story," Gracie said, handing Dean the box of tinsel and bumping her shoulder against his as they walked through the path of cleared boxes together.

"Nope. No story," Dean said, shaking his head furiously.

"I think there's a story," Gracie said with a grin.

"Okay, so there is a story," Dean conceded. "But I'm not telling it. It's embarrassing."

"Tell me," Gracie insisted.

"Too long," Dean claimed. "And look, here's the door." He shifted the box to one arm and reached out to turn the doorknob, but it wouldn't budge. "It's not turning."

"Let me try," Gracie said, reaching out with her own hand. She got the same result, though. The door refused to open. "I think we're stuck."

"Is there a lock?" Dean asked.

Gracie sighed. "Yeah, it locks from the outside."

Dean groaned, setting the box down on the floor and sitting next to it.

After a moment, Gracie joined him on the floor. "We'll just have to wait for someone to open the door," she said. "Someone will realize that we're missing soon. We won't be stuck here for long."

Dean nodded, his gaze drifting to the door.

"Hey, you know what this means?" Gracie asked with a smug grin.

"What?"

"Story time."

☆☆☆

Dean groaned, but running over the story in his head, he found that he didn't really mind telling it to Gracie. "It was a dark and stormy night," he began.

"No, it wasn't."

"Okay, it wasn't," Dean said reluctantly. "It was actually the day before Easter, four years ago."

"Is that important?" Gracie asked. "That it was the day before Easter?"

Dean tilted his head. "Yes, but not for this story," he said finally. "And stop interrupting. I'm talking."

"Sorry," Gracie whispered, before slapping her hands over her mouth.

"It was the day before Easter," Dean repeated, pausing to glance over at Gracie and check that she was staying silent. "And I woke up that morning to peace and quiet, which was very strange for the day before Easter. Put your hand down," he said sternly. Gracie meekly lowering her hand. "I was in Theo's room for the night, and though his bed was rigged with seven different colors of silly string, mine was completely clean. I checked everything. I checked my slippers, I checked under my pillow, I even checked the drawer where I had hidden my stuffed animals for the night."

"You have stuffed animals?" Gracie burst out. She shot a quick glance at him, and Dean glared. "Sorry, sorry, I'll be quiet now."

"Yes," Dean said haughtily. "I do have stuffed animals, and I'm quite proud of them. There's Tiggy, Beary, and Pandy."

Gracie giggled quietly. Dean continued, "As you can tell, my five-year-old self was great with naming things."

"Now, there was nothing wrong with my stuffed animals, which was good, because they were my off-limits items for the year. And nothing came up in the rest of the room either, so I decided it would be safe to go take a shower. I walked across the hall, walked into the bathroom, drew back the yellow shower curtain with the little ducks, and turned on the shower. Then, I stepped into the bathtub," he said dramatically.

Gracie waited, but Dean had finished speaking. "So what does this have to do with tinsel and confetti?" she asked.

"Oh, right," Dean realized. "The bathtub was filled with tiny pieces of confetti, and when I turned on the water, the color stained my skin pink for days."

Gracie started laughing. "You are not very good at telling stories," she remarked after a minute.

"I am great at telling stories!" Dean exclaimed, running a hand through his hair. He snuck a peek at Gracie, wondering if he should tell her the rest of the story, and the significance of the day.

"Whose prank was that?"

"Zar's," Dean responded. "But don't worry, I got her back good. I made her favorite cake the week after and put broccoli in it."

"Zara hates broccoli," Gracie said, her eyes sparking mischievously.

"Exactly," Dean said with a smirk. "I'm sure you can imagine her reaction when I told her what was in that chocolate cake."

"Did she kill you?" Gracie asked.

"I'm still here, aren't I?" Dean asked, spreading his arms. "Nah, she just hid all of my clothes. Except for one shirt."

"That's not that bad," Gracie said with a shrug.

Dean winced. "It was a neon yellow shirt, and she had cut holes in it."

"Regina George Shirt," Gracie realized. "She's brought that prank up before, but I never knew it was one she played on you."

"Oh, that was me," Dean said grimly. "Me and Jesse. Theo was smart enough to have a hidden shirt to wear. Actually, he had a whole stack of clothes, but it was every man or Zara for themselves. I only know because I was looking for the perfect place to hide a glitter bomb."

"So you were snooping," Gracie said with a nod.

"Essentially."

"And a glitter bomb?"

"Hey, I was thirteen," Dean protested. "Besides, it was basically all we had. Glitter, silly string, confetti, and whatever we could find in the kitchen. It's in the rules—we each get 25 dollars and whatever we find in the house. No permanent damage to anyone or anything, and it lasts from midnight of the day before Easter until midnight of Easter."

"Did you pick that day for any reason in particular?" Gracie asked curiously.

Dean looked down at his feet. "Yeah," he said after a minute. He wasn't ready to tell her what had happened. Hopefully she would take the hint that he didn't want to talk. That was the day he had lost the last adult that truly cared about him, and while he was extremely grateful that his aunts and cousins tried the best they could, bringing it up would be an instant downer. The Adams household was busily decorating for the holidays, and he didn't want to ruin the Christmas spirit by bringing up his dead grandmother.

"Okay," Gracie said simply, scooting a little closer to him. "If you want to talk, I'm here."

"Thanks," Dean replied. He didn't take her up on her offer, but it was worth considering in the future.

## Chapter Twenty

On Christmas Day, Dean woke up to Zara jumping on top of him in his bed. He knew it was Christmas because she was also shrieking, "It's Christmas! It's Christmas," but Dean chose not to dwell on the fact that he would be losing his hearing for the next day.

Dean rubbed his eyes and looked past Zara to where Gracie was leaning against the door, arms crossed and an amused expression on her face. He momentarily admired her legs in her pajama shorts before Zara jumped on his upper body and he started coughing. "A little help, please?"

Gracie laughed, stepping forwards and gently pulling Zara off of Dean. Zara struggled for a second, pouting, before she relaxed and Gracie let her go.

Dean eyed his sister warily as he pushed back the covers and climbed out of bed. His gaze drifted back to Gracie, who either hadn't realized or didn't care about how short her shorts were. She probably also didn't know how good she looked in them, but Dean would never tell her that. He wanted to live until the end of Christmas.

"Put on some clothes!" Zara exclaimed, and Dean looked down.

He only wore his boxers, as he normally wore to sleep. He shot a quick glance at the girls. Zara had her hands covering her face entirely, but Gracie was only now making a move to look away, her cheeks stained with a bright red blush.

Dean grinned, but pulled on a shirt anyway. He'd unpacked before falling asleep last night, leaving a set of clothes for today on top of the nightstand. "Okay, you can look now," he reported. Dean glanced at the clock before spinning back to face his sister. "Care to explain why I'm awake at six in the morning?"

"Because it's Christmas, Dean!" Zara exclaimed, a childish expression of glee on her face.

"And it's also six in the morning," Dean repeated. He yawned, wondering if he would get a chance to use the bathroom before Zara dragged him into whatever maniacal scheme she was no doubt planning.

"Yeah, yeah," Zara waved it off impatiently. "We're all going downstairs. Gracie's mom is already awake and making hot chocolate."

Dean stopped short in his quest to find a sweatshirt. "Hot chocolate?"

Zara grinned triumphantly. It was no secret that Dean was absolutely obsessed with hot chocolate. Whenever he left school, he would stock up on the little pouches and have one daily with his breakfast. It was the best incentive to wake him up in the mornings. In fact, Dean was so used to having his daily hot chocolate by now that if he skipped a morning, he felt overly tired until he found a chance to eat a piece of chocolate or some other sugar.

"Fine," Dean relented. "Just give me a minute to finish getting ready. I'll meet you both downstairs."

"Works for me!" Zara beamed, grabbed Gracie by the arm, and dragged her out of the room. Dean shook his head at his sister before pulling on his hoodie, intent on taking at least ten minutes to get ready so he could have a few peaceful moments before the chaos of Christmas descended.

Gracie smiled gratefully as her mother handed her a present. "Thanks, Mom."

"You haven't even opened it yet!" Her mother grinned.

Gracie opened the present, tearing into the paper as she knew her mom wanted. If it were up to Gracie, she'd take her time carefully peeling the tape off, but her mom preferred to rip the paper off as fast as possible.

Gracie unwrapped a stack of books, grinning widely when she realized they were the *Caraval* trilogy. "I love this series!" she exclaimed.

"I know," her mom laughed. "Did I do good?"

"You did great," Gracie agreed. She glanced around the room, taking in the mess of wrapping paper with various gifts lying in random places. A jacket from one of Zara's relatives was somehow twisted in the tree, and Gracie's new set of pliers was on top of one of the couch pillows. Dean and Zara had disappeared to exchange gifts in private, but the rest of their presents were stacked haphazardly beside the couch. "Oh," she blurted. "The other day, Mom, I forgot to mention it, but Dean and I were up in the attic and the lock jammed."

"The lock jammed?" her mom repeated.

Gracie nodded. "Yeah, we tried to get out, and it was locked, but when we tried it again later, it opened easily."

"Oh, the lock wasn't jammed," her mom said with a chuckle, standing up and dusting off her pants. She shot her daughter a wink before nodding to where Dean was approaching. "Go hang out with your boy. We'll talk more later."

"He's not my..." Gracie tried to protest. She cut herself off when she realized Dean was in earshot. She shook her head at her meddling mom, who was sitting down with Zara on the couch, before admiring the covers of her new books.

"What'd you get?" Dean asked, plopping down beside Gracie on the floor.

Gracie looked over, pretending she hadn't realized that he had re-entered the room. "*Caraval*," she showed him the cover before flipping the book open again.

Dean laughed before reaching out and covering her hands with his. "Come on, Gracie, take a break from reading and enjoy Christmas," he teased.

Gracie looked longingly at the book for another second before closing it and turning to face Dean. "Okay, here I am," she said. "What now?"

"Well," Dean said thoughtfully, making a show of scratching his head. "I was thinking we help your mom clean up…" his voice trailed off as the grin returned to his face. "I'm just kidding, Gracie. I have a present for you."

Gracie's eyes widened in surprise, though she had gotten him a present as well. She hadn't placed it under the tree with the other gifts since she didn't know whether Dean would get her something.

"I have something for you, too," she replied. Gracie glanced at where her mom and Zara were whispering on the couch, the pointing fingers making it very clear who they were gossiping about. "Do you want to go upstairs?"

Dean followed her line of eyesight, noticing her mom and Zara. He nodded. "Yeah, that might be best," he said with a grimace.

The two headed upstairs to Gracie's room, Dean leaving the door half-open as he came in. Gracie fidgeted on her bed nervously, pulling out her small present from her nightstand drawer.

"Should I open yours first?" Dean asked curiously, examining the present from all sides.

"If you want," Gracie said. She watched as Dean eagerly tore into the paper, pulling out the small mirror she had found at the Dollar Store. It had already been bedazzled with the word "cutie," and Gracie had used some of her own rhinestones to add the word "pie" to the bottom.

"Aww, Gracie, you noticed." Dean grinned at her, flipping the mirror open. He eyed himself in the mirror, sticking out his tongue and wrinkling his nose.

Gracie laughed. "It's so you can stare at yourself all day long," she joked. "But seriously, I also got you jelly beans."

"My favorite." Dean grinned at her.

"They actually are," Gracie said mysteriously. Smiling at Dean's confused face, she walked over to her duffel bag and pulled out a package of Berry Blue jelly beans.

"They make these?" Dean exclaimed. "Gracie, this is amazing. I hope you got the store name because I'm going to need a million of these."

Gracie looked away, blushing. "My turn," she said, fighting to get her face back to its natural color.

Dean handed her a wrapped present that looked as if it had been attacked by an entire roll of tape. "I wasn't sure how much was necessary," he said sheepishly.

Carefully, Gracie began to peel away each piece of tape. Once she was halfway through, she snuck a glance at Dean, seeing his fingers tapping his arm impatiently. Gracie pulled off one last piece of tape before ripping open the wrapping paper, the paper falling away to reveal a dark blue hoodie.

"A sweatshirt?" she asked, holding it up.

Gracie wasn't sure whether she imagined the faint blush on Dean's cheeks or not. "You're always falling asleep in the common room," he said, quickly and quietly. "It's cold in there. Now you can be warm."

Gracie looked down at the sweatshirt again, then back at Dean. It looked similar to one that Zara had, with her last name written on the sleeve. But Dean wouldn't have given her a sweatshirt with his name on it, would he? A thrill rushed through her body at the thought. She didn't have time to examine it now, though. "Thank you," she told him. "That's really thoughtful of you."

"It was nothing." Dean waved it off.

Gracie leaned forward and hugged him before taking her new sweatshirt and carefully hanging it over her desk chair. She wanted to put it on right away, but her house was already warm enough, so Gracie cast the sweatshirt one last glance before following Dean downstairs.

☆☆☆

Dean looked around the marketplace in amazement, taking in the small cheerful stands that adorned the street. Pine trees decorated the square; little kids chased each other, shrieking with laughter. An ice rink was partially hidden behind a giant Christmas tree covered with colored lights and handmade ornaments. His eyes caught on a stand selling hot chocolate, and Dean made a mental note to come back later. "Where to first?" he asked, turning to Gracie.

"Let's get tickets," she replied, motioning to a small stand that groups of people were crowded around. "Do you see Zara or my mom?" she asked as they joined the end of the line. Dean shook his head.

As soon as they had reached the square, Zara had run off with a girl she met at the entrance, and Gracie's mother had told the trio earlier that she had plans to meet up with a friend for the morning. He blinked, noticing that Gracie had disappeared. She came back a few minutes later, holding a handful of tickets in her fist.

"Can we go to the games?" she asked eagerly.

Even though he wanted a cup of hot chocolate, Dean nodded, following Gracie to a group of stalls to the left of the ice rink. She handed three tickets to the pre-teen standing in front of a booth, and the boy gave her three rings in return.

As Gracie prepared to throw, Dean caught the boy looking her up and down and shot him a glare. The boy looked away immediately, and Dean had to hold back a smirk. He might not be dating Gracie for real, but that didn't mean he wanted some acne-ridden, mop-haired kid hitting on her. Although he didn't blame the kid for staring—Gracie looked adorable in her layers, and he wished he had a fuzzy scarf like the one wrapped around her neck. She looked extremely cozy in her pom-pom hat and purple gloves. But despite her winter accessories, Dean spotted a pink flush to her cheeks.

"Ugh, nothing!" Gracie sighed, rubbing her hands together. Dean jerked his gaze back to the game, noticing that she had missed all three.

"Let me try," Dean offered. He accepted the rings and carefully tossed them toward the poles, one by one. Dean watched, smirking, as all three fell over the same exact pole. Gracie clapped her hands.

"Not bad," Gracie said admiringly. "What are you going to pick?"

Dean scanned the prizes, his eyes settling on a small plush white tiger. "That one," he said, pointing to it. The teenager handed it to him, and Dean gave it straight to Gracie.

"For me?" Gracie asked in surprise.

Dean half-shrugged, half-nodded as he shoved his hands in his pockets. Gracie stammered out her thanks before asking where he wanted to go next. "Can we get hot chocolate?" Dean asked.

"Yeah," Gracie said, tucking the tiger into her bag before leading the way to the food area. While the games were on the left of the ice rink, the food and drink stalls mirrored them on the right. Dean inhaled deeply, enjoying the sweet smell of caramel apples and cotton candy. The hot chocolate booth was directly behind a stall selling warm sandwiches, and Dean cast an admiring glance at the perfectly cooked breads before turning his attention back to his precious hot chocolate.

Gracie smiled at the woman behind the counter. "Hello, Mrs. Leigh."

"Hello, Gracie," the older woman beamed at her. With gray curls, short stature, and smile on her face, Dean did a double take at how much Mrs. Leigh resembled his grandmother. He blinked rapidly, suddenly overcome by a rush of feelings. At his second glance, he could spot a million differences, but there was something about the woman's warm expression that brought Dean right back to his childhood. "You look so grown up!" the woman exclaimed. "How's school going?"

"It's going great," Gracie said sincerely. "Can we have two hot chocolates, please?"

Mrs. Leigh's eyes went wide before an enormous grin stretched across her face. "Of course, dear," she said happily before turning around to get the cups.

Dean snaked an arm across Gracie's shoulders while they watched Mrs. Leigh pour the hot water. "What are you doing?" Gracie hissed at him.

Dean flashed her a grin and whispered in her ear, "Well, she already thinks we're dating. Might as well sell it."

Gracie flushed but didn't try to push him away. "Mrs. Leigh was my old babysitter," she told him. "She used to take me along to her weekly book clubs at the library, so she'll be spreading the news tomorrow that I have a boyfriend."

"A couple of old ladies won't hurt," Dean said confidently. "The entire school already believes we're dating. What harm could a couple more people do?"

Gracie shrugged her shoulders. "If you say so," she said, accepting the cups that Mrs. Leigh held out to her. She handed one to Dean before curling her fingers around the other; Dean couldn't tear his eyes away as she blew lightly on the drink.

Gracie and Dean wandered around the square for a few minutes, drinking their hot chocolates and visiting all the stands. At some point, they ran into Zara, handing her the rest of the tickets so she could go play some games with a pretty blonde girl.

"Mine is better than yours," Gracie argued. Dean looked up from where he was sitting across from her, carefully funneling colored sand into his plastic ornament.

"No way," he disagreed. "Mine is Christmas colors. Christmas colors make the best ornaments."

"All ornaments are ornaments," Gracie said, picking up a bag of blue sand. As Dean watched, she poured a bit of the sand into her funnel before exchanging the bag for one that was filled with pink sand.

Dean shook his head as he dumped red into his ornament, using a plastic spoon to level off the top. He screwed on the cover and turned to Gracie triumphantly. "Done!"

"It's not a competition." She rolled her eyes.

"Everything is a competition, Gracie Adams," Dean said seriously.

Gracie laughed as she tightened her own cap before grabbing both ornaments by their strings. "Come on, let's hang them on the tree."

Dean followed her to the center of the square where the enormous Christmas tree stood. He watched as Gracie said a few words to a man standing by a ladder before she handed him the two ornaments.

"Watch," Gracie said as she rejoined Dean, nudging his side.

Dean obliged, turning his face to the tree just in time to see their ornaments being hung about a foot from the top. "It looks great," he said happily.

"It does, doesn't it?" Gracie sighed contently, leaning her head against his shoulder. Dean looked down at her for a second before wrapping his arm around her shoulders once more and pulling her closer.

"You know," Dean said quietly. "I think I like not being at war with you."

"What a coincidence," Gracie said. "Because I think *I* like not being at war with *you*."

Dean stood silently as Gracie admired the tree, not daring to move for fear that she would split apart from him. At some point, his hand slipped into hers, and when they had grown tired of standing, they moved to a nearby bench to watch as groups of kids ran up to get their ornaments hung.

"You think we should keep this truce up at school?" he finally broke the silence.

Gracie glanced up at him, and it took all of Dean's effort to stop himself from leaning closer. "I think it's a lot more fun when we're not in a truce," she answered.

Dean's heart sank. Would this be the end of holding her and spending time with her? For some reason, the idea bothered him, but Dean couldn't pinpoint why. If someone asked, he wouldn't be able to tell them the exact moment, but sometime in the past month, Gracie had become one of the most important people in his life, and he looked forward to seeing her every day.

If she stopped their budding friendship and had them just continue their charade in school, well, Dean didn't know if he could handle it. He would take what he got, of course, but the past couple of days had been great, and he genuinely enjoyed spending time with Gracie when they weren't arguing or kissing.

"I also think it's fun when we are in a truce," Gracie said softly, so soft that he had to strain his ears to hear.

Dean cleared his throat and stood, holding out a hand to Gracie. "Well, it's almost time for us to meet Zar and your mom," he said. "Do you want to go ice skating?"

Gracie looked at the offered hand, and then back at Dean. "I'd love to," she replied, placing her hand in Dean's and letting him pull her to her feet.

## Chapter Twenty-One

After break, things returned to normal. Gracie's war with Dean continued, but she conceded the next round to him when she got drenched one morning walking into his dorm. A balloon had been rigged above the door and despite being in the room at the time, Dean had claimed innocence. Seeing as Gracie's white shirt had been soaked, she had no choice but to wear one of his sweatshirts back to her room to get a change of clothes. Of course, Annalisse and Juliet had been in their dorm at the time; coincidentally, they were taking pictures of each other. Gracie didn't know whether or how Dean orchestrated the whole thing, but gave him the win nonetheless.

She and Dean had continued being friends at school, in addition to their war. The library became their "truce zone"—they had an unspoken agreement that there would be no funny business in the library. Other than one time where Dean had kissed Gracie when they were searching for a book, the truce was upheld.

"Hey," Dean said, sitting down next to Gracie.

Gracie glanced up from her book, though she hadn't read a single word in the past fifteen minutes. She frowned upon noticing that every other student had left the library. "Hi. What time is it?" she asked, rubbing her eyes.

"It's almost dinner," Dean replied. "Want to come?"

"Sure," Gracie decided. "Just give me a second to put all this away." As fast as humanly possible, Gracie placed her books in the shelving cart before returning to Dean, who had slung her bag over his shoulder. "I can take that," she protested.

"But as your boyfriend," Dean raised his voice slightly as they passed a group of girls on their way out of the library. "I'm going to carry your bag."

Gracie hid her smile as they walked into the cafeteria, stopping to grab food before heading to what had become their usual table. Like most days, Zara and Theo were already there, bickering over something Gracie was sure they would forget about in five minutes. Raina and Nicole sat on either end, both girls eating slowly. Jesse was alone on the other side of the table, morosely picking at his dinner.

Gracie raised her eyebrows at Zara, who stopped arguing with Theo long enough to shake her head. There had been no change in Jesse and Raina's relationship, but judging by the scene in front of her, Gracie was quickly losing hope that they would ever be friends again.

"—cie. Gracie."

"Sorry, I spaced out," Gracie said, blinking a few times. "Repeat the question?"

"I asked if you heard about the latest round of chemistry thefts," Zara repeated.

Gracie frowned, sitting down in between Jesse and Dean. Zara had told her before break that the chem leak had been a cover story, but she hadn't mentioned anything since. "I don't think so? Remind me."

Jesse leaned forward. "It happened yesterday," he reported. "Someone swiped a teacher key chain and snuck into another lab."

Dean shook his head sadly. "What does this make, the second one in a month?"

"Third," Raina spoke up, all eyes turning to her. She blushed and Gracie smiled to herself, happy that her friend was talking during meals again. "One happened sometime before break. Someone went into one of the labs and left with a bunch of chemicals."

"But who was it?" Gracie asked, confused.

Raina shrugged. "They don't know. They don't even know when the second one happened. The cameras weren't taken down this time, and nobody unknown went into the lab."

"So it was a student or a teacher," Jesse said, his eyes growing wide.

Raina shot him a glance, turning away quickly. "Seems so. It wasn't explosive chemicals or anything. It was just a group of random ones missing, as if someone had grabbed the first things they saw."

"You can't force them to be friends," Dean murmured in Gracie's ear as the table fell into silence again.

Gracie startled, smacking Dean on the arm for scaring her. "I know," she whispered back. "I'm not going to lock them in a room together for twenty-four hours or something."

"Good," Dean said softly, his eyes trained on the two. "Because they need to work this out themselves."

Gracie sighed. "Let's hope that they can do that."

☆
☆ ☆

Dean glanced at his sister out of the corner of his eye before returning his attention to his uncles. "Did you need something?" he asked politely, knowing that Zara would only continue glaring. She had made a New Year's resolution to be nicer to her uncles, but clearly that wasn't lasting more than two weeks considering they were barely halfway into January.

Uncle Aaron cleared his throat, taking something that Uncle Alex handed him. "Yes. Ahh, Dean, I'm afraid I must be very honest with you today."

Dean gripped the armrests of his chair a little tighter. "Is everyone okay?" Dean had just seen both Theo and Jesse at breakfast, so unless something had happened to them in the past hour, he assumed they were fine.

"Everyone is fine," Uncle Alex spoke. "We would just like to speak with you about a matter that came to our attention recently."

Uncle Aaron placed an open envelope on the table. Dean eyed the expensive-looking paper, his eyes taking in the return address. "This is from my mom," he said slowly. "Is she alright? Why is she in Verona? Wasn't she in England for Christmas and the month after?"

Uncle Aaron winced. "Yes, well, as you know, we cannot control your mother. She left England early and, ahh, traveled to Italy."

"That's bullshit," Zara spoke for the first time. "Mom's favorite place in the world is London. She wouldn't leave early. If anything, she'd extend her trip."

"Language, please," Uncle Alex said sternly. "And that is because she did not leave England alone."

Dean frowned. "She found a boyfriend?"

"Not quite," Uncle Aaron said disapprovingly, sliding the card out of the envelope and handing it to Dean.

Dean took the paper hesitantly, tilting it so Zara could see as well. His sister swore, earning a reprimand from Uncle Aaron, but once Dean got a good look at the card, he cursed as well.

The card was an invitation to his mother's wedding, to some guy with a long name Dean had never heard of before. The invitation itself was embossed with gold leaves and swirls, but Dean only had eyes for the name of the bride. Still staring at the card, Dean reached out and blindly groped around on Uncle Aaron's desk for the envelope. He flipped it over and read the name on the front.

"Did she send another one?" Dean asked his uncles, hope creeping into his voice.

Uncle Alex hesitated before shaking his head. "I received one, and your uncle received one. I haven't spoken to Jonas today."

"Oh," Dean whispered, the envelope still clutched in his hand.

His mother hadn't even bothered to send her own children an invitation to her wedding—a wedding neither Dean or Zara, nor any of her family knew anything about.

"Where is it?" Zara asked, reaching for the card. Dean handed it to his sister. "Are we going?"

"Do you want to go?" Uncle Aaron asked.

Dean and Zara exchanged a glance before Dean nodded. "She's our mother," he said firmly. "She may not want us there, but we wouldn't want to miss her wedding."

"And Dean's bringing a date," Zara said quickly.

Dean turned to glare at her but stopped at the pleading look in her eyes. He understood immediately. Gracie would come as his date but would really be Zara's moral support.

"Yes. I am," Dean said, trying to sound as if this wasn't news to him.

"Fine," Uncle Alex said. "We'll leave tomorrow morning."

Dean's mouth dropped open. "Tomorrow morning?" he exclaimed.

"Did you check the date?" Uncle Alex asked, raising his eyebrows. "The wedding is tomorrow night."

Dean scrambled to grab the invitation again. He would have to check that Gracie had a passport right away. She needed to get permission from her mom, of course, but Dean knew that her mom would say yes. Zara needed her there, and Gracie's mother considered Zara to be a second daughter. "When did you get this?" he demanded, looking up at his uncles once more.

"A couple of days ago," Uncle Aaron answered reluctantly.

It was Zara who stood first. "We're leaving, Dean. It's clear that they don't deem us old enough to deal with this information." She sneered, spinning around and exiting the room without waiting for a response.

Dean offered his uncles an apologetic smile as Zara slammed the door behind her. "We'll see you tomorrow," he said, his voice devoid of any emotion as he followed his twin out.

Gracie glanced nervously at her friend as they entered Principal Ashcroft's private jet, the redhead practically fuming as she stalked through the plane. "Zara, you need to calm down," Gracie said, keeping her voice gentle.

"Just leave her," Dean muttered in her ear, causing Gracie to shiver. She looked down to see Dean holding her overnight bag. "Come on." Dean guided Gracie to a seat and seated himself next to her. "We'll be taking off in a few minutes. Uncle Aaron's plane is always fully stocked with the best snacks. He could decide to go on a flight at any minute, you know."

Gracie laughed. "Life of a rich kid?" she teased.

"Ugh, it *sucks*." Dean rolled his eyes dramatically, relaxing in his seat.

Gracie looked up in surprise as a neatly dressed woman stepped next to her seat, several papers in her hand. "Good evening," the woman said. "My name is Valerie and I'll be your flight attendant today. Here are the snacks that we have on today's flight, along with a list of flight safety instructions. I will be back in a few minutes to take your orders and answer questions."

Gracie turned to Dean. "This is incredible!" she exclaimed in amazement.

"You haven't seen the best part yet," Dean said, smirking as he motioned to the menu.

Valerie returned a couple minutes later, a pad of paper in her hand. "Now, the prepared lunch today is fettuccine alfredo," she said pleasantly. "Would you both like it, or should I have them make something else?"

"Sounds great," Gracie said with a nod.

"For me too, please," Dean agreed. He glanced back down at his menu. "I'll also have some chips and guacamole, and we'll have a platter of assorted cookies and candy to share. Any will do."

"Yes, Mr. Ashcroft," Valerie said, scribbling on her pad of paper. "And what would you like?" she addressed Gracie.

"Just water, please," Gracie said politely. "I'll share his snacks."

"She'll have strawberries and whipped cream," Dean said as Valerie turned to leave.

"They'll be out shortly," Valerie said, taking their menus before she walked away.

"How did you know that?" Gracie asked, turning to Dean.

Dean shrugged. "You had them all the time during Christmas, and whenever there are strawberries on the table, you always grab some," he said, a tone that Gracie couldn't recognize in his voice.

Gracie ducked her head, not sure why she was blushing, but trying to hide it all the same. "Oh. Thanks."

"No problem."

"I'm going to watch a movie," Gracie said suddenly, showing him her phone and then mentally smacking herself because he probably knew that she would be watching on her phone.

"Okay," Dean said, the amused expression back on his face.

"Okay," Gracie repeated.

"Bye, Gracie," Dean murmured as he stood up, always one to try and get the last word. Gracie watched as he stretched and went to join Zara across the plane, only tearing her eyes away once Valerie returned with their food.

✭
✭ ✭

Gracie hadn't been to many weddings before, but she figured this one was a bit more extravagant than the average wedding.

Dean and Zara's mom had spared no expense, flying in top photographers and caterers that were now milling around the hotel grounds. Apparently, Alexandra had rented out the entire hotel for the week, and from what Gracie saw on the way to the hotel, it was the nicest one in town. The ceremony itself was in the hotel's luxurious garden—a maze full of gorgeous flowers that were somehow all in bloom despite it being January. Tulle canopies were stretched across ribboned poles, creating a cloud-like effect. It was a sunny day, and Gracie had happily dressed in a long-sleeve silky dress that Raina had lent her. The pale purple dress flared out at the waist and danced around her knees as she walked. She finished the outfit off with a pair of silver wedges and silver jewelry; Gracie thought she looked rather pretty all dressed up.

Dean sided up to her, dressed in a sleek black tux.

"Wow," Gracie murmured to herself, unable to tear her gaze away. If she was pretty, Dean looked extremely hot in his tux.

Dean's mouth dropped open for a second, but he closed it quickly. "You look amazing, Gracie," he said sincerely.

"Thank you. You do too," she replied, proud of herself for making it through the short sentence without stuttering or forgetting what she was going to say.

Dean grinned shyly, a look she wasn't used to seeing on his face. "Should we go find our seats?" he asked, holding out a hand.

Gracie took the offered hand, gripping it as they weaved through the crowd of people. She moved closer to Dean as they passed by a group of perfumed women, clutching his hand tighter. She glanced around, looking for anyone familiar. Principal Ashcroft was on the other side of the tent with a woman she assumed to be his wife, but Blake was nowhere to be seen. Dean had mentioned that neither Jesse nor Theo had received an invitation, so she figured Blake hadn't gotten one either.

Dean tilted his head to look down at her. "You good?"

"There are a lot of people here," Gracie explained quietly. "And they all like to pinch my cheek and tell me how grown up I look. I hate that, but they're mistaking me for Zara, and she'd absolutely flip out at them."

Dean nodded, drawing her closer to his side. Once they were directed to their seats—between a snooty-looking couple and a group of people Dean vaguely recognized as distant relatives—he wrapped his arm around Gracie's shoulders, his fingers traveling up and down her arm.

Zara turned around in her seat in front of them, her eyes brightening when she saw how Gracie and Dean were sitting. "Having fun?" she asked slyly.

Dean scowled. "Why are you here?" he asked. "Shouldn't you be with Mom, walking down the aisle or something?"

A flash of a frown appeared on Zara's face before it was smoothed away. "Nah, I didn't want to hang out with a bunch of middle-aged women," she said casually, her face not betraying any emotion. "Too much perfume."

Gracie translated this to *I was there but Mom didn't want me to be there, so I agreed to go back to my seat instead of walking with my mother down the aisle at her wedding.* She shot Zara a sympathetic smile, but her friend pretended she hadn't seen it and turned around again.

Dean leaned in closer, his face only inches from Gracie's as he spoke, "Keep an eye on her later, okay? I know you're officially here as my date, but Zara was the one who asked if you could come. She needs you more than I do."

Gracie nodded slowly, careful not to bump her head against his. "And what about you?" she asked. "How are you doing?"

Dean pressed his lips together firmly, entwining his fingers with hers. "It hurts," he admitted. "It hurts that my mother is getting married and doesn't want her own children to be at the wedding. It hurts that she didn't bother to tell us or send us a wedding invitation. It's not that hard to email or text or keep in touch with your children. I don't get why she can't comprehend that."

"I'm sorry," Gracie murmured, squeezing his hand to offer him comfort. Dean squeezed back. "I can't pretend to know what it's like or tell you that everything's going to be okay, but I'm here if you ever want to talk about it."

"Thank you," Dean said quietly. "Really. It means a lot that you're here for Zara."

"And for you," Gracie corrected, meeting his gaze. Her eyes strayed down to his lips for a second, but Gracie shoved down all the feelings that told her to kiss Dean and instead returned his stare. "I'm here for you too."

The music started and everyone turned to the back of the room, but Gracie's hand stayed locked with Dean's. As the bride and groom walked down the aisle, as a man in a suit droned on about marriage responsibilities, as the entire ceremony went on, they remained close to each other, only letting go when everyone began to clap at the end.

☆☆
☆

Gracie washed her hands in the sink, marveling at the ornate mirrors and stunning marble countertops. The ceremony had been lovely, and there had been a short break before the reception so the bride and groom could have some time alone. She had excused herself to the bathroom, leaving Zara and Dean sitting at one of the back tables together.

Gracie carefully turned the water off before looking around for paper towels. There was a stack on the other end of the counter, and Gracie dried her hands quickly. As she took a step away from the counter, a woman bustled into the bathroom, instantly recognizable in her long white dress. Elegant, extravagant, and expensive looking, Alexandra somehow managed to pull off having an entire garden on the A-line skirt. It was stunning embroidery, but the dress couldn't hold a candle to the woman herself.

"Hello," Gracie offered to Dean and Zara's mom. "Congrats on your marriage."

Alexandra turned toward her. "Thank you," she said, glancing towards the mirror and fluffing her hair. "You're Dean and Zara's little friend? Greta?"

Gracie smiled politely. "It's Gracie, actually."

"Yes, we met at the reunion. It was lovely, although not as nice as this." Alexandra gestured around her, derision evident on her face. "It's too bad Zara couldn't be bothered to wear one of the dresses I picked out for her. They were *very expensive* and a waste sitting in her closet."

"I guess so," Gracie said uncomfortably. She shifted her weight. "She's showed me some of the dresses, and they weren't really her style. Zara likes dark blues and greens, not purples and yellows."

"The colors I choose go great with her hair," Alexandra said in a haughty tone. "Well, it was nice seeing you, Gracie."

"Wait," Gracie said hurriedly. Alexandra paused, and beneath her layered dress, Gracie could see a tapping foot. She swallowed hard, before words came flying out of her mouth. "I think you should talk to Dean and Zara. Like really *talk* to them, not just send them gifts every so often. They're both amazing, and I'm not just saying that because Zara's my best friend and Dean is my—something," she stumbled over the last word. "They deserve so much better. And you should just, um, talk to them," Gracie finished weakly, her voice growing lower with each word.

Alexandra stared at her for a moment before turning and leaving the bathroom without another word.

Gracie let out a shaky breath, leaning against the counter for support. Her heart beat quickly as she tried to calm herself, dabbing a bit of water on her face. How would Dean and Zara react when she told them that she'd confronted their mother? No matter how hard she'd tried to hide it, Zara had been heartbroken when Alexandra kicked her out of the wedding. She had pretended to be okay, but Gracie was furious on Zara's behalf. And while she might not be a violent person, if someone hurt Zara, Gracie would charge at them with fists flying.

*And Dean.*

Gracie breathed deeply, checking her pulse by placing two

fingers on her neck. She counted her breaths for a minute before opening her eyes and seeing a composed face staring back at her.

"You're going to go out there and be happy for Zara and Dean," she told her reflection. "You can overanalyze every detail of this conversation later, but right now, they need you."

Gracie tucked a strand of hair behind her ear, mentally shoving her thoughts to the back of her mind. Judging from their earlier reactions, Dean and Zara would happily avoid Alexandra for the rest of the night. She could unpack her conversation with Alexandra later, along with her sudden affection for Dean.

Pasting a smile on her face, Gracie straightened her dress and headed back to the party.

## Chapter Twenty-Two

The day after the wedding was a Sunday, and Dean happily returned to school. Zara had tried to extend their stay by a couple of weeks, especially after finding out that Alexandra immediately jetted off to Spain for her honeymoon, but Dean hadn't even attempted to argue for a few days' vacation.

It wasn't that the wedding wasn't nice or anything. He was just worn out by the day's events and ready to be far, far away from anything that had to do with his mother. Hopefully he wouldn't see her again for a couple of months. Sure, she was polite and all; she even asked him and Zara a couple questions about school during the reception, but she wasn't warm compared to the way she was when her friends came over, or the way Mrs. Adams was with Gracie. Their mom's new husband had seemed friendly, but Dean had barely spoken to him for more than two minutes. It was a large wedding, and every time he tried to start a conversation with either his mother or new stepfather, someone had interjected and whirled the newlyweds away. The most he had seen his mother was at the end of the reception when she had given him and Zara incredibly awkward hugs.

Dean hadn't grown up with hugs and physical affection, but he was fine with that. He had never been a very touchy child—unlike Jesse, who went through a phase where he absolutely *had* to give everyone a hug every five minutes. His mom's sudden hug had been weird and unexpected, and Dean found himself comparing it to the hugs he got from Gracie. He would never have guessed, but the brunette was very touchy and rarely an interaction went by without her poking him or tapping his arm.

In fact, the past month or so pretending to be Gracie's boyfriend had been the most physical contact he had ever had with someone. He would never admit it to anyone, of course, but he'd enjoyed hugging Gracie and holding her hand and sitting with her against his side.

But he didn't *like* Gracie.

She was just a girl who he liked hanging out with and who he had fun with.

There was absolutely nothing going on between them.

Right?

Dean sat up in bed, his mind moving faster than a roller coaster. He kicked the covers off his legs as he replayed the past few weeks in his head. Was it possible that he *did* like Gracie?

Their entire relationship had started off as a joke. He had wanted to tease his sister's best friend for a couple of days, rile up Zara, and then fall back into their regular pattern. But then Zara and Gracie and their friends had started sitting at his lunch table regularly, and now Dean couldn't imagine a time when they had been separated for meals. Gracie Adams was part of his life now in a way that she hadn't been a few months ago. Sure, Dean had known who she was, but he hadn't really known her.

And now, Dean did in fact know who she was, and he really, really liked her.

"Damn," Dean said aloud, staring blankly at the wall.

Could he tell her how he felt? She probably didn't feel the same way, considering she had called him her best friend's brother. He definitely considered her a friend—one of his closest friends by now.

Did she even feel the same about that? Was he deluding himself into thinking that all the flirting and touching and looks from the past couple of months were just part of their game?

Dean sighed loudly, covering his face with his pillow. He let out a muffled groan before pulling the pillow away and glancing at the clock that sat innocently on his bedside table.

*2:27*, the clock read.

Dean groaned again, this time scooting back so he was leaning against the wall. He clearly wouldn't get any sleep tonight, so maybe he should just grab a book and head down to the common room to read.

Deciding to do just that, Dean picked up *Shadow and Bone* from the nightstand and quietly crept out of the room, careful not to wake Theo or Jesse. A lone light flickered in the common room, and Dean hesitated on the bottom step, unsure whether or not he wanted to interact with someone right now.

"Aww, I love you too," he heard a girl's voice cooing. She sounded familiar, but it was hard to hear since she was speaking quietly. "And I can't wait to see you! Only three more months!"

Dean made a move to turn back upstairs, not wanting to interrupt some love-struck girl's call with her boyfriend. The girl laughed, and he froze.

Dean recognized that laugh.

"What do you mean I won't be the most important girl in your life anymore?" the girl said with a teasing chuckle. Dean silently stepped into the common room, letting his gaze wander in search of the girl. She was standing by one of the large couches, walking around as she held a phone to her ear. "I thought I was your favorite!"

Dean took another step closer. So what if the girl had wavy brown hair that fell just a little bit past her shoulders? So what if the girl was just about the right height and had the exact same laugh?

"I really miss you too," the girl said earnestly. "And I'm coming to see you the very first day that we've got spring break. I have the perfect day planned out already. It's going to be awesome."

Dean's heart sank as the girl moved towards the light, and he quickly ducked behind one of the couches.

Gracie Adams laughed again as he peeked out from behind the upholstery, her face illuminated by the light. "I should go," she said reluctantly. "I know, I know, I don't want to. I barely get to speak to you as it is. I'm just really busy here, and you're busy too. We haven't had much time to talk between the time change and all of my school work, especially since you've been away for the past couple of weeks." She listened for a few seconds before nodding. "Okay, I'll call you again in a few days. No, there are no boys you need to worry about here. I don't even hang out with boys, really. So there's nothing for you to worry about."

Dean swallowed hard. Had the past two months been a lie? Did Gracie really have a boyfriend and a whole other life that he knew nothing about? Was she pretending to like him, while having a good laugh that she was pulling the wool over his eyes and making plans with her real boyfriend?

"I love you too," Gracie said again, and with his heart broken, Dean slunk upstairs before she could figure out that he had been eavesdropping. Dean clenched his fists as he climbed the stairs. How could he have been so stupid this whole time?

He had underestimated Gracie, that was for sure. Was this her real plan? To get him to underestimate the bookish girl who spent most of her time studying, genuinely like her, and then break his heart when he tried to confess his true feelings?

Dean threw open the door to his room, then slammed it shut with more force than necessary. "Wake up!" he ordered loudly, stomping to Jesse's bed and throwing the blanket off of his cousin. Dean did the same with Theo, tossing his blanket into a pile at the end of the bed.

Theo blinked at him groggily as he sat up, rubbing his eyes the entire time. "Wha goin on?" he mumbled, sleepily.

"War," Dean declared, striding over to his desk and grabbing a large poster board he had been saving for his upcoming English project. He angrily picked up some tape and stuck the poster to the wall, waiting for Jesse to join Theo on the bed. When his cousin finally arrived, half-tripping over with every step he took, Dean tapped the poster on the wall.

"Revenge," he began, uncapping a thick marker and writing Gracie's name across the top in thick, bold letters. "This girl had been playing us for weeks," he said firmly, pointing to her name and glaring at his cousins. "She has been lying, playing on my feelings, and is one of the most sneaky, devious, deceitful, calculating, conniving, sly girls I have ever met!" With each word, Dean stabbed the poster with his open marker.

"So this is why I will get my ultimate revenge tomorrow," Dean growled, a gleam in his eye as he drew a circle around Gracie's name. "Gracie Adams will rue the day she decided to cross me!"

As he spoke, Dean drew diagrams and arrows, writing out all the important words and then drawing more circles. He connected points that he thought of, underlined ideas that had been brewing in his mind for the past couple of minutes, and filled nearly the entire poster board with his thoughts.

When he had forcefully scribbled a period at the end of his last sentence, Dean took a step back to admire his work. "Any questions?" he asked, turning around, a smug look on his face as he glanced expectantly at his cousins.

Dean frowned. Theo lay with his head hanging slightly off the bed, and Jesse lay partially on top of Theo, hugging a pillow to his body. Both boys were fast asleep, with Jesse snoring softly, his mouth open as he clutched the pillow tighter.

Dean grumbled to himself before he caught sight of the clock again. "Oh fuck," he swore, all of his previous energy disappearing. "I'm going insane." Swaying slightly on his feet, Dean stumbled to the nearest open bed, passing out as soon as his head touched Jesse's pillow.

"I don't know," Zara said solemnly. Gracie looked up at her best friend before sneaking a glance at the table in the corner of the lunchroom.

"Did I do something?" Gracie pressed. "Because there's no other reason for Dean to be avoiding me."

"*Did* you do something?"

Gracie threw her hands up in resignation, almost knocking her bowl of pasta over. "I don't think so!"

Zara winced as people turned around to look at them. "Lower your voice. Has something happened in the past week or so that could cause Dean to avoid you for two days?"

"Two and a half," Gracie muttered bitterly. "And no. I haven't done anything."

Zara shrugged. "Then I have no idea. I can try to talk to him, though."

"No," Gracie said hurriedly. She cleared her throat. "Thank you, but I think I need to figure this out by myself."

"Your call." Zara popped a grape into her mouth, smacking her lips together. "Have you seen Raina?"

Gracie glanced around the lunchroom again. "She's not with the boys," Gracie reported. "I don't see her. I see Nicole sitting over there, though." She nodded toward another table.

"It's good that she's making new friends," Zara remarked.

"I think the break will really help her. And when she's ready, she'll come back. I know you miss her."

"I do," Zara said. "But as much as I miss her, she needs to do what's best for her."

Gracie's eyes widened as she stared at her best friend. "When did you get so smart?" she teased.

Zara flushed. "It was maybe Dean," she admitted, her voice low.

"I may have been pouting, and he may have come up to the dorm and yelled-but-not-yelled at me for half an hour."

Gracie laughed, ignoring the pang in her chest when Zara said Dean's name. Her eyes instinctively sought out the table where the three Ashcroft boys sat before she quickly lowered them back to her bowl of food. Sticking her fork in the pasta, Gracie took another bite. "I'm done eating," she said. "I think I'm going to go find Raina."

Zara put down the grape she was holding, a concerned expression on her face. "Gracie, you've eaten like four bites."

"I'm not hungry," Gracie told her friend. "It's fine. I'll eat something later."

Zara hesitated before nodding. "Okay. I'll see you in class."

Gracie waved goodbye before shouldering her bag and leaving the cafeteria. She headed to the library, glancing around the corridors in hopes of spotting a certain Ashcroft. She had been watching for Blake for the past few days but hadn't seen him since they returned from winter break. Gracie shrugged it off as she entered the library, figuring he was probably busy with schoolwork and hadn't had time to visit his dad lately.

Gracie quickly found Raina huddled in a corner of the library, alternating between reading her book, taking quick glances at the librarian, and sneaking bites of the sandwich that was in her lap.

Gracie cleared her throat. "Are you eating in the library, Ms. Cohen?" she drawled in a passable attempt of Mrs. Dixon's voice.

Raina jumped, her face paling as she whipped her head around. Spotting Gracie and not the English teacher, she relaxed. "Not funny, Gracie," she huffed. "I am most definitely not Mrs. Dixon's favorite person right now. She would totally say something like that."

Gracie just had to laugh. "So funny," she said, taking a seat next to her friend. "So why are you hiding out in the library? Come join us for lunch."

Raina looked away. "I don't really want to be there if they're there," she mumbled, Gracie's ears straining to hear.

"Well, they're not," Gracie said, a slightly bitter tone in her voice. "Nicole's been sitting with some other friends, and Jesse's been sitting with his cousins."

Raina frowned. "What do you mean? Don't you guys sit together?"

"We used to," Gracie said with a sigh. "But Dean's been avoiding me for the past two days, and he's started sitting at another table. Theo and Jesse sat there too."

"Zara?"

"Still at ours," Gracie said. She sighed again. "I don't know what to do. I don't know *why* Dean started avoiding me, or how long he'll keep this up, and I don't know if I can just go and talk to him."

"Why not?" Raina asked.

Gracie shrugged helplessly. "Are we friends? I don't even know the answer to that question. This whole thing wasn't meant to be serious or even real. It was all a joke. How can I tell him that—" she cut herself off. "I don't even know what I want to tell him," Gracie confessed. "Part of me wants things to go back to the way they were, but a part of me *doesn't*. I don't know what I want to happen."

Raina looked at her hesitantly. "Do you think it might be because you like him?"

"I do like him," Gracie said. "I like hanging out with him and I like spending time with him. I thought we were friends. And it hurts that he's suddenly ignoring me."

"No." Raina shook her head. "I meant, do you *like* him?"

Gracie stared at her before laughing. Had Raina mixed the two of them up? Because she was the one with a crush on an Ashcroft, not Gracie. "No, that's ridiculous. I don't like Dean like that. We're just friends, or at least I thought we were."

"Whatever you say," Raina said with a shrug. "But I think you need to talk to him."

"Well, you need to talk to Jesse," Gracie pointed out. "When's that happening?"

"It's not," Raina said darkly, crossing her arms and scowling at some point over Gracie's shoulder. "He won't talk to me, look at me, sit near me, or do anything else involving me. He doesn't even want to be my friend. There's no use trying to fix anything when he's made it clear that he wants nothing to do with me."

"I'll talk to Dean when you talk to Jesse," Gracie offered, knowing full well what Raina's answer would be.

Raina scoffed. "So you're not going to do it," she stated, the words ringing through the air.

Gracie looked down at her lap. As much as she wanted to pull Dean into an empty room and demand answers, she refused to chase after him when he wanted nothing to do with her. "No."

## Chapter Twenty-Three

A clanging noise drew Dean's attention away from his dinner, and he, along with everyone else in the cafeteria, turned to the teacher's table. Uncle Alex was standing in front of it, a glass in one hand and a spoon in the other. Dean exchanged curious looks with his cousins, taking their shrugs to mean that no one had any idea why their vice principal was about to address them.

"Thank you," Uncle Alex said to one of the teachers, who took the two items from him and carefully set them down on the table. He turned around and cleared his throat, facing the students again. "A-hem. If I may have your attention, please?" he asked, before waiting a couple of seconds as the last few conversations died down. "Thank you. I will make this brief, as I know you are all eager to get back to your dinners. As of this morning, Principal Ashcroft has returned home for a couple of weeks to deal with a private family matter. I will be the acting principal until he returns. Nothing will be changing from our usual routine, however."

"Is everyone okay?" a student called out and Dean glanced that way.

"Everyone is fine," Uncle Alex said. "Principal Ashcroft is simply dealing with a personal matter. He decided it would be best to take a short sabbatical rather than commute back and forth. Thank you for your concerns."

Jesse tugged on Dean's sleeve. "Do you think everyone's alright?" he hissed.

"I'm sure everyone's okay," Dean responded. "But we can go check if you'd like."

Jesse bit his lip before nodding. "Yeah. Uncle Aaron is listed as my parents' emergency contact, so I'd feel better if we went over and made sure that they're okay."

Dean didn't voice what they were all thinking. His uncle hadn't told them about his mother's wedding until the day before it occurred. If something had happened to Jesse's parents while they were traveling, could he be trusted to tell Jesse right away?

"Aaron is fine, and so are your parents, Jesse," Uncle Alex said when they approached him at the teachers' table. "And so is your mother, Dean, and my wife."

"Is Aunt Becky?" Dean asked with a frown, unable to let go of the feeling that something was wrong.

"Rebecca is also well," Uncle Alex reassured them. "Everyone is physically well and healthy. I promise, boys. I'm telling you the truth."

Dean and Theo shared a look. They both remembered the last time that their uncles had kept something important from them, and it hadn't ended well. In fact, if he recalled correctly, Uncle Alex had run screaming from the house with two bite marks on his leg.

"You said that last time," Theo pointed out.

Uncle Alex inclined his head with a wince. "Yes, and I apologize for that. However, it was the collective decision that you four were a bit too young to know about the cancer. This time, I am telling you the truth. And if you are still concerned," he added quickly, "you can simply call your parents and make sure they are okay. I would ask that you refrain from calling Aaron and Rebecca, however, since they are very busy right now."

"But they're both okay?" Dean checked one last time.

"They are both okay," Uncle Alex confirmed. He gave them a slight smile. "Go enjoy your evening, children. Theo, I will see you tomorrow in my room."

"See you then, Dad," Theo said, waving as the trio headed back to their table.

"Still doing those hebdomadal dinners?" Jesse asked as they sat back down. Dean and Theo stared at him. "Weekly," he said with a sigh.

Dean snickered. "Still using that dictionary Nicole got you?"

Jesse ignored him. "I'm going to assume that you are, Theo," he said dryly.

"You assume correctly," Theo agreed.

"And how are they going?" Dean asked cautiously. He didn't know whether Theo had come out to Jesse yet, but he definitely didn't want to reveal his cousin's secret.

"They're going fine." Theo brushed Dean's words off. "Can we join Zara at her table?"

Dean looked up, spotting his twin sister instantly. She was sitting with Gracie and Raina, and Dean knew he wasn't the only Ashcroft who was hesitating.

Theo huffed loudly when neither Jesse nor Dean responded. "Alright, we're going. You two need to get over whatever the fuck you have going on with Gracie and Raina. Dean, it's been a week and you haven't spoken to her or pulled off whatever the hell it was you woke me up at four in the morning to talk about. Jesse, just fucking man up and confront her," he declared, before storming off and sliding into a seat next to Zara.

Dean and Jesse exchanged looks before they too joined the girls at their table. Dean didn't know who wanted to avoid the girls' table more, him or his cousin. Jesse had refused to talk about Raina, but Dean knew that he was hurting. No matter what Raina had done, Dean was sure it couldn't be worse than flirting with someone for weeks, kissing them repeatedly, and playing with their feelings, all the while having a secret boyfriend on the side. He forced a blank expression on his face as he sat down, busying himself with arranging his utensils around his plate.

"Hello," Dean said, careful not to look at Gracie.

Zara turned to him and asked eagerly, "Did you hear?"

"Hear what?" Dean said with a frown.

Zara leaned in closer, dropping her voice a few octaves as she revealed, "They caught the chemistry thief."

Dean's eyes widened. "Who is it?" he asked. "Wait, does it have something to do with why Uncle Aaron's missing?"

"Oh yeah." Zara nodded furiously. She twirled a strand of spaghetti with her fork, clearly enjoying dragging this out as long as possible.

Gracie sighed from where she was sitting next to Zara. "I think you have it all wrong. He wouldn't do that. There must be a reason. Maybe you overheard wrong."

Jesse snorted. "So you were eavesdropping?"

"Maybe," Zara mumbled, her face flushing. Dean frowned at his sister, wondering who Gracie had been talking about. Zara quickly brightened again, gesturing for them all to lean in closer. "So I was in the principal's office last night," she began, and Dean groaned loudly.

"Zara, how many more times do you need to end up in there?" he demanded, a disapproving look on his face as he stared at his sister. "What did you do this time?"

"Nothing," Zara said airily. "Anyway, it's not important. I was waiting in the office area, and *clearly* Uncle Aaron and Uncle Alex forgot I was there because they were discussing the case. Apparently, it was solved earlier that day and they caught the culprit trying to steal a couple more chemicals. The teachers had set up a trap and rigged the room with hidden cameras—ones not connected to the main security network. So the thief was caught and he couldn't deny it."

"Who?" Jesse demanded impatiently.

There was a satisfied look on Zara's face as she said, "Blake."

"Voldemort?" Theo shrieked. He dropped the cookie he had just stolen from Jesse's plate, ignoring the crumbs that fell all over the table.

"Voldemort," Zara confirmed. "He was doing it to discredit Uncle Aaron or something. I don't know the details. But he was stealing chemicals and using them for vandalism and stuff, I guess. Nicole looked up the chemicals last night, and you could mix them with colorings to make a permanent spray paint."

✯✯✯

Gracie's face paled suddenly. "I helped him," she said frantically. "I was going down to the chemistry labs when they were under guard, and I ran into Blake in the hallway. He came down with me and went into the supply closet to get the beakers. I asked him if everything was all good, since he was taking a while. I didn't mention it since you hate Blake and don't like talking about him," she rambled, turning to Zara. "Oh my god, I helped commit a crime. Can I get expelled for that? Am I going to get expelled?"

Gracie whipped her head around the room, wondering if any of the teachers were coming to expel her. Everyone seemed busy with their own conversations, but Vice-principal Ashcroft was missing from the teacher's table. Was he coming to find her and kick her out of school?

"First, lower your voice," Zara said sternly. "Second, calm down. You're not getting expelled."

Gracie breathed in and out frantically, not believing her friend. How would Zara know the consequences of abetting a criminal? Out of the corner of her eye, Gracie noticed Dean rolling his eyes at his sister.

"That's not helping, Zara," he said, sounding exasperated. Dean said something else, but Gracie couldn't focus on his words. Her vision was fading in and out and her lungs squeezed tightly with each breath. Gracie clutched at the table to keep herself from falling over.

The next thing she knew, warm hands were covering her own.

"Take a deep breath," the person said gently. Gracie blinked, the world still a blur, but she obeyed. "Good. Now take another one."

Gracie gasped slightly as the world swarmed back into focus, and she saw Dean's worried face mere inches from hers, her hands clutched in his larger ones.

"Good. One more," Dean coaxed. "It's okay, it's all going to be okay. Can you focus on me for a second?"

Gracie gave him a small nod, not trusting her voice. They were outside of the cafeteria now. How had they gotten there?

"Can you hold your breath for a few seconds?" Dean asked her, his voice steady and calm. Gracie nodded again, taking a deep breath and holding it until he nodded at her to let it go. She breathed out, feeling a little better.

"What do you need?" Dean asked gently.

"I don't know," Gracie whispered.

"Okay, do you want to go outside?"

Gracie considered this for a second. Right now, they were standing to the side of the cafeteria doors and people were passing by. She gave a small shrug and nodded at the same time. Dean must have realized what she meant though. He let go of one of her hands and led her outside by the other.

Gracie shivered in the cold as they stepped onto the cobblestone patio.

"Wait here for one second," Dean said, stretching out the *one*. He guided her over to a wicker bench, making sure that Gracie was settled before running back inside. He returned with a hoodie, handing it to her. She pulled it on, noticing that it was nearly identical to the one that Dean had given her.

"Do you have two of them?" she asked, clutching part of the fabric in her fist.

"I have a ton of them," Dean said with a laugh. "We made them one summer and ordered too many, so now Jesse, Theo, Zara, and I have a million each."

Gracie nodded. She'd noticed his last name sewn into the sleeve of the hoodie. She'd seen Zara wearing the same sweatshirt once or twice but had assumed they had just gotten the same hoodie. She ran a hand over the soft fabric again, staring down at her lap.

☆☆☆

Dean glanced worriedly at Gracie, unsure whether or not to sit next to her. He decided in favor of the idea, sitting down carefully so as not to spook her.

Thankfully, he had known what to do when she started hyperventilating. Theo had gone through a phase in middle school where he freaked out at the slightest mention of being social with someone other than his family. He had outgrown it during eighth grade, but it had worried the entire family. Dean had never forgotten what his aunt and uncle had taught him in case Theo started panicking and he was the only one around. To the best of Dean's knowledge, Zara had been unaware, as she spent most of her time playing with Jesse and Nicole. Dean was glad that he had pestered his aunt and uncle to tell him why Theo would start panicking or else he wouldn't have known how to help Gracie.

"What do you need?" he asked again, making his voice as soft as possible.

Gracie glanced up at him through her eyelashes, and Dean swallowed hard. She shrugged again and Dean made a split-second decision, scooting closer so he could wrap an arm around the shivering girl. Whether it was due to the cold or the panicking, he didn't know, but Gracie's body stilled as he held her.

"How are you feeling?" he asked after a few minutes.

"Better," Gracie replied. He was glad that she seemed able to speak again. "How did you know what to do?"

"I've had some experience with panic attacks," Dean said vaguely, not wanting to tell her about Theo's past. If Theo wanted her to know, he would tell her at some point, but for now, Dean would keep it to himself.

"Okay," Gracie whispered, snuggling closer.

"Gracie, you know you didn't do anything wrong, right?" Dean asked her. "Blake stole the chemicals, not you. You had no idea what he was doing, and if you had known, you would've stayed far, far away from him."

"I looked for him," Gracie admitted. She shivered and Dean wrapped his arms around her more tightly. "I wanted to ask him about Zara and why he would treat her so horribly. It was like the Blake you were telling me about and the Blake I knew were two very different people, and I just wanted answers. But...you guys were right. He wasn't actually my friend. He was just using me. I mentioned Zara in our first conversation, and he was really interested in you guys. I don't know why I didn't see it sooner."

"Blake is really good at making you think you're his best friend," Dean said gently. "Absolutely none of it was your fault, and I hope you know that."

Gracie just sniffed, closing her eyes. She looked so innocent when she was like this, all cuddled in his arms. But if she really had a boyfriend, then why was she all curled up with him? Was it because of the panic attack? He opened his mouth to confront her about the conversation he had overheard but took one look at the still pale girl and decided against it.

He would bring it up tomorrow, or even the day after. Dean would make sure that Gracie was feeling okay again before he accused her of lying to him and tricking him. Even after his impromptu planning session a week ago, he still had no idea of the best way to get her back. Dean had woken up the next morning to see the dorm room a wreck with random scribbles and meaningless words scrawled on a posterboard. He wasn't able to make heads or tails of the mess and, after about an hour of trying, had given up.

Dean had to face the facts—he could no longer come up with a way to get Gracie to admit that their relationship was fake because he didn't want the relationship to be fake. He wanted to be Gracie's boyfriend for real, to be able to hang out with her and kiss her without some ulterior motive.

She stirred against him, and Dean glanced down to see Gracie disentangling herself from his arms. "Sorry," he muttered, letting her go.

"It's okay," Gracie said back. "And, um, thanks."

"Of course," Dean said, his voice sounding distant to his ears. "I should go now."

"Wait!" Gracie called as he rose. Dean turned around to face her. "Yes?"

Gracie swallowed. "Did I do something? Is there a reason you've been ignoring me? Is something wrong or did something happen? Is it something that I did?"

Dean blinked, trying to wrap his head around her questions. He debated the best way to answer her, wondering if he should just tell her now.

"I overheard your phone call," he said finally.

A confused look spread across Gracie's face. "What phone call?"

"The one from a week ago," Dean replied shortly. "It was early in the morning and I couldn't sleep, so I went downstairs. I accidentally overheard your phone call. I didn't mean to, but I'm glad I did. It's nice to know how you really feel."

Gracie shook her head. "I don't get it. What do you mean, how I really feel?"

"It's okay, Gracie," Dean said, shrugging slightly. "Look, I get it. I won't bother you anymore. I'll let you live your life and not keep playing this game or whatever it is."

"Wai—" Gracie started to say, but Dean didn't want to stick around to hear whatever excuse she would come up with. Not even bothering to ask for his hoodie, he quickly hurried across the lawn, leaving Gracie alone on the bench.

## Chapter Twenty-Four

Gracie dropped her head into her hands, groaning loudly. When Dr. Jameson had first announced their canceled class, she had been excited to go back to her room and take a nap. But the minute she had walked into the room, thoughts of Dean had flooded her mind. She had tossed her bag on the bed and flopped down on the floor, unable to move an inch.

"Will you stop that?" Zara sighed from where she was lying on her bed.

"I can't," Gracie said miserably. "Dean hates me and I don't know why."

Zara sighed again, sitting up. "Okay. You and my brother have been moping for the past week. One day was fine, but this is getting ridiculous. Just talk to each other!"

"That would be hard," Gracie said glumly. "Dean has absolutely no interest in talking to me. Aaaaaand," she said, dragging out the word, "I have no freaking idea why."

"Why do I need to do all the work?" Zara mumbled to herself. Gracie got the sense that she wasn't supposed to have heard that, so she pretended that Zara hadn't said anything as the redhead climbed off of her bed and sat cross-legged on the floor opposite Gracie.

"Look, Gracie," her friend began. "I think you need to talk to him. Sit him down in a place he can't escape and tell him that the two of you need to talk. See, with the boys, you have to tell them what to do and they'll listen. How do you think we ended up playing princess dragons for most of my childhood? Because I told Dean, Jesse, and Theo what we were doing and didn't give them a chance to complain. Granted, Theo actually enjoyed the game, but I doubt the other two enjoyed dressing up as princesses while Zara-dragon attacked them."

Gracie managed a smile. The story was amusing, but she didn't think that it would work for her. "Zar, Dean won't even look at me. How do I get him into the same room, let alone get him to agree to talk to me?"

"Tell him what to do and he'll listen," Zara insisted.

Gracie shook her head, skeptical of her friend's advice. "I think I'm going to give it a few more days and see how he behaves. Maybe I'll talk to Theo or Jesse and see if they know anything."

"If anyone does, it'd be Theo."

"I know." Gracie nodded. "But for now, can you just let me be miserable in peace?"

"No," Zara said determinedly. "We're going to talk about this, Gracie. Now. Why are you so upset?"

"I have no clue," Gracie said with a sigh.

Zara frowned. "You and Dean are friends, right?"

"I think so. Or at least I *thought* so. I don't know. I have no idea of anything anymore."

"So would you say that you miss him as much as you would miss a regular friend who stopped talking to you?"

"Yes. Wait, no. I don't know."

"Progress," Zara declared. "Remember the time when Nicole yelled at you for no reason and you were really upset?"

"Zara, that was like two weeks ago."

"So do you remember?"

"Yes, I remember."

"Good. Because if I recall correctly—and my memory is amazing—you weren't as upset then as you are now."

"So? Does it matter?"

"Yes. It very much matters. Now, onto the next question. Why do you think you're so torn apart over this?"

"I'm not torn apart," Gracie tried to argue, but Zara was having none of it.

"Gracie Adams, you have spent the past three days either in bed or in class," Zara said seriously. "You haven't spoken to anyone other than me, Raina, and Nicole. You burst into tears last night when Raina asked what book you were reading."

"It was Dean's book. He let me take it from your aunt's house," Gracie mumbled in her defense. She was perfectly entitled to cry over it.

"Doesn't matter," Zara said firmly. "Have you ever stopped to think *why* you're affected so much by this?"

"Why?" Gracie asked grudgingly.

"Must I really have to put all the pieces together?" Zara lamented. "Why do you care so much about Dean?"

"I don't know!" Gracie cried. What was Zara trying to do? Confuse her even more?

"Why do you care so much about Dean, Gracie?" Zara demanded.

"Because he's my friend!" Gracie tried, her voice getting higher.

"Why do you care so much about Dean, Gracie?" Zara demanded for the third time, emphasizing each word.

"Because I like him!" Gracie screamed, before clapping her hands over her mouth as she realized what exactly she had said. Her eyes widened as she stared at Zara, whose shocked expression mirrored her own. "Because I like him," she repeated weakly, sinking back against the floor.

Zara joined her, a grin spreading across her face. "You actually admitted it," she said approvingly. "I didn't think you'd actually admit it."

Gracie paid no attention to her friend. "I like Dean," she repeated to herself. "I, Gracie Adams, like Dean Ashcroft."

"My brother," Zara added unhelpfully.

"Who hates me," Gracie finished. She looked mournfully at Zara. Zara winced. "Yeah, that too."

✯✯✯

Gracie took a deep breath as she stepped into the common room; she spotted Dean instantly. Her fake boyfriend was sitting by the fire, sharing a couch with Theo as both boys read. Nervously, she walked over and tapped Dean on the shoulder.

Dean glanced up. "Can I help you?" he asked, closing the novel loudly and turning to face her. Gracie winced at the tone of his voice. It was the voice you used when talking to a stranger—polite, but unfamiliar and a slight hint of "I don't really want to be part of this conversation."

"Yeah, um, yes," Gracie said, stumbling over her words. "Um, can we talk? Please?"

Theo looked up from his book, and the two boys exchanged a glance. Gracie waited, holding her breath, until Dean gave her a short nod.

"We can go up to my room."

Gracie nodded, following Dean up the steps. She rubbed her palms together, trying to get rid of the nerves that had appeared as soon as she had decided to talk to Dean. He held open the door for her and she stepped inside, curiously glancing around the room. Gracie had been in the Ashcrofts' dorm a couple of times over the years, mainly with Zara when she wanted to wake the boys up or grab something from the room. Contrary to popular belief, the room was pretty neat, with only a stray t-shirt lying on one of the beds. Dean led her to another bed, motioning for her to sit down.

"What did you want to talk about?" he asked.

Gracie swallowed. She had almost forgotten that she had been the one to ask to talk, and therefore, she was the one who needed to begin the talk. "Right. I wanted to talk about us, I guess."

"You guess?" Dean repeated.

"Yes," Gracie said, her confidence growing a little. "You've been ignoring me for no reason, and then there was the outside thing, and I still have no idea what's going o—" her voice caught as her gaze latched onto a poster hung on the wall.

When she had visited Disney World with her family, Gracie had gone on the Tower of Terror ride. She had traveled up with her mom, clutching her hand tightly as the floor dropped and they shot down over a hundred feet.

This drop was worse. Her heart sank like a stone tossed into a river, and Gracie froze in place, unable to reach down and fish it out.

"Gracie," Dean said, his voice slightly impatient. Gracie tore her gaze away from the poster, turning back to Dean. Why had she even come in here in the first place?

"Um, yeah. So that was it. I just wanted to talk," she said quietly, wringing her hands. She waited, hoping that Dean would say something, but he was silent. "You know what? This was a bad idea. I'm going to go." Without waiting for Dean to respond, she hurried out of his room.

Gracie rushed down the steps, intent on making it to her own dorm before the tears started falling. She told her mind to stop thinking about the poster she had seen, but her traitorous brain kept going back to that moment.

The poster board itself had been plain white, but it was covered in rainbow scribbles. At the top, the words "REVENGE ON GRACIE" were scrawled in big block letters. She hadn't stayed long enough to get a good look at the words below, but Gracie assumed they were all various plots and plans Dean had to win their game. The content didn't matter, really. Gracie was more focused on the title.

Of course, Dean didn't like her. This was all just a game to him.

She had wanted to talk to him, hoping that they could repair their friendship, and if the topic of an actual relationship came up, she would have confessed her newly discovered feelings.

Now, Gracie was glad that she didn't go through with her plan. She could almost kick herself for being so stupid. Why would Dean ever like her? She had clearly deluded herself into thinking that the past couple of months were something more than they actually were, while Dean was just laughing everything off and coming up with new tricks and jokes. Had he ever really cared about her, or was everything he did leading up to some master plan?

Gracie hurried into her room, still lost in thought. What part of this semester was real? What was fake? What was acting and what was how Dean truly felt? She collapsed onto her bed, a tear sliding down her cheek.

A weight on the bed next to her made Gracie look up to see Zara settling herself on top of the covers. "He rejected you?" she asked quietly.

Gracie shook her head, another tear falling. "I didn't get the chance. He doesn't like me. Not even as a friend. It's all a game to him." The tears were falling faster now, and Gracie hiccupped.

"I'm going to kill him," Zara muttered, putting an arm around her friend.

Gracie managed a shaky smile. "I thought we weren't allowed to kill Dean?"

"Oh, you're not," Zara said, her face set in determination. "But he hurt my best friend. Brother or not, he's gonna pay."

"Don't kill him," Gracie mumbled, leaning into Zara. "For some reason, I like him."

"Well, either way he's an idiot," Zara declared. "Just making sure you know that."

"Oh, believe me, I do." Gracie grabbed the tissue box from her nightstand, placing it in her lap. She pulled out a tissue and wiped away her tears, clenching it in her fist.

"I can go talk some sense into him," Zara offered. "He *really* needs some sense talked into him."

"Zara, you'd just prank him or yell at him the entire time, and that's not really helpful right now," Gracie said. "But thank you anyway."

Zara shrugged. "It's your loss. He'll probably do something kill-worthy within the next couple of days anyway, so if you want in, just let me know."

"I don't want to kill anyone," Gracie said in an exasperated voice.

"*Yet.*"

☆☆☆

Dean looked up in surprise as Zara stormed into his room, slamming the door behind her.

"What did you do?" she demanded, glaring at him furiously.

"Nothing!" Dean was quick to say, even throwing his hands up in innocence. "I haven't done anything!"

Zara scoffed. "Dean, I'm your twin sister. I know you. You can't lie to me."

"No, seriously," Dean insisted. Then he sighed miserably, knowing why she was here. He didn't want to have to deal with it now, but Zara was never one to take no for an answer. "I have absolutely no clue what I've done."

"You did something."

"No, I did not," Dean argued. "Gracie was the one who wanted to talk to me. Gracie was the one who ran out. I barely even got two words in!"

"So you know what this is about then," Zara said, levying Dean with a stare.

"Not really," Dean said. "Gracie said that she wanted to talk, but then, before we even started, she said that this was a bad idea and ran out."

"Are you sure you didn't do anything?" Zara pressed.

"I'm sure!" Dean exclaimed. "Look, we were just sitting on my bed, staring at nothing really..." his voice cut off as he sat down and mimicked Gracie's position, realizing where she had been looking. "Oh."

"*Oh* is right," Zara said sarcastically, moving to stand beside Dean. She, too, peered at the poster. "What the hell is that?"

"It's old!" Dean defended himself. "Back from when I didn't like Gracie, and we were just arguing."

Zara opened her mouth to say something but closed it before Dean could even finish speaking. "What did you just say?"

"It's old?" Dean said hesitantly.

"No, after that," Zara insisted. Dean looked warily at his sister, suddenly scared of the gleam in her eye.

"Back from when I didn't like Gracie and we—"

"Stop," Zara interrupted. A grin spread across her face. "You like Gracie!"

Dean fought to hide his blush. "No," he attempted to protest, but even he could tell that it wasn't going to work.

"Finally!" Zara exclaimed, throwing her arms around him in a hug. "Finally, finally, finally!" She cheered, letting go and dancing around the room.

Dean crossed his arms over his chest. "Either way, it doesn't matter," he said defensively. "Gracie doesn't like me back. She has a —I heard her talking on the phone. She doesn't like me."

"Yeah, but that's because she's still in denial," Zara corrected him. "Come on Dean, I know my best friend and I know my brother. Neither of you are going to take that first step."

"Because she doesn't like me back!" Dean cried.

Zara scoffed. "And I'm the Queen of England, right."

He thought about telling Zara about Gracie's secret boyfriend but figured that it wasn't his secret to tell. Since Zara was so insistent about him and Gracie getting together, she probably didn't know that

Gracie already had a boyfriend. Dean had no idea why Gracie would hide it from her best friend, but she probably had a good reason, and so he said nothing.

"Look, it's just not going to happen, okay? It's fine, really, Zar. You don't need to keep pushing this. So please, please, please, can you just let it drop?"

"No." Zara shook her head determinedly. "You like Gracie, and Gracie likes you, and this relationship *is* going to happen."

"It's not even your relationship!" Dean protested.

"Yes, but it's my best friend and my brother, so by that logic, I've been involved since day one." Zara shrugged. "You guys are really cute together, and you seem happier when you're with Gracie. I want to see you happy."

"Aww, Z, you care," Dean teased.

"Yeah, yeah." Zara waved it off, shoving his shoulder gently. "Let's never speak of it again. Now, I have a plan. Are you ready to hear it?"

"Do I have a choice?"

"Nope."

## Chapter Twenty-Five

"This is never going to work," Jesse declared, throwing his balloon to the ground. He cast it a disgusted look and Dean stifled a laugh.

"Well then, what do you suggest?" he asked, crossing his arms over his chest. "This is the only plan we've been able to come up with, and it took us an hour and forty minutes. Do you really want to go back to brainstorming again?"

Jesse winced, likely recalling the morning. Zara had shepherded the three Ashcroft boys into an empty room after breakfast, locked the door, and sent them a text telling them they weren't allowed out of the room until they had come up with a suitable plan to get Dean and Gracie together.

Naturally, all the plans had sucked, and Zara grudgingly chose her favorite—the one that involved filling the entire common room with balloons.

"No, but this is ridiculous," Jesse shot back, Theo nodding beside him. "We don't have enough balloons, and it'll take forever to blow them up considering we don't have a pump."

"You don't think I know that?" Dean snapped. "I know that! I'm not the one who's insisting on this, though, so I'm the wrong person to be talking to!"

Theo frowned. "You mean you aren't excited about this? Don't you like Gracie?"

"I do." Dean sighed. "But like Jesse said, this is ridiculous. I have no clue if Gracie even likes balloons or not. We could be doing all this for nothing."

"Well, that's stupid," Theo declared.

"Tell me about it," Dean rolled his eyes. "Or more accurately, tell Zara about it so we can do something else. It's Sunday. I'd rather not spend all day buried in balloons."

"Literally." Jesse snickered. "But if you're not happy about this, do something else," he added. "It's your possible future relationship, Dean, not Zara's. You should do something that you know both you and Gracie will appreciate. I don't know her very well, but she doesn't strike me as the type of person who would like a room filled entirely with balloons. That's more Zara's thing."

Dean nodded slowly. "Yeah, you're right. But what should I do? We spent nearly two hours trying to think of a good idea, and we got nothing."

"That's because you were trying to think of a big idea," Jesse explained. "Try thinking of something small. Something that you know Gracie would like."

"Right," Dean said. Jesse was right—big declarations weren't Gracie's style. Zara might prefer flowers and chocolate when she was pissed off, but all Gracie needed was a sincere apology. He tossed down the half-deflated balloon he was holding, wondering why he had just wasted an hour tying balloons. "Thanks, Jesse."

"Hey, I've got good advice every once in a while," Jesse said with a wink.

Dean laughed. "Alright, noted. Now, get out. I have to come up with a speech that'll make Gracie forgive me."

"And so I said to her, 'I don't see the point of working with you if all you're going to do is put your name on the project,'" Zara said, lounging on her bed. "And Maya just sat there with her mouth open. I found another partner, of course, because there was no way in hell I was doing that entire project by myself."

Nicole laughed, nudging her friend's shoulder. "There's a reason Maya ends up working alone for most projects," she stated. "Everyone hates working with her because she never does anything. The only reason she'd work with someone is if they're too nice to say no. And most people have at least some sense, so that would never happen."

Gracie flicked her eyes up from her laptop, glancing toward where Raina sat at her desk, studiously staring at a textbook. She didn't think Nicole knew it, but Raina had worked with Maya on their last English assignment for that very reason.

"So I ended up working with Liam, and it went fine," Zara continued. "We split the work equally, so we just did it by ourselves," she said, smirking. "But we met up after school for some *study sessions*."

Nicole sighed lazily, dropping backward to lie on Zara's bed. "Zara, have you ever had a history partner you haven't made out with?"

Zara scoffed. "Give me some credit. There was—" She paused, tilting her head. "I worked with Theo once."

"That's not related to you," Nicole corrected herself.

"Oh, well, no one," Zara answered flippantly.

Gracie shook her head, amused. "Do you *really* choose your history partners based on their attractiveness?"

"No," Zara protested. "Sometimes I pick them because they're good students, and then we just end up making out *because* they're attractive. I don't choose them because they're hot. That's just a bonus."

Both girls laughed. Gracie caught Raina glancing over her shoulder to see what was so funny before pretending to work again. She frowned, wondering if the other girl was lonely now that Nicole was hanging out with Gracie and Zara regularly again. Nicole had taken a few days to hang out solely with her new roommates but had soon slotted back into their evenings as if she had never left.

"Ahh, I missed you!" Zara was saying when Gracie turned her attention back to the two girls on Zara's bed.

"Clearly not enough to work with me on our history project," Nicole teased, playfully kicking her friend's ankle.

Zara laughed. "Hey, you're not my type."

"Girl, I'm everybody's type!" Nicole exclaimed, pretending to be offended. They laughed again.

"Hey guys," Gracie said suddenly. She snapped her laptop shut. "I'm going to run down to the common room. I think I left my math textbook down there while studying last night."

"No!" Nicole and Zara cried in unison.

"I'll go!" Zara offered quickly, shooting off of the bed.

Gracie frowned, looking at her friend suspiciously. "Okay, who are you and what have you done with Zara Ashcroft? Because my friend never does anything for someone else unless there's a reason for it."

Zara gave her a sweet smile. "I'm just being nice," she protested.

Nicole snickered and Gracie whipped her head around to stare at her other friend. "Zara, you don't *do* nice," Gracie said, exasperated. "So please tell me what's going on."

Zara and Nicole exchanged an uncertain glance. "We can't," Nicole said finally. "But trust us, there's nothing to worry about."

"Yeah, stay up here with us," Zara chimed in. "I want to rehash all the details of Voldemort finally getting what he deserves!"

Gracie hesitated. Raina had turned around, a curious expression on her face. Clearly, she hadn't been allowed in on the secret. Zara probably had some sort of surprise waiting in the common room. That, or she was pulling some prank and didn't want Gracie to get caught in the crossfire.

"Fine," Gracie said after a minute, even though discussing Blake was one of the last things she wanted to do. "I won't go downstairs, but I'm watching the two of you."

Zara glanced at her phone, then popped her head right back up. "Actually, it's fine. And hey, while you're down there, can you get my sweatshirt? I think I left it on one of the chairs."

Gracie eyed her innocent-looking friend. She had no idea what Zara was going for, but she was absolutely not in the mood for it at the moment. "If it's a prank..." she began slowly.

"It's not a prank!"

Gracie glared at her. "Zara."

Zara sighed loudly. "Fine, fine. Dean wants to talk to you but he didn't know how. He was supposed to set something up in the common room, but knowing him, he's just pacing around nervously. If you want to talk to him, you should go downstairs because he's really, really sorry and just wants to talk to you."

Gracie blinked twice. "I'm sorry, what?"

"Dean's really sorry," Zara said softly. "And I know that he's an idiot and hurt you, but I think you should give him a chance."

"I can't figure him out," Gracie admitted. "He confuses me. There are times when I think he likes me and wants to be my friend, but then the next day he's cold and won't talk to me."

"You confuse him just as much," Zara told her. "And even if he won't admit it, he's my twin brother. I know what's going through his head and I know how torn up he is about you. He really likes you, Gracie."

"Do you think I should go down?" she asked quietly.

Raina chose that moment to speak up, rising from her desk and joining Gracie on her bed. "I think that when you have the type of relationship that you and Dean have, you'll regret it immensely if you stay up here and refuse to see him. You may have started your relationship as a joke, but it's pretty clear to everyone around you that it's not a joke anymore. That's why you and Dean are taking the 'breakup' really hard, *and* that's why you both confuse each other. You set these rules at the beginning and now your feelings are changing and you don't know how to act."

"Raina's right," Nicole added, looking like it physically pained her to agree. "You haven't been sleeping or eating well recently. This whole thing with Dean is killing you. You need to talk it out and figure out what's going on between you."

Gracie curled her knees up to her chest, alternating her gaze between her three friends. If Zara was right, then maybe this was all one big miscommunication. Hope filled her chest as she thought about what they had said. Could there still be a chance for her and Dean?

"Okay," she said after a minute.

"Okay?" Zara confirmed. "You'll go?"

Gracie let out a deep breath, wondering if she was making the right decision. "Yes."

※ ※ ※

Dean paced around the common room, running a hand through his hair every few steps. He glanced at the clock hung over the fireplace, wondering why it moved so slowly. It was already eleven thirty and the last student studying had gone upstairs twenty minutes earlier. Dean had been downstairs trying to figure out what to say to Gracie for nearly an hour but had only texted Zara the go-ahead five minutes ago. A tapping on the steps drew his attention, and he turned to see Gracie carefully descending.

"Hi," he said nervously. Dean's fingers itched to shove his hands in his pockets, and not for the first time that evening, he cursed having forgotten his sweatshirt in the dorm.

Gracie, on the other hand, had most definitely not forgotten a hoodie. Dean's eyes widened at seeing her in the blue sweatshirt he had given her. He hadn't thought she could be any more attractive than she already was, but he made a mental note to give her more of his clothes in the future.

"Hi," Gracie responded, taking a tentative step toward him.

Dean swallowed, nodding to the couch. "Do you want to hit down? I mean, sit down!" he quickly corrected himself. "Sit down."

Gracie gave him a shy smile. "Okay," she said softly.

Dean sat down next to her, wiping his sweaty hands on his pants. He wasn't sure how to start the conversation, but what ended up coming out was: "Zara said we needed to talk."

"She told me the same thing," Gracie said, glancing over at him.

Dean looked down, then back up at her. He let out a breath, considering his words carefully. "I think we should talk because we want to, not just because Zara likes to meddle."

"I agree."

"Do you want to…not talk?"

"No," Gracie said immediately. She looked down, a slight blush staining her cheeks. "I do want to talk."

Dean nodded. They sat in silence for a minute, both of them sneaking glances at the other and quickly looking away when their eyes met. "Why didn't you tell me you have a boyfriend?" Dean blurted out.

Gracie jerked her head up, her eyes wide as she stared at him. "I don't have a boyfriend," she said, confused.

"The person you were talking to that night last week," Dean clarified. "It was around two in the morning. I heard you. You were telling him you missed him and loved him and making plans to see him when break starts."

The puzzled look stayed on Gracie's face for a few more seconds before slowly turning into one of understanding. She laughed and Dean clenched his fists tightly. "I don't have a boyfriend," she managed to get out. "That—that was my brother!"

Dean's anger disappeared instantly. "Your brother?"

Gracie nodded, still laughing. "He's currently in California. I haven't seen him in forever and with the time difference, we don't get to talk as much. Did you hear me talking about how I can't wait to see him in a few months?"

"Yeah," Dean said, biting his lip. "That was the first thing I heard. I wasn't eavesdropping, I swear. I couldn't sleep, so I came down to read."

"I didn't think you were," Gracie assured him. "My brother had put his wife on the phone. They just got married last year; she's pregnant and due in a couple of months. I was talking to the baby."

"So you weren't talking to your boyfriend?" Dean asked. Gracie nodded. "I feel pretty stupid now," Dean muttered.

"It's okay," Gracie said with a shrug. "I would have thought the same thing."

"That's why I was avoiding you this week," Dean said slowly. "But why were you avoiding me the past couple of days?"

"The poster in your room," Gracie told him. "I saw it, and, well, I thought we were friends, at the very least. I didn't think you took this game so seriously."

"Every game should be taken seriously," Dean said. "But I actually made that the night I overheard your conversation with your brother. I was upset and ended up waking Jesse and Theo to rant at them for an hour. I figured that stabbing a poster board was better than stabbing actual people."

"You Ashcrofts and your violent tendencies," Gracie teased. "I should have just asked you about the poster. I took this seriously too, I guess. I don't know."

"You thought it was just a game to me," Dean said quietly. "But you genuinely liked hanging out with me and were worried that I didn't feel the same."

Gracie turned to look at him again, a shocked expression on her face. "*Yes*," she said empathetically. "Just *yes*. How did you know?"

Dean took a deep breath. "Because that's exactly how I've been feeling."

Gracie stared at him, stunned. Was Dean saying what she thought he was saying? Gracie decided to take a chance. "And how you've been feeling," she asked, slowly, hesitantly, "is it...maybe...more than friendship?"

Dean's eyes fluttered closed, an indescribable look on his face. "Yes," he said finally. "I think so."

Even though Gracie knew everyone was saying that Dean liked her back, and her assumption from the previous conversation was that he did, his words still knocked the wind out of her. She slumped against the back of the couch, suddenly unable to support her weight. "Oh."

"Just oh?" Dean asked. He stood, looking away as he wrung his hands.

Gracie shifted her weight off the couch to stand too, her hands unconsciously reaching out for him. "I think I feel the same way," she said, answering the question he hadn't asked.

A sharp intake of breath was the only indication that Dean heard her words. He turned around slowly, his head tilted to the side as he stared at her, as if daring her to take another step.

In that moment, there was nothing that could stop Gracie from moving closer to Dean. Her insides fluttered with happiness, and she glanced down at her hands to find them shaking.

"What are we doing?" she whispered, tilting her head up to look at him. Her eyes met Dean's, hazel staring into deep brown. It was an odd feeling, a little hard to describe, but Gracie would happily feel this way for the rest of her life. It was almost as if months of tension and anticipation had all led up to this moment, and now that they had both admitted their feelings, neither of them knew what came next.

"I don't know," Dean confessed. "If you'd asked me this two months ago, I'd have a completely different answer for you."

Gracie laughed lightly. "I know. I would too."

"Two months ago, you were nothing to me," Dean said honestly, taking a step closer. "You were my sister's best friend and nothing more."

Gracie bit her lip. "And now?"

"Now," Dean said with a sigh, shaking his head. "I honestly have no idea what you are. You're so much more than Zara's best friend, and you're also my friend, but—" Dean shrugged. "I also don't want to be your friend."

"I don't want to continue the way we are," Gracie said softly. "I know we started this as a game, but it's become real to me."

"It's become real to me too," Dean agreed.

The two stared at each other for a moment, neither of them speaking. The fire in the common room crackled behind them, but neither Gracie nor Dean acknowledged its presence.

"Zara will kill you if you ever hurt me," Gracie said finally.

"Well, it's a good thing I don't plan on doing that." Dean chuckled. "She would also hurt you if you ever hurt me."

"Well, it's a good thing I don't plan on doing that," Gracie teased, throwing Dean's words back at him.

Dean swallowed hard. "So do you think we can give this—give *us*—a try?" he asked tentatively.

Gracie ran her hands over the sleeves of her hoodie, the same one Dean had given to her for Christmas. The movement helped calm her down, but Gracie's heart was still beating quickly as she answered. "I think we can."

Dean grinned slowly as he leaned down, his face hovering over hers. "Can I kiss you?" he asked quietly, as if he didn't already know the answer.

Gracie nodded, bringing her lips up to meet his. Unlike their previous kisses, this one was slow and sweet, Dean's hand snaking into her hair to pull her close. When they broke apart, Dean pressed a kiss to the corner of her mouth before taking Gracie's hand in his.

"Can I call you my boyfriend now?" Gracie asked. "Like actually, for real, this time?"

"You better," Dean teased. "Because I don't just kiss anyone, Gracie Adams."

"What about your girlfriend?" Gracie breathed, wrapping her free hand around the back of his neck. Her fingers trailed across his skin, and that mischievous grin that she loved danced across Dean's lips. "Do you kiss her?"

"Most definitely," Dean agreed before leaning in to kiss her again.

☆☆☆

Gracie looked around the table the next day, unable to keep the smile off her face. The boys had joined them at their regular table, with Dean sliding in beside Gracie and grabbing her hand like it was the most normal thing in the world. She was sure that it had been annoying for him to eat cereal left-handed, but Dean had managed without a complaint.

Annalisse and Juliet attempted to press her for details as to why the group was sitting together again, but Gracie refused to tell them even a single word. They had then tried to squeeze information about her and Dean's relationship, but Gracie wasn't budging on that either. Other than the Ashcrofts, Gracie, Raina, and Nicole, not a single person would know the story of how Gracie and Dean got together.

"Your roommates are staring at us." Dean leaned over to whisper in Gracie's ear.

Gracie grinned up at him. "Let them."

Dean squeezed her hand under the table, and Gracie leaned her head against his shoulder. Zara made a disgusted face but shot Gracie a smile to let her know she didn't really mind the PDA. Giving her best friend a smile in response, Gracie returned her attention to her breakfast, happy that everyone was finally back where they belonged —together, without a fake relationship as the catalyst.

Because this relationship was most definitely real.

# Epilogue

"Oh, Dean!" Gracie called in a sugary-sweet voice. "I need your help!"

Dean ran up the steps to Gracie's dorm, taking them two at a time. She had texted him only a minute ago, claiming she needed him *right away*. "What's wrong?" he panted, bending over.

"Nothing," Gracie said innocently.

Dean sighed. "I was in the middle of a card game."

"You mean you don't want to spend time with your girlfriend?" Gracie pouted. She smirked, watching Dean hurriedly try to take back his words. It was surprisingly easy to play him at times, and she was counting on that for her plan to work. Casually, Gracie set her phone on her nightstand, propping it up against a stack of books. She motioned for Dean to sit with her on the bed.

"Can you believe that we've been together for two weeks now?" she mused.

Dean shook his head. "Sometimes it feels like it's been a lot longer."

"Well, we *were* dancing around each other for a while," Gracie said with a shrug. "So I'm not surprised. Zara says we fight like an old married couple."

## The Gossip Games

"Zara doesn't have a girlfriend, so she gets no say." Dean smirked. "And I win. Again. Always."

Gracie threw her head back and laughed as she lied, "You know, Zara actually predicted that we'd end up dating. She was so thrilled when we started."

Dean looked surprised. "Back when we were faking it or when we actually started dating? Because she didn't seem thrilled that first day at breakfast when I pranked everyone and told them we were dating."

Gracie leaned back against her pillow, crossing her legs. She had Dean exactly where she wanted. Now, it was time to go in for the kill. "Oh, she was all like, 'are you two actually dating or is this just some joke? Because I think you and my brother would make a great couple. Seriously, you're both extremely annoying'. Except she used other words that I'm not going to repeat."

"What did you tell her?"

"The truth."

Dean raised an eyebrow. "You told her that we weren't actually dating and were just fooling the school because it was amusing?"

"You thought it was amusing," Gracie pointed out. "I was pissed."

"It was pretty hilarious," Dean agreed. "And hey, it's a good story to tell our kids. 'So, once upon a time I faked a relationship for the whole school and let them all believe it was real.'"

Gracie smirked. "Sorry, what was that? Want to say it again?" Without breaking eye contact with Dean, she reached out and grabbed her phone. She had set it to record right before Dean walked in and now played back the video. "Hmm, who should I send this to?"

Dean looked at her admiringly. "You are the most devious girl I have ever met."

"Don't forget it."

"And you're mine," Dean concluded, drawing closer. Their faces were inches apart. Gracie swallowed.

"Oh, am I?" she whispered.

"Yes," Dean breathed, before he leaned in and kissed her.

Gracie stabbed a few buttons on her phone, before closing her eyes and giving her full attention to the kiss. Dean's fingers had just twisted themselves in her hair when an ear-splitting shriek came from outside the door. Gracie recognized Juliet's voice instantly and she pulled back to smirk at Dean.

"I win."

Jesse's story will continue in Book 2

# Book Playlist

Listen to the book playlist on Spotify

# Ashcroft Family Tree

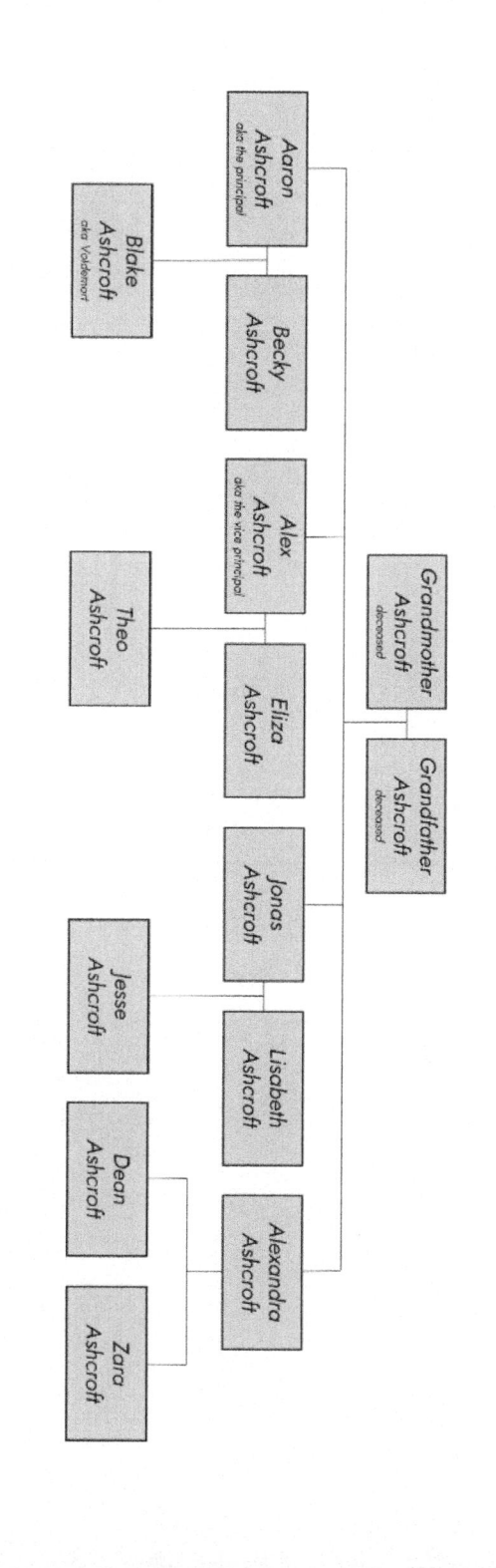

- **Grandmother Ashcroft** (deceased) & **Grandfather Ashcroft** (deceased)
  - **Aaron Ashcroft** (aka the principal) & **Becky Ashcroft**
    - **Blake Ashcroft** (aka Voldemort)
  - **Alex Ashcroft** (aka the vice principal) & **Eliza Ashcroft**
    - **Theo Ashcroft**
  - **Jonas Ashcroft** & **Lisabeth Ashcroft**
    - **Jesse Ashcroft**
    - **Alexandra Ashcroft**
      - **Dean Ashcroft**
      - **Zara Ashcroft**

# Acknowledgments

I started writing longer works with self-insert fanfiction, and four and a half years later, I'm holding my first published novel in my hands. I can say with 100% assurance that I had no idea that before I turned 19, I'd have written five books, signed a three book publishing contract, published one of those books, and amassed a whole lot of people that I need to thank.

Savanna, you took a chance on a girl who messaged you on Instagram, and I will forever be grateful for that. You're my publisher and my editor, and most importantly, my friend. I love working with you, and I don't think I could've asked for a better editor. I am so thankful for you and the entire SnowRidge team.

Sam, thank you so much for creating the gorgeous cover and bringing Gracie and Dean to life. I really appreciate how endlessly patient you were with my many changes, and how you were as enthusiastic about the cover as me. I adore it so, so much, and I am so excited to display it everywhere and stare at it for eternity.

Mariella, my favorite proofreader with absolutely hilarious comments. You left so many comments, I was nervous at first—until I saw that half of them were you telling my characters that they were idiots (they are, but we love them for it). Thank you for answering all my little questions and for being a part of this journey.

Mommy, Daddy, Carrie, Josh, and Emmie—you had no idea I was writing a book until I wrote it. According to my first grade report cards, I'd discovered my passion for writing a long time ago.

Carrie, Josh, and Emmie, the best thing I can tell you is that I hope that you discover your passions in life. Find something you truly enjoy and watch as your dreams come true. Mommy and Daddy, as soon as you knew about the book, you became my biggest supporters. Thank you for everything you've done, whether it's editing the book, suggesting cover details, or helping with all the behind-the-scenes. I love you all.

Auntie Sandy, you've always encouraged me to live life to the fullest and take advantage of new experiences. I think publishing a book certainly counts as a new experience! I can't wait for you to read it and in a few (or more than a few) years, for your girls to read it too.

Batsheva, we've shared so many romance stories with each other, and I can't wait for you to read this one. You're the Addie to my Lina, and I've never 'made the wrong choice' with you.

Christy, you told me you wanted an advance copy, and I told you that you were the first bookstagrammer on my list. Not only are you my number one bookstagrammer and a dear friend, you've been on my team—literally—since I was writing the first draft. I am so appreciative of every post you've shared, shop item you've photographed, and message you've sent me.

Tati B. Alvarez, Sara Confino, Jessica Costello, Cookie O'Gorman, Pixie Perkins, A.J. Skelly, my favorite authors who I am so lucky to call friends. You've made this publishing journey so much easier with your words of advice, encouragement, and endless support.

I wrote part of this book with my laptop resting on a laser cutter in a woodworking lab. A bit of a strange place to write, considering all the chaos happening around me, but I was surrounded by all my friends, and I took all their positive energy and put that in my book.

To Addie, Eitan, Emma, Ilan, Max, Michael, Mia, Micha, Moshe, Nadav, Richie, Tzipora, and Zack — you've provided me with so much inspiration over the past few years, whether knowingly or unknowingly. I hope you enjoy this Idiots in the Lab production.

To Mr. Preston, thank you for creating a space that I felt comfortable in. A desk may not have been the intended use for the laser cutter, but I loved every second I spent in the Fab Lab.

To Daphna and Addie, my two romance lovers. You had a front row seat to the writing of this book, and I hope you enjoyed the random quotes, pictures, and frantic texts that I still keep sending you today. I love you more than I love my book boyfriends.

Zack, despite having no interest in romance novels, you've always supported me and my writing. Thank you for letting me talk plots and characters even when you have no idea what I'm talking about.

Micha, as much as I told you that you weren't a character in my book, all of the best parts of you are in this one. You've always been there for me, and I don't think I could write a friend as amazing as you.

Mia, you are my best and most dearest friend, and this book would not exist without you. Our first writing was absolute pandemonium, but I love it because we wrote it together. You may not have helped me write this one, but you've been there every step of the way. You're the person I go to with a new idea, the first person I want to share news with, and no matter how far apart we are, you're always in my heart.

To every bookstagrammer, booktoker, reader, writer, author, and friend who has expressed excitement for this book—there are no words that can describe how grateful I am to all of you. I adore both the Bookstagram and Booktok communities, and I am so honored to be a part of them. Seeing all the love you guys have for The Gossip Games really just floors me, and I don't know how to express my gratitude. Special mentions to @carmennorriswrites, @chicklitistheshit, @love.them.fictional, @maya.m.reads, @rose.colored.books, @the_book_tale & @raenydayreads.

To everyone who has texted, dm'd, liked, commented, shared, and wished me congratulations, thank you from the bottom of my heart.

I hope you enjoy The Gossip Games as much as I do.

# About the Author

Allie Sarah is a New Jersey based writer who is studying creative writing. When not working on her next book, she can usually be found obsessing over Broadway musicals, beading for her Etsy shop (The Shop of Starlight), or curling up under blankets with a romance novel. You can find her online at @authoralliesarah (Instagram) and @the.book.princess (TikTok). The Gossip Games is her debut novel.

# SNOWRIDGE PRESS

### **FANTASY**

Dark Affliction

Peaceweaver

Grimkeeper

The Depths of Atlantis

Persuasion of Deceit

Persuasion of Destiny

Claervont Captive

Claervont's Cost

### **DYSTOPIAN**

Smoke and Mirrors

Thief

Merry Men

Archeress

Defender

### **CONTEMPORARY**

Je Te Veux

Made in the USA
Monee, IL
10 April 2023